SU

CAYE

Lloyd
Christensen

outskirtspress
DENVER, COLORADO

Outskirts Press, Inc.
http://www.outskirtspress.com

ISBN: 978-1-4327-8859-9

Outskirts Press and the "OP" logo are trademarks belonging to Outskirts Press, Inc.

PRINTED IN THE UNITED STATES OF AMERICA

Acknowledgements

I would like to thank my friends at the real Sunrise Caye. I hope that I have accurately reflected "George's" love for "Kim" and the island.

I would also like to thank Christine DeSmet at the University of Wisconsin @ Madison and Robin Smith of Robin Smith Ink! for their honest critiques, suggestions, advice, and lessons.

I would like to thank my friends at the Writer's Bloc of Granbury, Texas, and especially Peggy Purser-Freeman, for their support.

I also want to thank Luke Anderson for the drawing of Katie's cabana.

And I can't forget the folks I've worked with, peers and clients, that encouraged me.

Chapter 1

Saturday, December 30th, 1:30 P.M.

"I know that look, George. You're trying to come to grips with having killed someone. You have to remember, you had no choice."

"Glenn, I'm not really all that concerned with killing a couple of thugs. Maybe I should be, but I'm not." *Besides, it wasn't my first time.*

The leaves of a palm tree brushed against the thatched roof of my cabana, making it difficult to hear if anyone inside called out. I climbed a couple of the porch steps, stopped and, deciding I hadn't heard anything, came back down.

"George, are you trying to determine the body count?"

I stopped pacing, turned toward the beach, wondered if I heard a boat coming, and turned to face him.

"Yeah, I've been trying to do that." An iguana skittered out from under the cabana, crossed five feet of a hard-packed, sandy trail, paused for a second, and climbed onto a small table below another tree to bask in the sun blasting through a break in the clouds.

"George, I've been in the FBI for ten years. I was an Army Ranger for ten years before that."

I darted from the bench below my living quarters, where FBI Agent Glenn Kline rested, and the stairwell. I strained to hear sounds from my living quarters, to hear Kim, my wife, if she called out. The Caribbean breeze picked up enough to cause ripples in the water of the lagoon.

"So?"

"It's just that I've been there, okay? I know what it's like to kill someone—you had to do it."

"Right. I had to do it." *Unlike the last time when it was pure vengeance. Calculated, planned, well executed, but still vengeance.*

"Okay, George, what's the count?" He didn't look at me.

"Good guys: four dead, six injured enough to need hospitalization. Two of the injured are upstairs. The rest are on my boat somewhere between my island and the Belize mainland. Where the hell is the rescue helicopter?"

"I'm sure they had to find another senior Belizean police officer. Captain Black was—hopefully still is—the head of their investigation division, and he's on one of the boats headed for the mainland." The Belizean officer had been in a police helicopter that had been shot up pretty badly and he was badly wounded.

❧❖❧

I climbed the stairs to my office, taking two at a time, and walked across the short bridge to the cabana's open door. My wife, Kim, and Larry—one of my resort's guests—were each wrapped in blankets. They were sleeping, fitfully, but at least they were breathing. Even here in the Caribbean, spending a couple of hours drifting, immersed in the water, can cause hypothermia. I peered through a gap between palm leaves, looking for signs of another boat before going back downstairs.

"Okay, that count works for me. Don't count the bad guys, George. They don't count."

"I've already counted them. Three dead, two missing. The two missing are the only ones that do count." *They got away. They might be found. They might come for us.*

"We'll find them. The FBI is already contacting the State Department. They'll put pressure on Honduras. If they show up there, we'll get them."

"They've probably already gotten to one of Martinez's Honduran resorts. He's got several resorts along the coast. Their helicopter should have made that trip in less than thirty minutes."

"If so, we'll find them, George. They killed a couple of federal agents in the States. They killed a U.S. district attorney too. We'll find them."

"They could be on their way elsewhere by now. They could have banked west and gone to one of his Belizean resorts. He's got two or three here in Belize too."

I went up the stairs again. Kim and Larry were just as they'd been two minutes earlier. I, on the other hand, was tiring fast. The adrenalin was wearing off.

"George?"

"Yeah?"

"I've been here, at your island resort, and to mainland Belize, just the one time, the year before last. Please tell me this was *not* just another week in paradise."

I looked at him, wondering if he was serious or if he'd been hit in the head. I decided he was joking but I felt like slapping him sensible.

"No, Glenn, it was not just another week in paradise, but it did start out like one. Let me tell you about it..."

Chapter 2

A week earlier
December 23rd,
10:30 A.M.

"Sticks, can we talk for a few minutes?" I asked.

Sticks lifted the front end of his sea kayak and pulled it out of the water. His real name was Peter Griffin but he was tall and skinny, like a stick, and he played the steel drums. So he'd been "Sticks" ever since we met.

"Sure, George, but I only have a few minutes. The ship is coming soon." The ship had to wind its way through a mile or two of coral heads.

The sun was high and bright, and it was a warm day. The turquoise water that makes up Glover's Reef Atoll was smooth, with barely a ripple in the water of our lagoon. The breeze blowing in from the mainland some thirty miles to the northwest was just strong enough to make the diver-down flag at the end of my dock stand out. It had all the makings of another day in paradise, another day on my island, Sunrise Caye.

I helped Sticks suspend his kayak on hooks in the kayak palapa, a structure with eight support columns and a thatched roof. Sticks always hung his boats upside down to ensure birds didn't nest in them and any water could fall out. We hung his kayak next to his other personal boat: a canoe made of a clear acrylic that allowed passengers to see the fish and coral below.

We sat on a couple of Adirondack beach chairs, stretching our legs out in front of us. I rubbed my hands along the smooth, well-polished mahogany.

"So, George, what's up?"

"I'd like this to be between us, okay?" I reached down, picked up a fallen coconut, tossed it out into the lagoon and watched it float.

He leaned forward. "Is everything okay?"

"I've been here, at Sunrise Caye, for twenty years. Kim's been here for fifteen," I said.

"I remember the day she stepped off the boat. It was my week to go for the best-looking single woman on the trip. You were the manager and pulled rank." He grinned. "I have to admit, it worked out pretty well for you."

"As I recall, you got along real well with her best friend."

"Yeah, I guess you can say that. It was a fun week, and a great way to start my first season here." He chuckled a little.

I paused, maybe two minutes, watching as the incoming waves pushed the coconut toward shore. Some shad darted about, hiding from a barracuda watching from less than two feet of water.

"Sticks, it's been a long time. It's been long enough. Kim and I are putting the resorts up for sale."

"You're selling? Both resorts, Mountain To Sea and Over The Edge?"

"Both, if we can find buyers. Ideally, someone will buy both and operate them as one resort."

He looked stunned, taking a minute for it to soak in. The waves were rolling the coconut along the beach. "Got any buyers lined up?"

"No. I wanted to talk with you first."

"Are you open to selling them separately?"

"Sure. It'll probably be easier that way."

"Do you have any idea what they're worth?"

"My first guess would be five-hundred thousand U.S. I bought Mountain To Sea from Carey and Lucy a couple of years ago for one hundred and fifty thousand. Those assets haven't changed much." I'd done the math dozens of times. It doesn't seem like enough given how much of my life has been invested here.

"We've added three cabanas since you bought Mountain To Sea," Sticks said.

"The kayaks, canoes, and windsurf boards are probably worth about thirty-thousand. The kitchen equipment, solar panels and windmills and other infrastructure would be another forty to fifty-thousand. I figure Mountain To Sea is worth somewhere between what I paid and two hundred thousand dollars."

"What about Over The Edge?"

"The buildings, generators, and kitchen equipment might be worth one hundred thousand. The two dive boats would be another fifty thousand. The *Sensencula* would bring about thirty thousand. All of the dive gear, scuba tanks, and the air compressor are probably worth twenty-five thousand."

The coconut was trapped along the shore where the small waves had tossed it against some fallen palm leaves.

"That doesn't add up to half a million."

"No, but they have a pretty reliable income stream with repeat guests. Plus, we've got eighty years left on the one-hundred year lease on the island, and our leases are transferable. Belize isn't letting any of the cayes go cheap like they did twenty years ago when they were just trying to get people to come here and invest."

Sticks gripped the front of his chair's arms as if to stand and looked at me. "I need to check the guest cabanas for stuff they might have left. Let's talk as we walk."

I knew that he'd be interested. He'd been here almost since the beginning and had a lot invested emotionally, if not financially. I saw the shad dart away from the shore, scared by the vibrations of our movement. The barracuda's patience paid off as he snagged his lunch.

"George, why are you looking to sell?"

We walked eastward on a sandy trail under a canopy of palm trees, across the narrow, thirteen-acre island while I figured out how to answer.

"Kim is getting close to forty now. She's starting to regret not having a family. This isn't the lifestyle for raising kids."

We came out on the open ocean side of the island near the southern most of the Mountain To Sea guest cabanas.

"Sticks, can you imagine trying to raise a family here? There's almost no electricity, just what we can generate with the solar panels and windmills plus the gas generator. We don't have running water. There are no schools. There are no other kids to play with."

"Is Kim pushing you to sell?"

"She isn't nagging me to move back to the States. It's just that every time we visit family, or they come here, or guests with kids arrive, I can tell she's ready to have one or two of her own. She can hear her biological clock. 'Tick-tock, tick-tock.'"

"Are you up for becoming a father again?" he asked.

"Again? You know about my first family?" I'd never talked with him about them.

"Carey told me about them many years ago. Not much. Just that you were married and had a son and that you lost them both in some kind of accident. I've always wanted to ask you about them but since you don't talk about them I figured you didn't want to."

"Carey knew her. He went to school with me at the University of Texas in Austin and was best man at our wedding. That's before he went off and turned windsurfing into a competitive sport."

"He didn't tell me much, but that brings me back to the question. Are you ready to be a parent again?"

"Yeah, but I'm getting old—at least for starting a family. I'm fifty-three years old. If Kim and I had a kid today I'd be sixty-nine when he got his driver's license, seventy-one when he graduated from high school. If we're going to start a family, it's got to be soon."

We walked northward as he checked each cabana. I made a mental note at Cabana Number Eight to have one of the maintenance guys fix a hole in the thatched roof over the porch. I made another note at Cabana Six to have the wooden shutters adjusted.

"George, I've got to make the trip into Belize City with this past week's guests. I'm off until next Saturday."

I could see a pod of dolphins, a few hundred yards off shore, making their way north along the barrier reef.

"Look, George, I'll give it some thought while I'm in town this week. I'm interested in buying Mountain To Sea, but I don't know if I can raise the money."

"You get the first chance to buy. I figure we've been friends too long not to give you that."

"Thanks."

"Sticks, with your permission, I'd like to talk with Beth when she gets here. She and Mike may be interested in buying Over The Edge."

"Yeah, that would make sense. The dive operation really ought to be run by a dive instructor."

I trudged back to my place on the Over The Edge side of the island, enjoying the gentle breeze coming in from the west. As I walked into our cabana I saw my reflection in the mirror. I loved this island, even as rough as the living conditions can be. I loved diving every day. Heck, I loved the way I lived. For a fifty-three-year-old man, I was pretty fit. The activity of island life and a diet of mostly seafood and root vegetables had kept me thin and fit.

I closed my eyes for a moment, only to see the same visions that have haunted me since I started thinking about having kids: the ghosts of my first family.

I opened my eyes and asked my reflection: "Okay, I've talked with Sticks. So, why do I still have this sense of dread?"

With no answer from the mirror, I headed down to the dock to greet the new guests.

Chapter 3

Saturday, December 23rd, 11:00 A.M.

Mountain To Sea, the larger resort on Sunrise Caye, had a dozen guests the past week. They'd already had an early lunch and now were milling about the island, just waiting for the ship to take them back to Belize City. A couple of guests, a young couple on their honeymoon, criss-crossed the lagoon on a pair of windsurf boards in an attempt to get every minute of their vacation in as possible.

The next group of Mountain To Sea's Island Week guests was on the *Tropical Breeze*. I saw the ship, now less than a quarter of a mile away, cautiously weaving through the last of the coral heads. Sunrise Caye was part of Glover's Reef Atoll, a collection of eight-hundred small coral heads off the coast of Belize, what in my youth was known as British Honduras. It's a Caribbean paradise, located south of Mexico and north of Honduras. My eco-friendly resorts, Mountain To Sea and Over The Edge Dive Shop and Resort, are on Sunrise Caye.

According to my manifest, the *Tropical Breeze* carried twenty-four new guests for Mountain To Sea, four more guides, a few more employees to relieve the ones that wanted to go home for the Christmas holiday, and Beth Sodd, one of my dive instructors.

The *Tropical Breeze* crew brought the fifty-foot cabin cruiser in easily, gently touching the dock. I leapt over the side rail and onto the ship's stern. Glancing over the guests, I wondered what kind of week we were in for.

About two-thirds of the guests were upper middle-class couples in their late forties or early fifties; usually there was at least one lawyer in the bunch. About half of the remaining third included younger couples, in their early to mid-thirties and on their honeymoons. The rest would be single travelers—for some reason there were often sisters—out for an adventure. Most were physically fit; however, there were a couple of overweight guests that would struggle with the demands of Mountain To Sea's activities. There were two young girls, the younger one playing with a doll and talking to a woman I assumed was her mother. The older girl leaned over the boat rail and stared at the fish. Both girls had shoulder-length blonde hair, like their mother's. I couldn't help but think of Jan and Cindy Brady. The younger girl even had the curls.

Oh well, time to introduce myself and get this started.

"Could I have everyone's attention?" I waited a few seconds and tried again. "Please, can I have your attention?"

The voices dropped off and most of the people looked at me. The ship's crew and Mountain To Sea staff shuffled toward the front of the boat and greeted the staff already on the island. The older girl stared intensely into the water.

"I'm George Schroeder. Welcome to my island. Here on the island they call me 'King George.' I think the people working for me came up with that because of my regal bearing. Either that or they think I'm a royal pain in the …well, never mind where. My wife, Kim, and I started the dive shop. It's called Over The Edge Dive Shop and Resort and we're located in that blue building at the end of the other dock over there." I pointed to the only other functional dock on the island. All of the adults turned their gaze toward my place for a few moments and turned back to me.

The older girl pointed to something in the water, and her little sister climbed up on the rail to see it and sat back down with her doll.

"We need to unload the boat quickly so the folks leaving can load it and get underway. What we've found works best is for you to form a chain and pass the bags and other stuff down the chain rather than each person picking something up and carrying it to the end of the dock."

A couple of the younger guys stood up. One climbed onto the dock and the other started picking through bags and handed one up to the first. The women all climbed out of the boat, leaving the men to lift all of the cargo.

"At the end of the dock are two concrete pads. Everything coming off the boat has to go on the pad to the left. You'll notice a pile of stuff already on the pad to the right. That stuff is going out with the guests leaving today. If you put something on that other pile you won't see it again—at least not until next week when you go back to the mainland. Alright, let's get started," I said.

They climbed out of the ship and stepped down onto the dock. They formed a very loose chain down the dock and passed the smaller, lighter stuff down. As always, there were a few people who would take their own bags to the end of the dock. Heavy bags and the crates holding beverages usually got the same treatment.

One of the younger guys, in his early thirties, carried a crate full of beer down the dock and walked back toward the boat, empty-handed. He stood still, on the edge of the narrow dock, to make room for a heavy set guy who looked to be in his early thirties too, with a duffle bag.

"Get out of the way," the heavier guy grunted, bumping his duffle against the thinner guy, sending him into the waist-deep water.

The thinner guy ran to the beach and shoved him, toppling him over. "What the hell's wrong with you?"

I watched as Vince "Gator" Pauletti, this week's lead guide, jumped in between them, holding the thinner guy back. "Dave, let it go. Kevin, you too, just let it go." Gator was built much like Sticks but not as tall, perhaps five foot eight. He had longer, black hair. Muscular, perhaps wiry was a better term. He was also seven or eight years younger than

Sticks. He'd been working here for six seasons, ever since he graduat-ed from the University of Florida where he'd be a solid, second-place finisher on their track team.

The one called Dave glared at the other guy, Kevin, but shook it off and went back to unloading the boat. Kevin, the guy with the duffle, got up, put his duffle on the pad with the rest of the stuff, and sat on one of the beach chairs.

❧❖☙

It took about twenty minutes to unload the boat. When the boat was unloaded I checked it once for items left behind before gathering up the new guests. I glanced over the rail to see what the two girls had been looking at. I saw a starfish. We don't have many of them around here.

"Alright, well, that could have gone a little more smoothly. What we're going to do now is take a tour of the island. While we're doing that the guests who are leaving will load the boat with their gear. Your stuff is safe where it is. Please follow me."

Dave, the thinner guy, was taking a little ribbing from his buddy. I had a feeling I'd have to keep an eye on Dave and Kevin. I'd think people that can afford to spend a couple of grand for a week here, not counting their transportation costs between the States and Belize City, could behave like grown-ups.

❧❖☙

I motioned for everyone to follow me. I sauntered sixty yards and stopped in front of Mountain To Sea's bathroom.

"Mountain To Sea and Over The Edge are eco-friendly resorts. We're on the outer edges of the world's second largest barrier reef. With that in mind, we do everything we can to protect the natural resources." They gathered in a loose circle, jockeying for a good look at me and the structure behind me.

"This is our pride and joy. I've been on the cover of *Outside* magazine with this. It's our composting toilet. The process doesn't really like ammonia. That can't be avoided for the women, but, men, there is a saying here—'Pee into the sea.' Seriously, you men, if all you need to do is whiz, please just go into the sea or behind a tree."

The two little girls giggled. They weren't alone.

"At the top of the stairs are a couple of stalls. It's a two-holer, but fortunately not an Aggie two-holer."

"What's an Aggie two-holer?" someone asked.

"I take it you're not a Texan. An Aggie, as in someone from Texas A&M University, two-holer is sort of like bunk beds. One stall is above the other. You don't want to be in the lower bunk." A couple of people laughed, politely. *Guess I'll never make it as a comedian.*

One of the middle-aged women turned to another, nodded her head toward two men, and softly said "What have they gotten us into?" I pretended not to hear.

"You'll notice a light switch at the top of the stairs. We don't have commercial electric power here. What we have are solar cells that feed batteries. There's not enough capacity in the batteries to light up the bathroom all night, so please remember to flip the switch when you're done using the facility."

Right about that time Lucky came by. The little girl saw Lucky. "Look, Mommy, a bunny!" and she bent down, calling the rabbit.

"That's Lucky. She belongs to, well, everyone here. She likes people, especially around meal time."

"She's big!" The girl had Lucky in her hands and was struggling to pick her up.

The girl's father knelt down and picked up Lucky, letting the girl pet her. "She's pretty well-fed, that's for sure. George, are rabbits native to the islands?"

"No, she's the only one here. One of the Mountain To Sea guides last season saw her in a market in Belize City. When she realized Lucky was being sold as food, and not as a pet, she opened her fanny pack and brought her out here. Lucky for Lucky, there aren't any predators out here. We have a couple of cats on the island now, too." The two girls were taking turns petting Lucky.

I led the group eastward along one of the conch shell-lined trails across the island, pointing out the walkways leading to Over The Edge's part of the island as we walked, and I showed them where Mountain To Sea's Adventure Week guests stayed. As we walked beneath the canopy of palm trees the breeze rattled the leaves. A coconut fell to the ground, startling a couple of the closest guests.

I could hear some of the staff members at Over The Edge, their voices muffled by the trees and distance. I got a whiff of our lunch: grilled chicken with freshly made salsa.

"Most weeks, the Adventure Week guests come out here on Wednesday and they sleep in tents on these raised platforms. All of you in the Island Week group get cabanas. There isn't an Adventure Week group this week," I said.

We continued walking east from the Adventure Week tent area and came to a trail along the open-ocean side of the island. A rock, actually coral, wall separated the trail from the ocean. Three big iguanas lay on the wall, basking in the sun's warmth. The iguanas didn't move. They weren't very skittish. You'd have to get within a foot or so for them to move away. The new guests gasped as they took in the immenseness of the Caribbean and the changes in water color.

"George, why are there these changes in color? I mean, we've got crystal-clear water here near the shore and then there's a turquoise streak, then dark blue." This question came from one of the younger guys. I guessed him to be about five foot, ten inches tall; a few inches shorter than me. He wore a pair of khaki shorts and an olive green t-shirt revealing well-defined muscles. With his crew-cut he belonged on a recruiting poster for the Army or Marines.

"I'll answer that in a moment. I'll ask each of you to introduce yourselves over lunch, and probably again at dinner tonight too, but may I ask you each to introduce yourselves when you ask a question."

"Sure. I'm Jack, by the way."

"Jack, that's a good question. The difference is water depth and vegetation. In close, the water is mere inches deep, maybe three feet or so. The turquoise ranges from three feet to about thirty-five or forty feet. The Wall is that line where the color changes to dark blue."

"The Wall? It's that close?" Jack asked.

"It takes our dive boats about two minutes to get to those buoys you see. They mark dive sites. The one straight out from you is Sunrise Caye Wall. Further down to your right you can see a buoy for one of our beginner's level dive sites, Beth's Garden. Y'all met Beth on the boat ride out here. The Wall is just that, a nearly three-thousand foot drop.

"Over here is the shower area. We use collected rain water for showers. This is fresh water, but it's not filtered. It's fine for showering. It's probably not fit to drink. We have bottled water and filtered rain water in the dining hall for you to drink. You should probably use the filtered or bottled water for brushing your teeth too."

We were still close to the shore and their attention was drawn to the rippling water. There was a lot of splashing.

"That was probably a school of jacks, going after some shad for lunch," I said.

"Next we come to the individual cabanas. They're numbered with the one closest to the showers being number Twenty-three and the one closest to the dining hall being Cabana One. There are fifteen steps from the ground to the porches, putting the floors about ten feet up. We have railings but you should be careful. You don't want to fall off."

"Listen to that surf," one of the younger women said. She was about five foot, four inches tall. She was a little pudgy, maybe one hundred and forty pounds. She had long blonde hair, worn straight.

"And look at the waves crashing on the rocks!" her husband, Jack, replied.

"Not rocks, the reef. We're still on the barrier reef. Belize has the second largest barrier reef in the world, second only to the Great Barrier Reef off Australia."

"George, what is that island out there?" Jack pointed across the break in the barrier.

"That's Tradewind Caye. There's a resort on that island, a very primitive one."

"Primitive? Isn't that the pot calling the kettle black?" said one of the older women.

"We're a five-star resort in comparison. They don't provide cabanas. They don't provide much of anything. Their guests are required to bring their own drinking water and food, tents and sleeping bags, basically everything they'll need. The owners don't offer diving, but guests there can snorkel and the resort does have a handful of kayaks. We often get their guests kayaking over here hoping to buy food or water."

"Oh my, why would anyone want to do that?"

"They advertise pretty heavily—especially in travel magazines in Europe—so most of their guests are European. Most of the guests there are really young, teenagers or early twenties. The owners are French and spend most of their time on that big catamaran you see anchored a little offshore. And they're cheap, about seven-hundred dollars US per week. But you get what you pay for, I guess."

The older of the two girls pointed beyond Tradewind Caye. "Is that a ship out there?"

To see it, I had to squint and hold my hand up to my forehead to shade my eyes from the blinding sun. The other guests took similar positions as they scanned the sea.

"You have really good eyesight!" I said.

She smiled.

"That looks like one of the cruise ships heading out from Belize City. We see them, and we see a cargo ship or two, almost every day. You can see them better at night because they're really well lit. Sometimes they're almost spooky, especially in foggy conditions. Kind of like pirate ships." I looked at the littlest girl. "Do you know what pirates are?"

"Uh huh," she said, nodding. "Like Captain Hook in *Peter Pan*!"

"A long time ago there were pirates around here. This whole area is called Glover's Reef. John Glover was a famous pirate that sailed these waters."

"Daddy! You didn't say there'd be pirates here. I want to go home." She began to sniffle as she buried her face in her father's leg.

Her father picked her up. "Katie, that was a long, long time ago. Before even your grandpa and his grandpa were born. There aren't any pirates here anymore."

"I didn't mean to scare you. I was just hoping you'd help me look for their buried treasure." *Man, sometimes I really step in it.*

The sniffles stopped. "Buried treasure?"

"Yeah, pirates always had, or were looking for, buried treasure. Maybe there's some here. Will you help me look for it while you're here?"

"Do you have a map?"

I couldn't help but laugh a little. "Maybe Santa Claus will bring us one." I turned to the rest of the group thinking Kim and I could have a lot of fun with these two kids this week.

We arrived at the dining hall. "If you look out that way you can see the hammock palapa. That's a great place to spend the late afternoon, especially if we have a breeze from the northwest like we do today. Beyond that is the kayak palapa. I'll let Gator talk with you more about the kayaks and other toys later."

"Can we go swimming now, Mommy?" the little girl asked.

"Not yet, honey. Maybe after lunch we can go swimming. Are you hungry?"

"I'm starving," she said. Several people laughed, and added "Me too's."

"A little bit of advice before I finish: drink lots of water while you're out here so you don't get dehydrated or constipated. If you have any illnesses or injuries, please let one of the guides know. They each have some basic medical training and have a first-aid kit. By the way, do we have any doctors or nurses with you?"

Most trips have at least one doctor, in addition to a lawyer or two. Mountain To Sea's trips were not cheap but no hands went up.

"If you're going into the water, please do so from the lagoon side. The island is made of coral and—especially on the open-sea side of the island—the waves knock you onto the coral and you'll get cut up. If there's something more serious, someone will notify me."

Dave asked, "Do you have more medical training than they do?"

"Yes, sir, in a past life I was a dentist in El Paso."

"That's a hell of a career change!"

"And one that's made me extremely happy. The barracudas and sharks might have sharper teeth but their breath doesn't stink near as much as some of my past patients. Anyway, it looks like it's lunch time. I'll let Gator introduce our chef."

Chapter 4
Saturday, December 23rd, 12:30 P.M.

With the guests at Mountain To Sea getting fed lunch and settling into their cabanas I walked to my cabana at Over The Edge. Back when Carey and Lacy still owned Mountain To Sea they didn't offer diving, only sea kayaking and wind surfing. Over The Edge didn't offer sea kayaking or wind surfing. Mountain To Sea guests that wanted to dive could walk down the beach to my place and we'd sell dive packages and training. I still operate the two resorts as separate businesses.

I woke up from a short, fitful, nap as our largest boat, the *Sensencula*, pulled up to our dock. Early this morning Kim had gone into Dangriga, a small town on the Belize coast, to pick up guests we'd be hosting this week at Over The Edge and to pick up supplies for our resort. Among the three guests she picked up were Terri and Joe Wright, a retired couple from Sioux Falls, who were spending the winter traveling through the Caribbean. From their earlier emails, they came here from Cancun and would be going to Honduras next.

The third guest was a repeat for us. Larry Carlson, a forty-five year old computer guy from Texas, had been here three times at Mountain To Sea and this was his second time with Over The Edge. On his first trip at Mountain To Sea he'd planned on just taking the resort course and making one or two dives. He wound up getting his PADI Open Water certification by the end of the week. Last year we put him through the Advanced Open Water certification class.

I walked down the dock and helped Terri and Joe climb out of the boat. Larry helped Jeremy, my boat captain, and Marcus, one of my dive masters, unload the boat before climbing up onto the dock. We shook hands.

"Man, it's great to see you, George. I miss this place."

"Larry, it's really good to have you back too. You look like you've lost some weight."

"I have. I've lost a little over fifty pounds since I was here last year," he said with a smile.

"That's great! So, how many dives can we put you down for?" I already knew. Larry loved the island and loved diving. Even having lost fifty pounds he was still significantly overweight. Judging from past trips he didn't have the energy to make a lot of dives. He typically made one, or at most two, dives a day and spent the rest of the day hammock surfing.

"Well, I signed up for the six-dive package but we'll see." He looked past me. "So, who's that?"

I followed his gaze. "Ah, that's Misty. She's one of the dive instructors here this season." Misty, wearing a pair of tight-fitting shorts and a t-shirt, was rinsing dive gear at the base of the stairs to my office. Her long dark hair hid the tattoo on her neck but the ones on her tanned legs were on view.

"Is Beth here this week?" He asked a little too anxiously, but we all knew he had the hots for Beth, and he knew she was happily married.

"She's here too. Actually, she just arrived on the Mountain To Sea boat a couple of hours ago. This is her first trip of the season. She came a week earlier than planned when she heard you were coming." I lied, but he'd get an ego boost out of it and that might get him to make a couple more dives. "But let me introduce you to Misty."

After introducing everyone I turned to Kim. The direct sunlight tinted her normally bronze hair a fiery, coppery red. "Honey, have you assigned them cabanas yet?" I asked.

"I have. Larry, you're in the White House again this year. Terri and Joe, you are in the Blue House. Larry, you know where your place is already. Do you need any help with your bags?"

"Nah, I can handle them. Thanks."

"In that case, Marcus, can you help the Wrights with their bags? Terri, Joe, if you'll follow me I'll show you around."

"You know, we've got plenty of time to get a dive in this afternoon," I said. I wanted to get Larry in the water as quickly as possible. His first few dives were always kind of shaky.

"I haven't made a dive in about six months, so someplace easy would be best," Larry.

"How about an hour from now?" I asked. "Beth's still unpacking but I'm sure Misty and Marcus are ready."

"That works for me." Misty was always ready to make a dive. She smiled at Larry, encouraging him.

"I'll bring my gear down in a few minutes and get it set up." At that, Larry set off for his cabana, dragging two heavy bags through the sand.

"Joe, Terri, how about you? Ready for a dive?" I asked.

"Sure. Our certification cards are packed away, and we've got some gear of our own: regulators and dive computers, fins and masks, but we'll need to rent vests and tanks," Joe said.

"No problem, Joe. Just bring your gear and your C-cards. We'll have some paperwork for you to complete first." Even in paradise, you can't get away from paperwork. We have to provide copies of our guests' passports to the government, along with Belize's hotel and resort taxes for each guest. For divers, we have to have the guest's certification number as well, along with some medical stuff, to satisfy our insurers.

⚜

The three of them were all suited up and ready to go in less than an hour. I watched from the porch of my cabana as Marcus and Larry went over Larry's gear.

"This is very nice equipment you have," Marcus said as he inspect-ed Larry's buoyancy compensator. The "BC" is what non-divers would think of as a vest.

"Thanks. The day after I got home from my first trip here, I guess that was four years ago now, I went out and bought the best I could afford."

"Why did you get the integrated weight pouches?"

He smiled shyly. "Well, as you probably have noticed, I'm fat. During that first trip here, when Beth and George taught me to dive, I wasted a lot of my time, and my air, because I was struggling with the weight belt."

"What kinds of problems?" Marcus asked.

"It would keep sliding down, off my belly and onto my legs. I think that had a lot to do with my buoyancy troubles that week and why I sucked down so much more air than anyone else," Larry replied.

"I am seeing more of our guests with these integrated pouches. I like how they slide into pockets on either side of the vest and snap into place. That way they stay put." Marcus pulled on one of the pouches, demonstrating that it stayed in place.

I consider them an extravagance, but if the integrated pouches helped Larry feel more comfortable in the water, well, that meant he'd spend more money on more dives. He enjoyed himself more and I made more money. I think that's known as a "win-win."

While Marcus set up everyone else's gear, Misty reviewed the dive plan.

"We're going to take it easy this first trip. We'll go around the south end of the island," she said, pointing in the direction the boat would travel, "and right after we pass through the break in the reef we'll head back north a few hundred yards. Joe and Terri, right out from your cabana is the buoy for Beth's Garden. That's the name of the dive site where we're going," Misty said.

"How deep is it?"Terri asked. Larry was on his back, floating in the water, trying to get comfortable and get the air bubbles out of his suit.

Misty looked at Terri and replied, "At the buoy, it's about thirty-five feet to the bottom. When we're down I'll give you a few seconds to adjust your buoyancy and check with each of you to make sure you're comfortable." She looked at each diver, making sure she had their attention.

Larry looked up, gave an "okay" sign, and put some anti-fogging drops into his mask. As he rinsed out the mask he smiled. "Beth's Garden is probably the perfect first dive. Not too deep and reasonably sheltered from the wind."

Larry hated floating on the surface, regardless of how gentle the waves were. He'd never learned to breathe through the snorkel and even gentle swells made him uncomfortable. Once he gets down ten feet or so he calms down.

"We'll take it easy, but in a minute or two we'll swim over the edge of the wall. We'll drop down a bit. For this dive, let's stay above sixty feet. We'll just drift with the current." Misty made sure to make eye contact with each of her charges, looking for confirmation they understood her.

"What about the boat? Does it come back in?"Terri asked, sounding a little nervous.

"No, Jeremy will stay out there. He's great at following our bubbles. When we come up, he'll be real close by," Misty said.

"That's good to hear. We had a bad experience with someone in Mexico last year."

"Well, don't worry about that here. Jeremy's the best," Misty said.

I waved as the boat pulled away from the dock, hoping Larry's first dive went well. The better his first dive went the better the rest of the week would go. Misty stood on the bow of the boat as it picked up speed, her long brown hair blowing in the breeze behind her. That image, the silhouette, would make a great ad in some dive magazine, but Kim kept telling me the cost of advertising in one of them wasn't worth it for our place. I trusted her judgment on company finances.

✖

They'd been gone about twenty minutes and I stood knee deep in the lagoon, doing some maintenance on the *Sensencula's* outboards, when Beth walked onto the dock, her short, curly hair bouncing. As long as I've known her she'd worn her blonde hair long, down to her shoulder blades.

"So, what's with the new hairstyle?" I asked.

"Oh, I was just ready for a change. I'm hoping it'll be easier to keep clean out here. Do you like it?" she asked.

I was having some trouble getting used to this new, shorter style but wisely said, "Yeah, I do. But how does Mike like it?"

"He's getting used to it. I cut it like this a month ago but it took him three days to notice. Men, you're all pigs." She laughed.

"But for some reason, you women like us anyway." We both laughed, knowing we'd had this discussion before.

"So, how has Misty worked out?" Beth leaned against one of the posts supporting our welcome sign.

"She's done a pretty good job. She trained a couple of dozen Mountain To Sea guests, as well as a couple of ours. The guys all like her, almost as much as you. It took her a while to get used to the Garifunda that the locals speak, and they still make fun of her at times. Would you please hand me that screwdriver?"

She stretched, waved at a couple of the Mountain To Sea guides leading their guests back from a snorkel trip, and handed me the screwdriver. I counted heads. Both of the kids were there but someone was missing. Since I hadn't counted heads as they left and Gator wasn't giving an indication of a problem I ignored it, thinking that maybe one of the adults wasn't feeling well.

"She told me she's leaving after this week. Any particular reason why?" Beth asked.

"Well, what she said is that she's ready for something different. She wants to see another part of the world. I guess paradise isn't enough. She said she has a job lined up in Indonesia, at one of the dive resorts there." I put the covers back on the outboards and pulled myself up over the edge of the boat, tumbling in.

I put the keys into the ignition switches. "But Kim doesn't think that's it," I added.

"What does Kim think?"

"Kim thinks Misty's lonely. Not enough guys out here for her." I turned one key and the right engine coughed, then started.

"There aren't a lot of them to choose from, at least among the staff. Then again, they're all young, muscular guys, and they're all single." She shouted to be heard over the second motor as it sputtered to life and she wandered off toward the Mountain To Sea dining hall to catch up with friends.

Beth, a native of Austin but year-round resident of Utah, spent every summer and fall in the States with her husband leading white water rafting trips in the Grand Canyon. Beth was in her late forties or early fifties. She hadn't aged in the ten years I'd known her. She still looked the part of the stereotypical Austin blonde, long legs, blue eyes, and what some of us used to refer to as "great hands." She was beautiful, to be sure. Nothing close to Kim, mind you, but I understood why so many of the guys that come here ask about her.

The dive boat was coming in. Kim walked out to the dock, handed me a beer, and waved at the boat. I watched a small southern stingray pass under the dock, looking for a snack.

As the boat pulled up on the other side of the dock from me Marcus was grinning. He'd been with us for three seasons now. Belizeans were not known for being quiet, or shy, but Marcus was about as reserved as any native I've known. He'd taken on the responsibility of maintaining all of my dive gear, and was very thorough, very detail-oriented. That wasn't a trait common in Belize.

"Marcus, what's that I see? A smile? A real, honest-to-God grin?" I asked. I took a long swallow from the Belikin bottle and stepped up onto the dock.

"Larry, show George what you found."

Larry looked up, poker-faced, and handed me a weight pouch, and then another.

I took them from him, not thinking anything of it except they had a lot of lead in them. Then he handed me another, identical weight pouch. It was covered in sand, and a few coral polyps were growing on it.

"You found another weight pouch? Wait, is this the one you lost out here last year?" I asked.

Larry yelped, "Hey, I didn't lose it. Jeremy did. He's the one that dropped it."

"No, sir," Jeremy, our boat captain, insisted. "You let it slip out of your hands before I touched it."

I remembered that dive. We'd done one of the underwater navigation tests for the advanced certification Larry was going for. When we came up he handed a weight pouch to Jeremy, but it slipped. I dove back down to look for it. We were in only about twenty feet of water but I hadn't been able to find it.

Jeremy had worked for me since I opened Over The Edge twelve years ago. He was born and raised in the waters along the barrier reef. He was in his late forties, thin, with short but graying hair.

I turned to Terri, extending my hand to help her out of the boat. "How was your dive?"

"I haven't made a dive in almost a year. I had some problems with my mask letting in water. But the view was just gorgeous."

"I'm sorry to hear you had problems with your mask. Is it a new one?"

"No, but I haven't used it in a while," she answered.

"How about you and Misty spend some time later figuring out what's wrong? We don't sell masks, but we might have a few around you can try."

Misty looked up, stopped disconnecting the scuba tanks, and said, "I might know what the problem is. I saw that you were usually exhaling from your nose, not from your mouth. When you'd exhale the lower part of the mask would pull out from your face as the air went through. That lets the water in."

"What should I do?"

"First, exhale through your mouth. Let the air go through your regulator, and if necessary, around it. You can also wear the mask strap lower on the back of your head. That will hold it tighter."

"I'll have to try that. The dive was just beautiful. When I was near the top of the wall, I was surrounded by these blue fish."

I said, "We call that 'a river of wrasse.' There are thousands of them, going somewhere together."

"It's amazing. They're so beautiful."

"I agree, it's always amazing to have that river of deep, almost cobalt blue surround me on a dive. That said, and not that I'm hungry or anything, but how do they taste?" Larry asked as he looked my way.

"I don't know about wrasse, but Annette is here this week and she's making your favorite dinner: fried grouper. It's almost time to eat. You've got time for a quick shower and to change clothes. Marcus and Misty will take care of your gear." I watched as the three of them left for their respective cabanas.

Chapter 5

Saturday, December 23rd, 5:15 P.M.

I walked down to Mountain To Sea. The 5:00 volleyball game was underway and the teams were evenly matched. Between points I got Gator's attention.

"Gator, I saw everyone coming back from the snorkel trip. When I counted heads I thought there was one short. All okay?" I asked.

"Yeah, boss. I didn't lose anyone. Antonio, the guy over there with the Hawaiian shirt, doesn't want to snorkel. He spent the afternoon on a hammock reading. Want to get in on the next game?" He pointed to a group standing near the dining hall doorway where there was one guy in a Hawaiian print shirt, completely buttoned down and tucked into a pair of white shorts.

"I don't think so. Tomorrow, for sure though."

I went into the dining hall and mingled with the crowd and checked in with Felicia, the Mountain To Sea cook. She had a creole snapper dinner going and a freshly made mango salsa. I sampled the conch fritters she put out on a dining table for snacks. Good, I thought, but not quite as good as Annette's.

One volleyball game ended and the players took a break to get a drink. I watched as Kevin bulldozed his way through a few people standing in the doorway. "Out of my way," he said, gruffly. He charged into the dining hall, got a beer out of the cooler, opened it, and chugged it down. He tossed the empty bottle into a trash can instead of putting it into the recycle rack and charged back out, shoving another guest to make room.

"Hey, knock it off," the guest, Antonio, said. His own drink got spilled.

"Then get out of the way, old man." Kevin gave him the finger.

Antonio looked at another man, one with whom he'd been talking, shook his head, and said, "There are jerks everywhere, I guess. You'd think someone who could afford a vacation spot like this would have some manners."

"Money doesn't equal class, I guess," the other man said.

I don't think Kevin heard their exchange. I eased my way through the group standing and sitting on the stairs and waited for the point to finish.

"Hey, Kevin, come here for a minute," I said.

I led him a few steps away from the court, toward the beach and away from the others. "Kevin, you're not the only guest here. You need to control your temper."

"What are you talking about?"

"I saw you push Antonio."

"So? He shouldn't stand there, blocking the path."

"Maybe so, but I don't appreciate seeing you flip him the bird either."

"Then don't watch."

"Everyone's here for a good time. If you're going to stop others from having fun I can send you packing. Got it? And the next time I see you give anyone the finger I'll break it." I hate having to be the heavy but some people just don't understand the basics of civility. I remember an uncle asking me once, when I was little, "ain't you got no couth, boy?" Apparently Kevin lacks it.

❧❦❧

I walked back to Over The Edge. Annette let me know that dinner was ready so I blew the dinner horn, a well-polished conch shell that emits a unique, low bass sound which can be heard all over the island. I blew the horn, instead of ringing a dinner bell, for each meal. Mountain To Sea uses an old west style dinner bell to let their guests know its mealtime. We sometimes have little kids here at Over The Edge and I'd usually have to teach them how to blow into the shell and let them call everyone to dinner. I grabbed another beer and headed for the dining hall where I found a couple of people already waiting.

"Hi, Erin. How you've been doing today?" I asked.

"It's been a productive day," she said, gathering up several dozen sheets of paper and closing her laptop. I sat across from her, wrapped my beer bottle in some napkins so I wouldn't leave a moisture ring that might damage her papers.

"Are you going to make your deadline?"

"Oh, I think so. I'm mostly doing some editing, trying to double-check my continuity. You know, making sure the character I called Ricky in one chapter isn't called Ricardo in another. This is probably the eleventh draft."

"I'm not familiar with the process of writing books. I barely even read them. Do you have an agent already?"

"I do. I wrote for *The Village Voice* for more than twenty years before editing it for the past dozen years. I had a book deal before I started writing."

I'd been wondering how she and Larry, a somewhat vocal conservative, were going to get along. I was about to find out.

"Larry, pull up a spot on the bench. I've got someone for you to meet."

He sat down next to me and surveyed the quantity of papers, a notebook, and Erin's laptop. "Hi, I'm Larry Carlson."

"I'm Erin, Erin Walker."

"Erin is a writer. She's been here a little over a week, working on a book," I said, taking another slug from the beer.

"Oh yeah? What kind of book?"

"It's a murder-mystery, with a bit of techno-thriller in it," Erin said.

"Set here?" Larry asked.

"No," Erin grinned. "It's set in Bosnia. I spent a few years there covering the peacekeeping mission."

"Erin, are you a reporter?" Larry asked.

"I was. I worked for *The Village Voice* as an international war correspondent."

"That's interesting. I'm not real familiar with that publication. It's got a pretty liberal slant, doesn't it?"

"Some people think so. Those of us with the voice think we're neutral," Erin replied.

"Sorry. I get most of my news from TV and the local newspapers."

"Tell me, Larry, which papers are local to you?"

"I live near Fort Worth. When I'm hope I read the *Dallas Morning News* and the Fort Worth *Star-Telegram*. I spend a lot of my time working in Chicago and there I read both *Tribune* and *Sun-Times*."

"Two papers? That's a bit unusual."

"Yeah, well, so am I, although I prefer the term 'abnormal.'"

"You mean like 'Abbie Normal'?"

"Exactly! But not everyone catches the *Young Frankenstein* reference." Larry took another sip of his beer.

"And you say you read two papers every day?"

"Yeah, I'm a conservative in most of my politics but I like to get multiple views. It used to be that Dallas had two newspapers and the *Dallas Morning News* was the more liberally slanted one while the *Star-Telegram* was more conservative. The other Dallas paper folded and the Fort Worth paper changed ownership. Today they're both kind of in the middle. Still, I like getting different views from different columnists. Plus, they have different comic strips." Larry grinned on that last note.

"Do you get different views on TV too?"

"Not really. I watch Fox News and occasionally CNN for national news and commentary. I think Fox does a fair job of balancing views from conservatives and liberals. I really can't stand some of the people on the other cable channels, especially those imbeciles on MSNBC."

"Would I be correct in saying you're a Rush Limbaugh fan?" Erin asked.

"No, actually I'm not. I don't hate him, or Beck or Hannity or any of the others for that matter, but he tends to be too partisan for me."

"Too partisan?"

"Yeah, Republicans don't screw-up in his world. They do pretty often in the real one. Democrats can't do anything right in his world. They sometimes do in the real world—usually by accident, I think." He took another drink from his beer.

I think Erin was about to say something when Beth walked in with another staff member, Dylan. Larry turned to Erin and asked, "Would you excuse me for a minute?" Without waiting for an answer he walked over to Beth with his arms wide open. They hugged briefly.

"Larry, have you met Dylan yet?" Beth asked, breaking their embrace.

He reached out a hand. "No. Hi, I'm Larry Carlson."

"I'm Dylan Bellamy."

"Is this your first season here?" Larry asked.

"Yeah, I got here about two months ago," he said as the three of them sat down at one of the tables.

"I referred Dylan to George a few months ago. Dylan used to be a park ranger in the Grand Canyon. Mike and I had to work with Dylan to clear our white-water rafting trips. You know, there's government paperwork in every job," Beth said.

"I've got a brother that's a park ranger in Maryland. They lived up in the mountains for years and always took their vacations at the beach."

"There's a comic, Steven Wright, that used to ask 'where do park rangers go to get away from it all?' For a lot of us, it's the beach."

"But Dylan's leaving here in a few weeks. He's going to take a permanent job with a resort in the U.S. Virgin Islands," Beth added.

"Too much excitement here for you?" Larry joked.

"I've had enough excitement for a while. Law enforcement in the Grand Canyon can be pretty scary. There are a lot of idiots with guns out there."

"When my brother worked in the state parks, the ones in the mountains of western Maryland, he did a lot of law enforcement. He spent a lot of nights looking for poachers and spot-lighters."

"Yeah, I've done that too. It's dangerous work."

"I remember calling him and my nephew answering the phone. Donny was maybe five then? Anyway, he'd say 'My daddy shot someone last night.' I asked my brother about it. It wasn't a frequent occurrence, but often enough," Larry said.

"Yeah, spot-lighters are out at night and shine a spotlight on their prey. Most animals freeze when the light shines on them. You do the same thing to the spot-lighter."

"Right, and yell freeze and they freak out. From what my brother would tell me, they're armed, and usually drunk. They respond by shooting at whatever spooked them in the first place," Larry said.

Dylan stood. "That's the kind of excitement I've had enough of. I've had a few experiences like that."

"Are there a lot of poachers in the Grand Canyon? I didn't think there was much game there."

"There's plenty of game, mostly elk and deer. But there are also a lot of illegal aliens traversing the park now. Some are led by armed escorts, known as coyotes, and are just trying to find a better life. Some are drug runners and they're too well armed."

"You've had encounters with the drug runners?"

"A while back one of my buddies got shot after stumbling across some smugglers. He shot back and managed to kill one of the guys and then the local district attorney started talking about prosecuting him, not the drug smugglers, for using excessive force. On my last encounter I ran into a group using fully automatic weapons. I was out there with a sidearm and a hunting rifle. I've had enough."

Larry just sat there, taking it in.

"Anyway, I've got to check the fuel supply for the generators. With Erin spending a lot of time on her computer we've been running the generator more than usual. Then I'll get another beer. Do either of you want one?"

Larry swirled the last little bit of his Belikin Stout and said, "Sure. I'll take one."

"Me too," said Beth.

❧❖❧

I was ready for a quiet evening. I'd spent the morning on paperwork and processing—shall we say "material?"—from the composting toilets. Such are the days of life in paradise.

I took a lot of pride in our composting toilets. As a diver and resort owner it was in my interest to be as environmentally friendly as I could. A few weeks ago an agent with the Belizean Department of the Interior came out to review our facilities. He took very detailed measurements. He was going to start manufacturing kits and make this the required standard for future resorts on the cayes. Of course, he'll be the only authorized source of the kits. Corruption and monopolies were common in Belize.

❧❖❧

Shortly after our dinner that evening, Beth, Misty, and I walked down to Mountain To Sea to meet their guests. I've learned I get more interest in my Discover SCUBA class when the girls are with me. We checked in first with Gator at his cabana first.

"Hey, Gator, how's it look so far?"

"About normal, I think." He looked up at us from his cot, sat up, and waved to a spot next to him while looking at Misty. "We've got three honeymooning couples. The older couples voluntarily gave up the cabanas with double beds and took the ones with separate bunks. The two single guys each have their own cabanas—at least for now. When the Adventure Week guests arrive on Wednesday we might have to give each a roommate." Misty sat on the cot, shrugged her shoulders and tossed her hair back.

"There's no need for roommates. The Adventure Week trip was cancelled for lack of participants. Is everyone getting along alright?"

"I don't know. One of the single guys seems to be a bit of a hothead." He scratched his chin.

"I'm guessing that was Kevin?"

"Right, on the boat coming out someone—Dave Cavuto—stepped on his toes, literally, and got an earful. The last five o'clock volleyball game got a bit carried away too, and I thought he and another guy might get into a fight. But everyone seems calm for now."

"The last volleyball game? After I'd already told Kevin to control his temper?"

"I didn't hear what you said to him, but, yeah, it was after you'd left."

"Let's see if we can keep everyone peaceful. Remember, we can always send someone packing if we have to."

He grinned. "Or feed them to the sharks."

"Let's hope it doesn't come to that."

Chapter 6

Saturday, December 23rd, 6:30 P.M.

The two girls, Beth and Misty, and I left Gator's cabana and walked to the dining hall. At the first table I found three couples, all in their mid-forties or early fifties. One of the couples had two young girls with them.

"Mind if we join you?"

"Please do. George, I'm Bernie Stamps. This is my wife, Helene. These are our daughters, Michelle and Katie."

Katie, the younger one, looked up when she heard her name, smiled, and went back to feeding Lucky. I watched Beth drift off to visit with one of the Mountain To Sea guides. Misty sat down next to Katie, leaned over and picked up Lucky, placing her on the bench between herself and Katie.

"So, Bernie, where are you from?" I asked.

"Spokane. Ever been there?"

"Actually, I have been there a couple of times. Kim, my wife, is from Spokane. She used to teach art classes at Riverside Elementary. She should be coming over here in a few minutes. How about the rest of you?"

"I'm Eric White. Bernie and I work together. This is my wife, Susan."

"I take it you're from Spokane too then?"

"Yes, well, a suburb called Cheney. Susan teaches history at Eastern Washington University."

"What do you guys do?"

Bernie answered, "We're lawyers with an environmental law firm. We're working with a Belizean firm in Dangriga to stop a new resort being proposed."

Yep, lawyers. At least two of them this trip.

"Is that the big one being talked about for Placencia? I think I heard something about two thousand rooms."

"It is even bigger than that, three thousand rooms. And the developer wants to blast a huge hole in the barrier reef to allow cruise ships to come in," Bernie said.

I whistled. "Three thousand rooms? I don't think Placencia can support that."

"The developer thinks they can. The investor's willing to put a lot of money into it. He's even talking about building a larger airport so American tourists can bypass Belize City. It would mean a lot of jobs for the economy," Eric said.

Bernie frowned, or maybe it was a scowl, at Eric's response.

"Do you guys know who the owner of that proposed resort is?" I asked.

"A guy named Carlos Martinez. I don't know much about him."

"Well, Bernie, he owns several smaller resorts. He owns one on Victoria's Caye. It's about three miles south of here." I looked around for a second to get my bearings before pointing in the right direction.

"Victoria's Caye? Yeah, Gator pointed it out to us on the boat coming over. He owns that?" Bernie asked.

"One of the two resorts there, yeah. I think he has more in Honduras than in Belize. Anyway, he even has small airstrips on a couple of those."

"Does he have an airstrip on Victoria's Caye?" Susan asked.

"No, Susan, it's too small, but he recently put in a helipad. I think he charges something like $950 U.S. for four people to fly to and from Belize City. It takes about fifteen minutes to fly here."

Eric said, "That sure beats the two-and-a-half hour boat ride."

"I take it that you didn't like the boat ride." On a clear, nearly wind-free day like today it should have been quick and smooth.

"No, I didn't. It wasn't too bad. I'll admit it was a smooth ride, but it was a long one, especially without a bathroom on the boat."

I ignored that frequent complaint and said, "Anyway, Martinez is a very wealthy and politically powerful man. I'm not sure I'd want him as an adversary."

"Do you know where he got his money? I've heard stories…" Eric asked, almost whispering.

"Let's just say that in the off season for tourism there are a lot of low-flying aircraft around Victoria's Caye."

"Drugs then? That's what I've heard," Eric said, again almost a whisper, as if suggesting he'd heard Martinez was involved with drugs would make him a target.

"Honduras and Belize are convenient drop-off points for drugs being smuggled to the States. He also owns one of the biggest lumber-yards in the country. A couple of years ago, as a hurricane was heading this way, a lot of boats traveled from the cayes, his resorts in particular, to his lumberyard. The DEA found railroad cars full of drugs in the yard."

"So why isn't he in jail?" Eric asked.

"He said it must have been the night security guard. Some poor guard, probably getting ten dollars a day at the time, was sitting on tons of drugs. That guy went to jail."

"Still, a three-thousand room hotel and a new airport capable of handling international jet traffic would be a huge boost to the economy," Eric said.

I got the sense Eric wasn't as opposed to the project as Bernie was, and they were about to rehash an ongoing argument about it. I turned toward the third couple and asked "So, how about you folks? Are you with them?"

The third couple introduced themselves as Antonio and Lisa Terrazzo. "No, we just met them last night in Belize City. We're from San Mateo, California. We own an Italian restaurant in Sunnyvale. We're giving our son a chance to run the restaurant for a week during the holiday to see how well he handles it," Lisa said.

"Or how badly he screws it up," Antonio said.

I've noticed that fathers are always more cynical than mothers. I think they also have more pride when the sons accomplish something but tend to be more critical in public.

"Are any of you divers? We have the best diving in the world right out there," I said as I pointed toward the ocean.

"Helene and I both dive. We got certified on a vacation to Hawaii a few years ago. We haven't made a dive in two, maybe two and a half years though."

"No problem. Do you have a PADI or SSI certification card?"

"We have them in our bag," Helene said. "I made sure to bring them with us."

I gestured toward Beth and Misty. "We also teach here. I've got two dive instructors here this week so we can do the Discover SCUBA class for anyone that wants to learn. Missy and Beth are great teachers. They teach kids too. Right outside your cabanas is a buoy that marks Jacques Cousteau's third favorite dive site. It's a two-minute boat ride. There's no better place to learn than here."

"Can I dive too?"

"Maybe. How old are you, Michelle?"

"Eleven."

"If it's okay with your parents we can teach you." I turned to her parents. "We can teach the Bubblemakers class. That's scuba diving but there's a depth limit of twenty feet."

"Me too! I wanna dive," Katie squealed.

"I don't know. How old are you?"

"I'm four." She held up her right hand, fingers displayed and her thumb turned inward.

I smiled at her. "I wish we could, but you have to be at least eight to dive. How about snorkeling?"

Helene said, "I think we'll need to talk about it. They're both pretty good swimmers and love to snorkel."

Bernie looked at his wife and he smiled at Michelle. I felt confident they'd let us teach Michelle. I could see that Bernie was a pushover for his kids.

I turned toward Antonio and asked, "Antonio, Lisa, how about you? Are you divers?"

Lisa shook her head. "I don't think I'd do well getting under the water. Today was the first time in many years I even tried swimming in the open water. I might try snorkeling again."

"Antonio? How about you?" I asked.

"Oh, no, no way. I didn't want to leave my restaurant this time of year but she dragged me. I'm here for the sun and sand. I'll probably spend most of my time sleeping in a hammock." He took a sip of his drink, a Cuba Libre. I could smell the cinnamon in the rum.

"I'm sorry you didn't want to be here," I said. I tried not to sound put out by his attitude. "At your restaurant, are you a chef?" I asked.

"When we first started the restaurant Antonio did most of the cooking. He's a great chef. These days, we've grown so much we've got three chefs working for us."

"I still get into the kitchen and create. All my chefs, they're all trained in the big culinary schools. Me, I learned as a child at Mama's side. Her's and Nonie's, my grandmother."

"How have you liked your meals here? Is Felicia making you happy?" Felicia is the Mountain To Sea chef. I brought her down from Miami this season to try and "Americanize" our menus.

"I'm very happy with our meals. I've been pleasantly surprised. I don't think they can go wrong with the freshness of the sea food," Antonio said. "I can't quite figure out what some of the ingredients are."

"You're free to ask Felicia. I'm sure she'd be happy to show you how she makes these meals. If not, c'mon over to Over The Edge and Annette will just blow you away with her cooking."

"Do you think they'd mind me being in their kitchens? A lot of chefs don't like an audience."

"I'm sure they'd be happy. They might want you to share some of your recipes with them."

"That could be fun for you, Antonio," Lisa said. "Just because you can't swim doesn't mean you get to lie around all day while we're here."

Lord, I hoped Kim never turned into one of those wives who told the world of her husband's weaknesses. I could see Antonio's face turning red, either from embarrassment about not being able to swim or anger that she'd tell us.

"I did my time in the Navy. I know how to swim. I just prefer not doing it," he said, a bit testy.

Chapter 7

Saturday, December 23rd, 7:30 P.M.

The most direct way back to my place from the Mountain To Sea dining hall is along the lagoon on the west side of the island. Tonight I walked the long way, passing behind the guest cabanas. There had been some dolphins swimming and playing along the breakers at sunset recently and I hoped they'd still be there.

I heard a woman shriek, and then a man laughing as I approached the showers. I shouted out, "Is everything okay?"

Laughter followed. The young guy, Jack Bunton, came out from one of the shower stalls wearing a pair of swim trunks and sandals.

"Hey, George, yeah, everything's fine." He was laughing.

His wife came out next, wrapped in a bath robe. "I'm sorry. First it was the cold water and then, as I was washing my hair I felt something. I looked down and a small lizard was running around my feet. That's what caused me to shriek." She was blushing.

I laughed too. Partly because they were laughing, partly because the story of the lizard was plausible, and partly because I think I interrupted an intimate moment. "Well, as long as you're okay I think I'll move along."

"Wait, George. Is there anything we can do to get hot water? I've gotten used to cool or lukewarm water for showers but I don't think Sherry here will," Jack said.

"That big black tank up there holds about seven hundred gallons of collected rainwater. The sun heats the tank during the day. Late in the afternoon it might get to about seventy degrees. Once the sun sets the water temperature drops. I usually take my shower right before dinner."

"Then that's what I'm going to do. Jack, don't worry. I can handle this for a week," Sherry said to him, still blushing. They'd both toweled off and moved onto the main pathway with me. With the bright moonlight I could see them clearly.

"You two are on your honeymoon, right? I think that's what Gator told me earlier," I asked.

"Our first anniversary was last week but this is our honeymoon," Jack said.

"Jack is in the Army. He had to ship out for a tour in Afghanistan the day after our wedding. He just got back last week and has to go back in two weeks." Sherry stood to his left, her right hand in his left.

It's just an observation I've made, a lot of military guys, and cops, seem to always have their right hand free. Their gun hand is always free.

"Is that what you meant by being used to cool or lukewarm showers?"

"Yeah. In Afghanistan I spend days at a time in the country where daily hygiene is limited to maybe rinsing off with a rag or something if we find a stream. At base we usually get warm water, but not hot water like we'd get at home."

"In the Army, what do you do?" I asked.

"In the real world, I'm a narcotics officer with the Boston Police Department. The National Guard paid my way through college, and I was called up for active duty. The Army has me training Afghan troops in drug interdiction."

"Wait a minute. I never served, but from what I've heard, the Army almost never assigns people to do what they know how to do."

"I hear it used to be that way. It isn't anymore. Most of the reservists I know are doing what they do for a living."

"How many tours have you made?"

"Just one. I'm going back, but it's supposed to be for four months, then my commitment is up."

I sensed he didn't really want to talk about his deployment.

Sherry sighed. "Unless they do another stop-loss."

"So you decided to spend half your leave in Belize?"

"My family wasn't happy with that but we never had a honeymoon. With the Army, and the uncertainty of service today, I, we, just thought it was the right thing for us. We'll have a few days with our family when we get back."

"We're honored you're here. Do you dive?"

"I do. I got my C-card in college. Sherry doesn't."

"Sherry, do you want to learn?" I asked. "This is the best place you'll ever find for learning to dive."

She looked at Jack. He nodded and said, "Babe, you'll love it if you try it. Just look how much you liked snorkeling today."

"Okay. Yes, I'd like to take the Discover class."

"Great. You're going to love it," Jack said.

"Cool. Jack, as a way of saying thanks for spending half your leave with us, Sherry's class is on the house. Please, though, don't let anyone else know I said that. Kim will beat me enough as it is."

"You don't need to do that. We're not a charity case," Jack said.

"I'm sorry if I offended you. You are, however, our guest this week and I really do appreciate your service."

"George, we went to out to dinner twice at home before coming to Belize. I was in uniform both times. Both times people, strangers, anonymously bought our dinners. I appreciate their gestures, and yours too. I'm an officer and get paid fairly well. The Boston Police also pays the difference between my Army salary and my civilian one."

"Well, just tip your instructors and the staff here well at the end of the week and we'll be fine. By the way, there's probably going to be a storm late tonight. This time of year we tend to have some pretty strong ones hit around two or three in the morning. They pass in about thirty minutes."

I got back to Over The Edge and heard conversation coming from our little patio area. I took a seat next to Kim, facing Larry. Beth and Misty were on either side of him.

"Hi honey, is everything okay at Mountains To Sea?" Kim asked.

"I think so. I just got Jack's wife, Sherry, to sign up for the Discover class."

"Great! I think that makes five students. Beth, Misty, are you girls alright with that many at one time?" she asked.

"I am," Beth said.

"Me too," Misty said.

"Good. By the way, I comp'ed her class," I added.

"George, why? We've got a narrow margin on the classes as it is," Kim asked.

"Jack's a Boston cop but he's been in Afghanistan for over a year and goes back in a couple of weeks. It's their honeymoon. It just seems like the right thing to do," I said.

"He's a Boston cop and he's working in Afghanistan? How'd that happen?" Misty asked.

"He went to college through the National Guard and got called up. You and Beth will get paid for teaching her."

Chapter 8

Sunday, December 24th, 5:30 A.M.

"You woke up a couple of times last night. Did you dream of them again?"

I looked at Kim. I knew it hurt her. God, I hated hurting her, but I'd never lied to her and didn't plan to start now. "Yes."

I stood and began to dress.

She sat up in the bed. "Was it just Grace?"

"No, she was holding Austin. He was still a baby, not even a toddler."

Austin's face, its angular lines and high cheekbones mirrored his mother's. His pale-white skin matched mine. His Comanche black eyes reflected his mother's contribution to his DNA. His pointed nose jutted out like mine. What little hair he had was jet black, like his mother's and her family, but much finer.

I put on my running shorts and a t-shirt.

She took my hand, pulling me down onto the bed. "You haven't had them in your dreams in years. Why are they back?" Her eyes glistened with tears she being held back.

"I think it's related to our decision to start a family. I just don't understand what it means."

"Do they speak to you?"

"No. The baby giggled, I think. I don't know. He could have just been spitting up."

"What about Grace?"

"She doesn't say anything. I can't make out the look on her face. I sensed sadness." I leaned over and laced up my running shoes. I gripped her hand tightly, briefly, and let go. "The sun's coming up."

❧❖❧

Sunday's sunrise was amazing. I'd been out here for twenty years and still loved watching the sun come up over the Caribbean. After a storm like the one that hit around three o'clock this morning the air is even more clear than usual. Beth joined Kim and me on our usual run around the island. We were on our last lap when I saw Gator heading toward Mountain To Sea's kayak palapa.

Kim and I stopped our run but Beth waved and kept going. "Morning, Gator. How's it going?"

He slipped his hand through his hair, brushing it away from his face. "Okay so far. There's almost no wind this morning and the sun is coming up. It's Sunday, and we have the kayak orientation session this morning. Several of the guests are experienced kayakers so the orientation and the snorkeling trip to the aquarium should go pretty smoothly."

"I guess that means no divers from Mountain To Sea this morning. I wonder how many of my guests will dive today."

Kim picked up some debris that had washed up on the beach. "Don't forget, we've got a Discover SCUBA class scheduled for this—"

"Gator! George! Come quick!" Gene, one of the other guides this week, yelled from near the dining hall. We started walking that way when he yelled again: "Run, man, we got trouble!" and he began running toward one of the guest cabanas.

We ran, looking at each other and the cabana. Several people gathered beneath the porch at Cabana Five. I called to Gator, while still running, "Who's in five?"

"Jack and Sherry."

The onlookers backed away as we approached. I could see someone lying on the rocks, beneath the porch: Jack. Sherry leaned over him, rocking back and forth on her knees. Sherry wore a t-shirt, one of Jack's I would guess from its length, over a one-piece swim suit.

"What happened?" I asked Gene as I knelt down and checked for a pulse. There was one. His heart was racing. He was unconscious but breathing in very shallow breaths.

"I don't know. I've got trash duty this morning. I walked past here not fifteen minutes ago, you know, clearing debris that washed up. Is he dead?"

I saw the trash bag off to one side.

"He's alive," I said. "Gator, run down to my office and get Dylan. The two of you need to bring the stretcher and first aid kit."

I stood to take a better look at how Jack was positioned. My guess was that he leaned his back against the railing and it gave way. He flipped and landed face down. I suspected a broken neck and had to act as if there were a break. His right arm lay beneath him, as if he might have been trying to break his fall.

Dylan and Gator arrived with the stretcher. "Want us to pick him up, boss?" Gator asked.

"Not yet," I said. I ran my hands along his body, working down his right side, feeling for any obvious broken bones. When I got to his feet I straightened out his right leg, then checked his left and straightened it out, placing his feet together. I worked my way up his left side. His left arm was outstretched, bent at the elbow. It was pretty obvious his left shoulder was out of place. It would hurt like hell if he was conscious, but I had to move his arm to line it up with the rest of his body. When I did I heard a moan, then nothing.

"Dylan, undo the straps on the stretcher. Then I want you to place one end on Jack's feet. We'll have to lay the stretcher on top of him."

Dylan did as I said. I dug my hands into the sand beneath Jack's lower legs, about half way between his ankles and knees, and pulled one end of the strap through the dugout sand. I pulled that end through the buckle mechanism until it was very snug around his lower legs. I repeated the process around his mid-thigh area and again at the waist and chest, keeping his right arm in place.

I positioned myself with Jack's head centered between my knees and looked around. My hands were bleeding from numerous little cuts, the result of digging through the coral.

"Dave! We're going to need your help. Take a spot near Jack's feet, facing me. Get on your knees."

Dave did as I said, water lapping at his feet and knees.

"Alright, this is going to be tricky but we have to roll him," I said.

"Tell us what to do, boss," Gator said.

"Gene, get on my right side. Dylan, stay on my left. What I want to do is roll him counter-clockwise. Dylan, you'll have to push this side of the stretcher into the sand like a pivot. Gene, you'll pull the other side of the stretcher up and over, toward you."

"What about me?" Dave asked.

"Dave, you can help both of them by holding that stretcher handle in your right hand still, but let it rotate, and use your left to help Gene pull the stretch over. I'm going to hold Jack's head still in case his neck is broken."

I looked each of them in the eye. Each understood.

"Okay, I'll count to three. On three, let's turn him over. One. Two. Three."

I heard Jack take a deep breath and a deep moan as we rolled him over. I checked his pulse again. It was still there but not racing as much. His pulse was stabilizing. He was still breathing. With him on his back I could see that his right arm was broken just above his wrist.

"Now what, boss? Do you want me to call the rescue chopper?" Gator asked.

Belize was still a protectorate of Great Britain. When England granted Belize its independence in 1972 there were concerns about long-time animosities between Belize and its western neighbor, Guatemala. Belize did not have its own military. The Royal Air Force kept a small base near Belize City on St. Georges' Caye. They had a rescue helicopter that could make it to Sunrise Caye in less than fifteen minutes.

"Not yet," I said. I rummaged through my medical kit and found a pen light. I checked Jack's eyes and found no signs of bleeding and his irises responded to the light. I put a splint on his broken arm. I checked his breathing and pulse again. They were getting closer to normal. I used a stethoscope and heard nothing suggesting fluid in his lungs, around his heart, or other internal bleeding.

"I don't think his life is in immediate danger. We'll take Jack and Sherry to Dangriga in the Sensencula."

Calling in the RAF rescue chopper is an expensive solution. If I believed he'd die if not taken to a hospital in minutes I'd have called the chopper. I thought a boat trip to Dangriga would be uncomfortable but sufficient. I didn't know if Jack was a member of DAN, the Divers Advisory Network, or not. DAN would cover the cost of the RAF air ambulance; otherwise, he'd be responsible for the cost. Taking the boat costs him nothing, I'd be out some gas money but that's chump change in comparison.

"Gator, you and Dylan carry Jack down to the dock and put him in the Sensencula. Be as gentle as you can. You may need to find some stuff to put under the stretcher to pad the ride," I said. "Have someone find Juan, he can drive the boat."

⭐

I stood and looked at the crowd. I was glad not to see the two kids.

"Did anyone see what happened?" I asked.

Gene said, "I was walking along the beach, doing my trash pick-up duties. I saw Jack coming back from the dining hall with his morning coffee. I got up to the last of the cabanas and turned around. I found him a few minutes ago—just like you found him. I didn't move him. Sherry was still upstairs."

I looked up at the porch. One of the railings was missing. That's not quite true. It was on the ground, beneath the porch. The railings were just branches or saplings, in this case a palm sapling about two inches in diameter. One of our coffee cups lay a few feet away. The sand beneath it looked wet.

Otherwise I got no response. A few people looked at Kevin, suspiciously.

Kevin said, "Hey, don't look at me. I just walked up to see what everyone else was looking at. I didn't do anything."

I looked at Kevin. He looked pale, like he'd never seen a seriously injured person before. I believed him.

"What do you think happened?" Eric White asked.

"I'm not sure. My first guess is that he leaned against a railing and it broke loose, causing him to tumble over. His neck may be broken. Beyond that, his left shoulder is dislocated and his right arm has a clean break."

"Do you think he'll be okay?" Dave Cavuto asked. His wife, Dagan, stood beside him.

"I didn't hear any fluids in his lungs or signs of other internal injuries. If I were more worried I'd have called in the rescue helicopter."

Before sending the Sensencula off to Dangriga I wanted to pack all of Jack and Sherry's things. While I didn't believe he suffered any permanent injury it was a certainty they would not be back at Sunrise Caye this week.

As I climbed the stairs to their cabana I grabbed the railings and shook them really hard. They seemed pretty secure to me. Once at the top of the stairs I looked into the cabana. There wasn't anything obviously wrong. The bed was unmade. Sherry was apparently asleep when Jack fell.

They didn't have a lot in the room. I guessed that Jack's military experience taught him to travel light. They had a single duffel bag and a rucksack. They'd hung their shirts, jeans, and swim trunks from a clothes line run along one wall in an almost military precision—two inches between each hanger. Their undergarments were all neatly folded and resting on a table made of two-by-fours. Also on the table was a clear, water-resistant plastic bag that held their passports, wallets, and two key rings. Each had a pair of sandals and a pair of sneakers placed neatly under their respective sides of the bed. I found a cell phone and a watch stuffed in Jack's sneakers.

Beyond the clothing the only personal items they had were a digital camera and a framed five-by-seven picture. I wondered if Jack carried it with him to Afghanistan or if Sherry brought it from home. My hunch was it was Jack's. He looked pretty sharp in his dress uniform. She looked beautiful in her wedding gown. She was easily twenty pounds lighter when the picture was taken. Her blond hair fell with a gentle wave off her shoulders. Here on the island she'd worn it longer and strait.

I packed their gear as neatly as I could, padding their valuables and the picture frame between clothing items in the rucksack. I lugged the two bags to my boat dock and handed them to Dylan who was in the boat, talking quietly to Jack. Jack's eyes were open.

"I think he's coming to," Dylan said. "He's been mumbling something but I can't make it out."

I climbed into the boat and sat next to Jack. I checked his pulse. It was steady and about what I'd expect for someone in serious pain. His breathing was fair, again what I'd expect given his pain.

"Jack, it's George," I said. His eyes shifted and seemed to focus on me. Maybe he had a concussion. "You fell off the porch and have been pretty well banged up. Your right arm is broken, your left shoulder is dislocated, and you may have injured your neck. Sherry is fine."

His lips moved but I couldn't hear what he was saying, if anything.

"Jack, can you move your fingers in your right hand for me?" I asked.

His fingers moved, one at a time starting with his little finger and working toward his thumb. That was a relief.

"Good, now can you do the same with your left hand," I asked.

He did, and I think he smiled a little in response to my smile.

"Alright, now, wiggle your toes for me. Don't worry about your legs, they're tightly strapped to the stretcher."

His toes all moved.

"Jack, I think you're going to be all right. You can move your fingers and toes so I don't think there is any reason to worry about paralysis. We've got your head strapped in place, with some padding, to keep it in the same position we found you in. I don't want to risk a neck injury but I think you're going to be okay."

Again, his lips moved but I couldn't make out any sound.

"Jack, we can't hear what you are trying to say but don't worry. You'll be on your way to the Belize mainland in just a few minutes," I said. I leaned in, trying to hear what he was saying. I couldn't make anything out.

Dylan looked at me. "Kim is on the phone making arrangements for the ambulance to meet us. At least it's a calm morning. The ride across should be relatively smooth."

"Good, keep talking to him. They'll be on their way in a few minutes. Kim will have to go along. I need you to stay here," I said before going into my office.

By the time I got out of the boat and climbed the stairs to my office Kim was ready to go. "The ambulance will meet us at the Riverside marina. We've got to get going," she said to me.

"I'll get Juan to drive the boat. Stay with Jack and Sherry until you get to the hospital and then stay with Sherry tonight in town."

"How's he doing? I could see through the window you were talking to him," Sherry asked.

I moved a step toward Sherry and took her hand in mine. "Sherry, he's awake. He can move his fingers and toes and understands commands. Keep his head strapped tight until he's in the hospital but I think he's going to be alright."

Juan is one of the maintenance workers here. Like most of my Belizean staff he lives in Dangriga.

"George, we've got to go to Southwestern Caye first," Kim said.

"Southwestern? Why?"

"I called the other resorts around here to see if there were any doctors or nurses staying there. Eddie called back. Would you believe there's a neurosurgeon on vacation there? Anyway, the neurosurgeon will ride with us to Dangriga."

"That was smart thinking," I said. One of the many reasons I love her is that she's every bit as smart as I am, and then some.

"George, I don't know when I'll be back. I'm afraid it won't be tonight," Kim said.

"I know. I don't want you to even try. Juan's not familiar enough with these waters to make the run in the dark. Spend the night in town. Tell the neurosurgeon we'll cover his hotel tonight too and bring him back in the morning."

"I already did."

"I told Juan to take our car and follow you to the airport. Whenever you tell him to, he can go home and surprise his wife by being home on Christmas Eve."

"We've been married for fourteen years. This is the first time we'll be apart on Christmas Eve."

"Yeah, but you don't get your present until you get back." I was trying to lighten the mood. She hit me.

"That's not what I meant!"

"Honey, I know, but it's unavoidable. Now, give me a kiss and get going."

We kissed. Softly, and apparently long enough for Juan to cough a few times to interrupt us. "I'll miss you. Hey, think of it this way. When was the last time you got to take a hot shower on Christmas morning?"

Chapter 9

Sunday, December 24th, 7:30 A.M.

Once the boat left Dylan turned to me. "George, do you know how it happened?"

"It looks like he leaned against the railing while drinking coffee and the railing gave way."

"Which cabana was that?"

"Five."

"Five? George, we replaced those railings the week before last. They were secure, I'm sure of it."

"Yeah, that was five. I want the two of us to check the railings on all of the cabanas so go grab your toolbox and meet me at Cabana Two in a couple of minutes."

"Sure. You know, Gene was here and helped us with those railings. Do you remember that he did some pull-ups, and then wrapped his legs around one of the railings and did a sit-up, suspended from the railing?"

"Yeah, we were kidding about the movie, *Rocky IV*, where Rocky did something like that. He's a big guy, too, easily two hundred and thirty pounds. Jack wasn't but one hundred and eighty, if that."

We went cabana by cabana starting with Number two and worked our way through the last cabana. Cabana One was where the lead guides stay and was built at beach level; there were no railings. We didn't find any railings that were weak or needing adjustment.

At Cabana Five we checked the other sections of the railing. They were all fine.

"Hey, George, look at this." Dylan was pointing to a lock washer lying on one of the deck boards.

"Where did that come from?"

"The bolt holding this end of the railing is gone. We put all of the bolt heads on the inside of the porch to reduce the potential for people to get snagged by the protruding bolt. What bothers me is that if this bolt worked loose and fell, the washer and nut would have fallen down into the sand and rocks below."

"Dylan, I agree there's no way it could have fallen and rolled over there. So, how'd it get there?"

"Beats me, boss, but the railing isn't broken. The whole section came off. The bolts on each end would have had to be missing, or at least the nuts, for that to happen."

"Hmm, even if the nuts were gone there's a problem."

"Yeah, we put the bolts in from the inside of the porch. Leaning against the railing would just push the bolt in further. They'd have to be reversed to allow someone to push the railing away from the cabana."

"I'd really wonder if we left the bolts off if it weren't for one thing."

"I know, George. This is the section that Gene did those sit-ups on."

"Then again, Gene wrapped his legs around the vertical supports. He didn't suspend himself from the sapling."

Jack leaned against the only railing in any of the cabanas that was installed backward and to top that the bolts were in place but the nuts weren't on? I didn't believe that but had no idea how else it could have happened.

Chapter 10

Sunday, December 24th, 8:00 A.M.

I went to the Mountain To Sea dining hall where the remaining guests were enjoying breakfast.

I rang a small cowbell we have in the dining hall. "Can I have everyone's attention, please?" I

"In case anyone here isn't already aware, Jack Bunton fell from his cabana's porch this morning. He and Sherry are in one of my boats and should be getting to the mainland about half an hour from now."

"Is he going to be alright?" Bernie Stamps asked.

"Jack was conscious before the boat left. He was able to move his fingers and toes. I don't think there is any reason to worry about paralysis. As luck would have it, there was a neurosurgeon on vacation at Southwestern Caye and he's on the boat too."

"So, now what?" Eric White asked.

"What happened to Jack was an accident. You're all here for another six and a half days. You can sit around and mope or you can have the fun you came for. Gator will be leading the kayak orientation shortly and we're planning to go on like normal."

I grabbed a cup of fresh orange juice and then sat down at Dave Cavuto's table. "Dave, I wanted to thank you for your help earlier."

"No problem. You think he's going to be okay then?"

"Yeah, I do. I don't remember, are you guys divers?" I wanted to get everyone thinking again about the fun they were here to have.

"I've been diving for almost ten years. So has Dagan. By the way

George, this is my wife, Dagan."

"Alright, two more divers," I said. "Ever been to Belize before?"

"We were in Ambergris last year. We've also been to Roatan."

"Roatan? Dave, how'd you like Honduras?"

I don't ask about my competitors in Ambergris.

"I loved it. We went to Fantasy Island. We were looking for Tattoo, I guess."

"Maybe you were, but I was looking for Ricardo Montalban." Dagan spoke slowly and dragged out the last syllable of 'Montalban,' making it sound like 'bahn', as in autobahn. Dagan smiled. She had a distinct, southern accent. One of those that makes men melt. Not the deep south, like the exaggerations from *Gone With The Wind* and others that distort the sounds of true Georgia peaches. Hers was tinted with something, maybe Appalachian? It reminded me of Jodie Foster's accent in Silence of The Lambs. Wasn't her character from West Virginia? I don't know, I'm not really an expert on accents. For sure, Dagan had a sexy voice, with a body to match. Tall and thin, with long black hair and a few streaks of grey she wasn't trying to hide and dark, dark eyes. Probably some Native American in her, I thought. Cherokee? Weren't they common in the western Virginia, North Carolina and Tennessee area a few generations ago?

"Dagan, honey, you were there with me. All of my fantasies were already fulfilled. Anyway, George, we went during whale shark season. We made a couple of dives with whale sharks. *That* was fun," Dave said.

"Yeah, they're fun to dive with. We make trips down to Gladden Split around the full moon each spring. They aren't usually seen this far up. We saw one a few weeks ago, between here and Dangriga, as we were coming back from a supply run. By the way, where are y'all from?"

"Boston, or close to it anyway," Jack said.

"Neither of you has a Boston accent. You both sound like you're from the south," I responded.

"I grew up in Atlanta and did my undergrad at Georgia Tech and then my graduate courses at MIT. We've been in Boston ever since," Dave said.

"That sounds right for you, Dave. It might explain the Yellow Jackets t-shirt too. I was trying to place Dagan's accent."

She blushed a bit. "Is it that noticeable? I'm from Bristol, Virginia. We met at Georgia when we were in college."

"I've driven through Bristol, I think. Isn't it the same city as Bristol, Tennessee?"

"Yeah, but we don't usually like to acknowledge them. Of course, they don't like to acknowledge us either," she said, with one of those killer smiles. I swear I saw a twinkle in her eye.

"So you live in Boston?" I just wanted to keep the conversation going, to hear Dagan's voice.

"No, we met in school but I got a job as an analyst in Boston with one of the big investment houses. I specialize in pharmaceutical company stocks," Dave said. He held Dagan's hand, not so much out of affection but as a reminder to me, man to man, that she was with him.

"And I've got a job as a financial reporter," Dagan said.

I looked at another couple at the table. "And how about you two? Right out there is some of the best diving in the world," I said.

"I dive. I got my C-card a couple of years ago in Hawaii. I'm Mindy."

"And I'm Rich Williams. I've haven't tried diving, but I'm willing to take the Discover class later this week."

"Great! We've got a class planned for this afternoon but we can do another later in the week if you'd like. We're pretty flexible around here. Rich, where are y'all from?"

"Chicago. I work for one of the credit bureaus as an I/T systems analyst," Rich said. He wore a teal colored golf shirt and khaki shorts, quarter-socks and deck shoes. If he had shaved this morning he'd almost pass as a model for a Tommy Hilfiger ad. Mindy wore an extra long yellow t-shirt with a *Far Side* cartoon of a pudgy guy pushing against a door at the *Midvale School For The Gifted*. The door had a sign that said "pull" on it. The t-shirt covered whatever else she was wearing. My guess was that they were both in their early thirties.

"Well, I'll check on you folks after your kayak orientation and snorkel trip. I have a couple of people at Over The Edge that want to make a dive this morning. Have fun!" I said as I stood and walked toward the kitchen to put my cup in the wash.

Antonio Terrazzo stood in the kitchen holding a knife and a bag of onions. He looked my way and said, "Felicia is going to let me help her make lunch today. I've never tried to fix Jerk chicken before. She said that if I want her recipe I have to chop the onions."

"Have fun, and be careful. I'm sure you know your way with these kitchen utensils but we don't need any more accidents today."

Chapter 11
Sunday, December 24ᵗʰ, 9:30 A.M.

All three of Over The Edge's diving guests wanted to dive this morning. Beth and Marcus escorted them to a site we named Hole Lotta Wrasse. Larry came back thrilled with pictures he took of a spotted eagle ray and a hawksbill turtle.

Terri was excited about a nurse shark. "Marcus spotted it first. He had me swim around this little coral head, and he got a bit closer, pointing excitedly at it, but I didn't see it. Finally the shark got up off the sand, looked my way, and swam off. That was really neat. I didn't know they could sleep."

Marcus gestured with his arms fully outstretched. "Yeah, it was a big one too. Bigger than me, even. It was six, maybe seven feet long. I don't see them that big out here very often."

I added, "Nurse sharks do sleep. They seem to sleep a lot. About all they do is eat and sleep."

"Sounds like they have something in common with our sons," Joe said. "They're both teenagers."

❧❖❧

I was doing some work in the office when Larry shouted up from the base of the stairs, "George, you have company coming."

I looked outside but didn't see any boats at my dock. I suspected Larry saw one of the boats from the Belize Maritime Police. They come by a couple of times a week to collect the taxes due and hope for a free meal.

I went down the stairs and saw Larry pointing toward a sailboat that had come into the lagoon and quietly dropped anchor a couple of hundred yards offshore. Three people were on a small skiff heading toward the dock. I walked down the dock to greet them. Larry walked with me. The skiff went past the dock and turned around like they planned to tie up facing their boat at the far end of the dock.

"I'm a typical American. I don't recognize most national flags. Isn't that the Swedish flag?" Larry asked.

"No, that's rectangular with a blue background and a gold cross running the length of the flag. This looks like the mirror image of the International Red Cross. It's a square cloth with a red background and a white cross. I think that's the Swiss flag. I haven't had Swiss stop in before."

"Do you get much traffic through here?"

"We're on the outer part of the barrier reef. Most sailboat traffic stays closer to the mainland, but it happens about twice a month. Usually it's a bigger boat like that one. She must be over fifty foot." We were about halfway down the dock when Larry stopped.

"Hello! Can I help you?" I asked as the skiff eased its way to the dock.

A tall man with short, blonde hair and a deep tan tossed me a line. "Yah, my family would like to do some diving and saw the diver-down logo on your building." He had an accent I couldn't identify, but it sounded like some of the exaggerated Swiss accents I remember from American television shows.

"Great! Come on up to the dining hall and we'll talk," I said while wrapping the line around one of the posts.

"I am Einar Boxler," he said, reaching up to shake my hand. "This is my wife, Frida, and our son Gunnar."

I helped each of them up to the dock and led the way to the dining hall. I had to look up to Einar. I'm six feet, two inches tall. Einar must have been at least three inches taller. I guessed he was in his late forties or early fifties. Frida Boxler was maybe five-and-a-half feet tall, thin, with blonde hair and also well tanned. Gunnar was about twenty, not quite as tall as his father, but still taller than me.

"You don't sound like you're from around here," I said, smiling.

Einar had a quizzical look until he realized I was joking. "No, we are from Switzerland. We are on holiday and doing a bit of traveling."

I showed them the way to the dining area. Erin, our writer, was working at one of the tables, her laptop open and a bunch of papers spread around with various items serving as paperweights. I introduced her to our guests and then the four of us sat at another table. Einar and I sat on one side of the table with Gunnar and Frida opposite us. Erin was working at a table on the opposite side of the hall, facing me.

"So, you're on holiday. What do you do back in Switzerland?"

"I am a lawyer. Frida used to teach." I noticed, across the hall, that Erin looked up, a surprised look on her face. She looked at me, shook her head a couple of times, and returned to her work.

"I retired last summer," Frida added.

"Gunnar is off to university in a few months. He completed his first term of military service shortly before we began this trip."

"Are the three of you divers? Do you have certification cards with you?" I asked.

"Frida and I have certification cards. Gunnar does not have one." Frida reached into her purse and retrieved two identification cards. They were NAUI certification cards. They were perfectly acceptable. Most of our guests were from the United States where PADI and SSI were the most prominent SCUBA certification programs.

"These are okay for us. When was the last time the two of you dove?"

"We made a couple of dives this past week, in Aruba, and the week before in the Bahamas. We dive every year."

"Gunnar, you haven't dived before?" I asked.

Kim and Misty came into the hall and sat down. I introduced them.

Misty's eyes lit up when she saw Gunnar.

"No, sir, but I have done a bit of snorkeling."

"Okay, well, we have an introductory course. It requires about forty-five minutes of class time and another thirty to forty-five minutes of exercise in the lagoon here before we go out to the dive site. We happen to have a class scheduled this afternoon."

After agreeing to the price for his training and for each dive, I walked the three of them back to their skiff to return to their boat for lunch. I went back to the dining hall.

Erin looked up when I walked back in. "George, can we talk for a minute?"

"Sure. Is there anything wrong?" I asked as I sat down next to her.

"You know that I worked in Europe for a long time. I spent much of the nineties reporting on human rights violations and some of the ethnic cleansing that took place in Bosnia."

"You've mentioned that before."

"I thought I recognized Einar when he came in. He might be a lawyer, but he wasn't always." She turned her laptop toward me. There was a picture of a tall man in a dress uniform. It sure resembled Einar. There was a caption under the picture. I guess it came from some magazine or newspaper. The caption identified the man as an officer of the Swiss Army and as military attaché to their ambassador to NATO.

"If my memory serves correctly, he wasn't just an attaché. He was involved in their covert operations group. He also got re-assigned suddenly. There were rumors he was involved in some kind of smuggling operation but I never heard what was being smuggled and there were never any charges."

"I wonder why he said he's a lawyer?"

"I don't know, but according to this bio I found, he wasn't married and didn't have kids.

Chapter 12
Sunday, December 24th, 11:30 A.M.

I think about problems the best when exerting myself physically. I have a Bowflex machine on a patio above the storage room where we keep all of our dive gear. I was working out, continually running through my mind how we'd replaced the railing at Cabana Five a couple of weeks ago. I just couldn't see any way we'd have put the bolts in facing the wrong way. Even if we did, I didn't see how both bolts could have worked themselves loose.

My workout was interrupted by the sound of a boat motor.

I looked out and saw the Maritime Police boat coming. I grabbed a towel, wiped down my face and arms and walked down the stairs and out along the dock.

"Charlie, how are you doing?" I asked as I grabbed the line he threw me. I made a loose figure-eight knot around a pylon as Charlie stepped off the boat.

"George, I am probably doing better than you today. I hear someone got hurt?" The boat had come from the south so I guessed he'd been to Southwestern Caye and heard about it from Eddie.

"Yeah, I'm afraid so. One of our guests fell from a porch. His neck might be broken. Kim and one of Eddie's guests, a neurosurgeon, took him into Dangriga."

"Guess I better have a look around, then."

"Why? It was an accident. It's not a crime scene," I asked.

"My bosses in Belmopan would not be happy to hear that a tourist got hurt and I didn't investigate."

Belize had a national police force but they didn't have boats and didn't travel to the cayes. The islands within the marine preserve were generally under the lazy but watchful eye of the Maritime Patrol. Mostly the Maritime Patrol looked for poachers fishing illegally and then accepted bribes to look the other way. But every organization has its own internal politics and Charlie was right, he might get in trouble with his bosses if he didn't at least take a quick look and file a report.

We walked down the beach and crossed to the foot of Cabana Five. Charlie's relaxed pace didn't surprise me. Belizeans are a very superstitious people. They'll go miles out of their way to avoid seeing where someone was hurt or killed. I'd only expect him to move quickly to leave.

"So, George, tell me what happened." He looked at the porch.

"We're not sure. Nobody witnessed it. Gene, you know Gene, right?"

"Yes, he's the big guy, the arrogant one, right?"

"I guess so. We refer to it as being cocky. Anyway, he passed by here as he picked up debris along the shoreline. He saw Jack—that's the guy's name—coming back from the dining hall with a cup of coffee. Gene kept on until he got to the shower area and then turned around. That's when he found Jack lying there."

"How long was that?"

"According to Gene, it was maybe fifteen minutes."

"Was anyone else there?"

"Jack's married. His wife, Sherry, was still asleep."

"Where is she now?"

"She's with Kim and her husband. They're probably in Dangriga by now."

Charlie took a small note pad and pencil out of his shirt pocket.

"When we get back to your office, can you give me their names and passport numbers?"

"Sure."

"George, how did he fall?" Charlie asked.

"I think he leaned his backside against the railing and it gave way. He tumbled over, landing face-down with his head facing the cabana. Right about here," I said as I stood about where Jack's head had been.

I lay down, trying to mimic how I found Jack. When I stood I saw a few Mountain To Sea staff members gathered near Cabana Four, watching.

"There were no witnesses?" Charlie asked.

"Nope, like I said, Gene had just passed by no more than fifteen minutes earlier and Sherry was apparently still asleep."

"Well, let's look upstairs." He climbed the stairs, shaking the railings thoroughly as he climbed. "They feel sturdy to me."

"We replaced the railings in this cabana two weeks ago. In case you're wondering, we've checked the railings on each cabana today to make sure they're all okay. They were all fine. We also already replaced the railing." I didn't see any point in telling him that when we did we found Dylan's ratchet wrench set was missing and we'd had to use more traditional wrenches.

At the top of the stairs he looked down at the coral and rocks below, where Jack had fallen. He stood back from the railings a little and gently pushed each of the remaining sections. "These railings are solid, too."

"Like I said, we checked them all after the accident and replaced the missing section. It was an accident and I didn't want to leave the section of rail missing."

"What can you tell me about this man? Jack, I think you said his name was."

"Charlie, he and his wife are on their honeymoon. They've been married over a year but he's in the Army and had to go to Afghanistan. He just got back to the States two weeks ago and has to go back to

Afghanistan in two more weeks."

"So, he is a soldier then."

"Not exactly. He's a police officer in Boston but is in the Army's National Guard and was called up for active duty."

"Was he worried about going back to Afghanistan? Any chance this was intentional? Could he have hurt himself to avoid being sent to combat again?"

"I don't think so. He and his wife seemed pretty happy. Of course, they only got here yesterday. He seemed pretty friendly last night at dinner and said his next tour was a short one."

"Very well, then. It sounds like an accident."

Charlie and I walked back to my office and as we got close we could each smell lunch. "George, when we walked down the dock a few minutes ago I could see Annette was fixing lunch. May I join you?"

"Sure, you're always welcome here, you know that." He was, but he's a bit of a mooch and I didn't want his presence here to spook the guests. They had enough on their minds already with Jack's injury. But I couldn't really say no; it could cost me later.

Chapter 13

Sunday, December 24th, 12:00 P.M.

I watched the Mountain To Sea guests paddling back from the aquarium, a small area within the atoll surrounded by coral heads. Their kayak orientation included learning how to get in and out of their kayaks with snorkeling gear. As part of the orientation they paddled to the aquarium, tied their boats together, and snorkeled for about half an hour. They'd have to get back into their boats and paddle back.

I walked to the kayak palapa and met the group as it returned. I helped a few of the ladies pull their boats up the beach to the palapa. As soon as they were back on the island they were ready for lunch and I followed them to the dining hall. At one table I found a pair of sisters, forty-seven year-old twins named Alicia and Carolyn, from Minneapolis.

"So, Alicia, how was your paddle trip?" I asked.

"Oh, that was fantastic. The paddling itself I don't much care for but the snorkeling was amazing. I don't know how deep the water is there but from the surface I could see the creatures on the bottom. The water clarity is amazing."

"That it is. The aquarium seldom gets more than twenty feet deep. Do you actually snorkel and dive, or just swim at the surface?"

"I can dive. My sister and I have made trips to the Caribbean every year for almost five years. I think our first trip was the year my youngest son, Michael, turned eleven and he's about to get his driver's license. Oh God, I hadn't thought of that. I'll soon have three teenage boys with driver's licences."

"Carolyn, how'd you enjoy your trip?" I asked.

"Like Alicia said, it was fantastic. I'm not much for kayaking either but it's a fun way to get to a snorkeling site. I saw a couple of lobsters. Is it legal to harvest them?"

"That depends. In the maritime preserve free diving, that is diving without tanks, is a legal way for citizens to harvest lobster but only what they will consume themselves. We don't usually allow anyone to do it here."

"Bummer, I was hoping for a lobster dinner sometime this week," Carolyn said. "I've got one teenage son and a ten year-old daughter. She has allergies and can't eat shellfish so I don't get shrimp, crabs, or lobster often."

"I'll think about it. I've got enough Belizean citizens working here that we could probably get a number of lobsters and maybe do something like a lobster roll. I'll ask Felicia and Antonio if they'd be interested in trying that." *We'd only need one lobster for every three guests to make a good meal.*

"Antonio? Lisa's husband?" Alicia asked.

"Yeah, he doesn't want anything to do with the water. He's excited now about learning how Belizeans prepare foods so he's helping out in the kitchen. Anyway, so you snorkel and have spent some time in the Caribbean. Do you dive?" I asked.

"We took a resort course once. I had fun. I might be willing to take another resort course. Carolyn, what do you think?" Alicia asked.

"Sure, but only the resort course. I don't want to spend all week in class."

❧❀❧

There was one pair of women from San Francisco who introduced themselves as partners. Neither expressed any interest in diving. And we had two men, both in their thirties and single. Kevin O'Reilly was one and I'd already gotten to know him better than I'd want to. The other, Jerry Douglas, was a commercial realtor from Atlanta.

"Jerry, have you ever dove?" I asked.

"I tried it a couple of times. The first time I was in my teens. My family took a vacation to Key West one winter and everyone else dove. I had some problems with nose bleeds. I didn't like it. I couldn't get my ears to clear either."

"You were a teen then. Have you tried it since?"

"About three years ago I went to Jamaica with some friends and tried it again. Same results: nose bleeds and I couldn't clear my ears. I'm not interested in trying it again. Snorkeling will have to do."

"I understand, and the snorkeling here is great. There are plenty of people to snorkel with. The only thing I ask is that you not go alone, ever, and always enter the water from the lagoon side of the island. I just don't want anyone getting cut up by the coral on the open ocean side," I said.

⁂

In all, we had five certified divers, a few more with some prior experience with a resort course, and three others who were interested in the Discover SCUBA class, plus maybe one Bubblemakers class for Michelle. This could be a busy week. I looked forward to busy weeks.

Chapter 14

Sunday, December 24th, 1:30 P.M.

After lunch Beth, Misty and I taught a Discover SCUBA class for three of Mountain To Sea's guests. We taught the class in our dining area so that the guests didn't get sunburned. The class was seated around one dining table. I introduced Gunnar to the other guests.

"Before we get started, can each of you tell me if you've ever dived before? Maybe give me a sense of how much time you've spent in the open water and how strong a swimmer you are," Beth asked.

One of the Mountain To Sea guests, Kevin spoke first. "I've never been in the ocean before. I swim a lot, mostly in the lakes and rivers near home. I'm big on water skiing. I've never tried diving and haven't snorkeled either, well, until yesterday anyway."

Kevin looked to be in his early forties or late thirties. He was overweight but not obese. He was the guy that pushed Dave off the dock Saturday morning and shoved Antonio during a break in the volleyball game last night. Diving is a sport for those with self-control. I worried about his ability to control himself. He seemed like a hot-head.

Kevin watched as Misty spread out equipment on one of the tables. Misty worked from Gunnar's side of the table. She leaned over and brushed up against Gunnar a few times.

The twin sisters from Minneapolis, Alicia and Carolyn, also took the class. Alicia, the older sister, spoke next. She looked at Carolyn. "We took a resort course in Nassau once. That was, what, maybe eight years ago?"

"Nine years ago. It was the year before Bobby was born."

"That's right. Anyway, I haven't made a dive since then."

"But we were in Cancun last May and did some snorkeling."

"Okay, so when you made that trip to Nassau, did you have any problems in the water?"

"No. We made several dives that week. I think I made six or seven. Carolyn, you made a couple more, didn't you?"

"I think I made ten dives. I didn't have any problems on any of them. We didn't go very deep. I think we stayed above forty feet."

"You probably did. The legal limit for the old resort course was supposed to be forty feet. Actually, for our PADI Discover class it's also supposed to be forty feet. We don't look too carefully, but we won't lead you down much below that this week."

Beth turned to Kevin. "Kevin, we don't require our certified divers to use snorkels, but in the class we do. We'll get enough practice out here in the lagoon that you'll be comfortable."

"How about you, Gunnar?" Beth asked.

"I swim frequently. I have snorkeled often, especially the past few weeks as we've sailed the Caribbean. I have friends that dive and they've tried to teach me. I have not taken any classes."

Misty patted his shoulder. "Don't worry, you're in good hands." She left her hand on his shoulder several seconds.

I was a bit worried by his tale. I know a lot of beginner divers have thought they knew enough to teach friends how to dive and loaned them equipment. Bad habits get picked up that way but not the safe habits.

⚜

The lecture part of the class ran about an hour and then they spent another forty-five minutes in the lagoon. I stretched out in a hammock suspended at the end of the dock and watched as they moved into the lagoon. The lagoon was seldom more than six feet deep. Anyone having a problem could simply stand up in most of the lagoon, but its deep enough for them to swim along the sea grass and get used to the equipment. Kevin and Gunnar worked with Beth while the two sisters worked with Misty. After a short break, Jeremy took the four of them to Beth's Garden, a dive site with a sandy area at about thirty-five feet, to drop into and practice some basic skills before moving out to the reef at the top of The Wall. Dylan went on the dive too, just as another pair of eyes to look out for anyone having trouble. Part of his compensation plan here is to make as many dives as he wants.

Glover's Reef Atoll is along the world's second largest barrier reef. The Wall is a severe drop off just a few hundred yards east of our little thirteen acre island. It was a nearly vertical drop to over 3,000 feet. Large animals including dolphins, sharks, and stingrays inhabited the area. The reef was also home to a variety of smaller fish, lobsters, crabs, and all the other Caribbean reef critters.

The dive boat came back about thirty-five minutes after it left. I was sitting on the deck above the room I use for storing the tanks and other dive gear. I was playing my guitar, and listening to a new CD, a gift from Larry. I was a big Beatles fan and generally prefer classic rock. This was country, a Texas artist named Brian Burns. Larry knew that Brian Burns has been to my resort once. More country than I usually like but the CD had one song with a guitar riff I liked and I was trying to teach myself. It was a remake of an old Uriah Heap song, "Stealin". It wasn't a particularly tough piece but I couldn't concentrate as thoughts of seeing Jack's body on the beach constantly ran through my mind. I couldn't see any way we'd have left the nuts off the bolts holding the railing in place. As the boat rounded the southern jetty I set my guitar in its stand and walked down to the dock.

"So, how was it?" I asked the group as Misty helped tie up the boat.

Carolyn stood, holding her hand up toward me. I took her hand and assisted her onto the dock. "That water's beautiful. I loved it. I'm ready to go again!"

"We can do that. You know, we can put you through the whole Open Water certification too, if you'd like. That way, when you come back here next year, or go someplace else if you insist, you won't have to go through a class again."

She laughed. "You're quite the persistent salesman, aren't you? Well, I don't think I'm interested in the Open Water class, but more dives are certainly on the schedule."

"Same here." Alison had done a backward roll off the boat into the lagoon and walked toward the beach. "I don't want to spend the week in class, but I'll definitely be making more dives."

"Did you see anything interesting?" I asked.

"I don't know what most of what I saw was. We saw a moray eel. It was big! And then there was that huge, I mean monstrous, fish. Carolyn, what was that?"

"I don't know, but it was bigger than either of us. It might have been bigger than both of us. Beth, do you know what that was?"

Beth and Misty were on the dock, working to straighten out the tanks and gear. "Yeah, we don't see them around here very often, and I don't think I've ever seen them at the garden. It was a goliath grouper."

"A jewfish? At Beth's Garden?" I was surprised; we'd never seen them there. "I only see goliaths a couple of times a year, usually near the Crack or on one of the other deep dives."

"Beth called it a goliath grouper. You just used the term 'jewfish'. Why?"

"I'm sorry, Alicia. That used to be what they were known as. Now, in the days of political correctness, everyone uses the new name. They are a type of grouper, and as you saw they can be very, very big, up to several hundreds of pounds. The old name is what I grew up hearing them called. There are people who claim that when Jesus fed the masses with just two fish and five loaves of bread, the fish were goliath groupers. They're some of the biggest fish in the sea, especially around here."

"Well, I don't know about that but they were huge."

Jeremy helped Kevin get out of the boat. "Kevin, how was it?"

"Not so good. I had a lot of problems down there and spent most of the time trying to adjust one thing or another. Either I was sinking or I was climbing. I was constantly adjusting the air in my vest, or having to clear my mask."

"New divers often have problems with getting and staying neutral. Beth can work with you some more on that and adjust your weights. I'm not sure about the mask, we don't keep spares. Is water coming in the problem?"

"No, well, a little. Mostly it just kept fogging up."

"Is it new?"

"Yeah, I just bought it the day before flying to Belize City."

"Okay, I'll get Marcus to help you prep it. Usually dive shops help people do that."

"I didn't buy it at a dive shop. I got it at the store I work in."

"Okay, if you didn't buy it in dive store then it's probably not one of the better brands. Did they tell you how to pick one that fit?"

"No, nobody in the department that stocks masks actually dives. I got one of the most expensive ones we carry so it should be a decent one."

"Why don't you come back a little later this afternoon and Marcus will help you with getting the mask prepped. I think the cooks at Mountain To Sea have snacks ready. The rest of the guests down there just came in from a snorkel trip."

"Okay, I'll see you after lunch." He walked off, without his mask.

"Gunnar, how did you like it?"

"It was fantastic. The clarity of the water is unbelievable."

"Like I said, we can put you through the full Open Water certification if you'd like."

"I want to make more dives; however, I do not think we will be here long enough to do a full course."

"Okay. We look forward to diving with you more while your family is here. Marcus and I'll be going out in a few minutes with your parents and a few of our guests. Now, your parents are in the dining room."

At that, Gunnar picked up two of the air tanks, placing one of the steel, 120 cubic foot, thirty-four pound empty tanks on each of his shoulders, and followed Misty, who was carrying several sets of regulators, to our storage area. He swung those tanks onto his shoulders as if he were familiar with them. Beyond their weight, most people tend to pick them up by the base and cradle them. He seemed to know that the valves are firmly attached. Most people treat the valves gingerly. Was he being reckless? Or did he have more experience with the tanks than he'd let on?

As he walked his eyes stayed focused on Misty. He dropped off the two tanks, getting a hug and peck on the cheek from Misty. Fuel for the gossip mill, I thought. He joined his parents in the dining hall. Misty returned to the dock, smiling.

The two sisters, Alicia and Carolyn, walked down the beach toward the Mountain To Sea dining hall. When they were out of hearing distance I asked Beth, "So, how was it?"

"The girls did fine. They took to the water like they were born for it. I checked their tanks and neither one used even fifteen hundred pounds of air."

"And Kevin?"

She shook her head. "Not so good. He was the first in the water and thrashed around. He clung to the buoy until everyone else was in the water, and on the way down he held onto the buoy line. I'm surprised the barnacles on the line didn't cut his hand."

Misty grabbed another empty tank. "He wouldn't do the exercises when we got to the bottom; you know, clear his mask, switch regula-tors, and stuff like that. Maybe his mask problems were a part of the cause, but he didn't seem to care where the others were."

"Yeah, if he wanted to see something he'd just barrel his way in to look at it, pushing the others out of the way." Beth put the last of the empty tanks on the dock.

"Misty, would you dive with him again?"

"I don't know, probably, but I'd rather dive with the two women and dump him on Beth and Marcus. I'll go down with Gunnar anytime though."

"With, or on?" Beth asked.

I figured I'd be better off not commenting.

"Anyway, about Kevin, I'd rather dump him on Marcus. Maybe he'd listen more to another man." Misty seemed to be blushing but it could have been the sunlight.

"Okay, why don't the two of you meet up with Marcus and fill him in. Maybe we should have Marcus work with Kevin in the lagoon before he makes another dive. So, how about Gunnar, how did he do?"

Beth looked up. "Like he's been diving for a long time. I mean it. There's no way he was that smooth on his first dive. He's done this before, somewhere."

Misty added, "Yeah, and his buoyancy control was perfect. Maybe better than Marcus, and that boy never seems to need to adjust the air in his BC."

"Marcus doesn't need a BC," I said. "He's that good, and that low in body fat."

"And there's something else. I checked all of the air tanks before and after the dive. Misty and I each used about a thousand pounds of air. Gunnar only used about twelve-hundred pounds."

"Twelve-hundred? Even Marcus would use that much," Misty ex-claimed, "and Gunnar probably has a hundred pounds on Marcus."

Chapter 15

Sunday, December 24th, 3:00 P.M.

Today was turning into a busy day. I wasn't complaining, mind you, since that means making money. With Beth and Misty just coming back from a dive they would need an hour's surface interval before their next dive to avoid nitrogen sickness, what most people know of as "the bends."

We had Gunnar's parents and another couple from Mountain To Sea wanting to dive. It was one of those times when I have to remember I was a dive master and instructor too. One of the problems with owning a resort was that Kim and I often had to concentrate on our business needs and we forget to enjoy the diving. I had Marcus lead the dive.

❧❖❧

We scheduled another dive for later that afternoon with the same three students, plus Larry from Over The Edge, and Bernie and Helene Stamps. Kevin was the first person from Mountain To Sea to come down to our dock. I invited him into our dining hall. Misty and Dylan were in there, having some juice. We each took a seat at their table.

"Kevin, what do you do for a living?" I asked.

"I'm an assistant manager for a sporting goods store. It's one of the largest chain stores in the country, one in which most customers become members." He shifted, as if he wasn't comfortable on the bench seat.

"Where in the Midwest do you live?"

"Illinois. Moline," he said, taking his eyes off Misty and focusing on me.

"Moline? That's pretty close to where you're from, right, Misty?" I asked.

"Yeah, only about ten miles or so. I'm from Coal Valley."

"Coal Valley? What's your name?" Kevin asked.

"Misty. Misty Lawler."

"Is that your married name?"

"I'm not married."

"That's interesting. I went to high school in Coal Valley. I lived just a few miles down the road, in Orion. I thought I knew everybody. You look like you're about my age."

"I'll be thirty next month."

"I turned thirty-one last month. Do you know Paul Roberts? He was a year behind me."

Misty momentarily lost her smile. "I know of him, but I didn't know him well. Well, I have to go check on the air tanks and get suited up."

⚜

From my office I watched as Marcus and Kevin spent some time in the lagoon, practicing skills. I could hear their conversation.

"Kevin, most dive shops recommend using toothpaste to wash the protective gel off new masks. Done right, that works, but all too often people scrub too hard and wind up scratching the face."

"So what do you recommend?"

"Let me show you." He took the mask from Kevin's hands, and reached up to the dock and pulled out a cigarette lighter.

"I start with the front of the mask. See, I hold one lens about six inches from the tip of the flame. If you look close, you can see a light-blue haze around the lens. That's the gel burning."

"How long do you hold it like that?"

"Not long over any one spot. See, in small circles, dipping closer and backing away. It's a dance, of sorts. Too close, or for too long, and you'll actually melt the lens." *I like that reference to a dance. Marcus really is more detail oriented than most Belizeans.*

Marcus waved the inside of the mask around the flame, kind of swirling it around the flame. Finished, he extinguished the flame, waved the mask around in the air for about half a minute to let it cool, and handed it back to Kevin.

"Now, Kevin, rinse it briefly in the water. Just dunk it into the water and bring it up, face down, and swish the water around."

Kevin did as he was told.

"What's that guy doing with his mask?" Kevin asked, motioning toward Larry.

"It's fake spit." Larry tossed a tube to Kevin. "Just put a dab on the inside of each lens, use your finger to get some all the way around the inside, including the sides, not just the face. Make sure to get some in the nose part of the mask. Then rinse it all out. When you can't see any more of the gel, you're about done."

"Why?" Kevin asked, doing as Larry told him.

"It helps to prevent the mask from fogging up. Do this before each dive. I usually do it before getting on the boat and give the mask one more quick rinse before getting into the water. You can keep that bottle."

"It feels like a full bottle. Are you sure you can spare this?"

"Yeah, I have extra. If you run out though, you'll have to use the real thing."

"Larry has duplicates of almost everything he needs for diving here. My guess is he has three or four bottles of that."

"Marcus, you say that like it's a bad to be prepared." Larry didn't really mind people kidding him about having extras.

"Um, what's the 'real thing'?"

"Well, I said it's fake spit, right? You can always spit into your mask and use it. That works just as well."

⁂

I listened as Marcus gave the pre-dive itinerary.

"We're going to a site called 'The Wild Side.' Don't let the name scare you. It's really a fun, peaceful dive. We'll do a backward roll off the side of the boat. Once in the water I want to see you give me the okay sign." He demonstrated by getting eye contact and placing his right hand on the top of his head.

"I want everyone to have some air in their vest before going into the water. So please, right now, put a little air into your vests. Give it enough that the BC feels tight."

Each of the guests did so.

"Good. That also shows there's air in your tanks and the air is turned on. So, once we're in the water we'll go down. Kevin, you and I will go in first and we'll swim down to the bottom together while the rest of the divers get in."

"The two of us go in first. Got it."

"Everyone else, just remember to stay upright and let the air out of your BC and clear your head every few feet. The bottom is at about forty feet. You should've cleared your head at least a dozen times by then."

He waited while each guest gave an indication they were listening. He was quite thorough.

"Kevin, when we're at the bottom, you and I are going to practice clearing your mask and changing your regulator while we wait for the others. I need you to understand that if you don't do the exercises, we come back up. No exercises, no dives. Understand?"

"I understand. No exercises, no dives."

"Larry, you, Bernie, and Helene will be the next in the water.

Once each of you has given her your okay sign, Beth is going to get in and she'll lead the three of you down to the bottom. And Larry, wait for Beth, okay? Put more air in your BC if you need to. I don't think there's much chop out there today. The winds are really calm." The diver down flag on my dock was hanging limp, no breeze blowing at all. He waited for all three to indicate they understood.

"Finally, you two ladies will get in, and once you've given her your okay sign, Misty will lead you down. All okay so far?"

The group nodded or grunted in acknowledgement.

"Alright, once we're all on the bottom, Beth will lead the dive. It'll mostly be a drift dive. We'll swim along the top of The Wall for a few minutes and then drop over the edge. There's a modest current near The Wall. It isn't much, but we'll let the current dictate our direction and speed. Now, let's go have some fun."

~✦~

With their departure, I grabbed my fishing gear and joined a few Mountain To Sea guests heading toward the south end of the island. Jerry Douglas, Antonio Terrazzo, and Rich Williams had all expressed interest in fishing. The waters around Sunrise Caye hold thousands of bonefish and they put up a great fight. I don't find them particularly tasty but they're edible. From our vantage point I could see the divers get in the water and watched Jeremy as he would get a little rest and every few minutes move the boat. From that far away, I couldn't see the trail of bubbles, but Jeremy always stays close to the bubbles, especially when Larry's in the water since we all know how much he hates being on the surface. I caught a couple of good bonefish before I saw the divers climbing back into the boat. I left the rest of the guys to fish and made my way back to the dock about the time the boat made its way through the jetty separating Sunrise Caye from Victoria's Caye.

Beth leapt from the bow of the boat onto the dock and began tying up the boat as Jeremy maneuvered it into place for the night. Marcus, on the stern, tied off that end as the guests began climbing onto the dock.

"So Kevin, how was it?" I asked.

"Overall, it was pretty good," he said as he gathered up his mask and fins. He didn't look at me as he answered.

"Did you have any problems with your mask fogging?"

"Not as long as I was wearing it." He gave Bernie a hard look and started walking down the dock and then toward his cabana.

I looked at Marcus for what that meant but it was Bernie who spoke up.

"Beth found a large lobster hidden in a small cave and pointed to it with her dive light. We all closed in to see it and got kind of bunched up. I was above most of them and dropped down to take a look."

"Okay..." I had a hunch I knew where this was going.

"I guess I was a bit too fast and was about to collide with Kevin, who was coming up from below. I used my arms to try to push myself off Kevin, but I accidentally knocked Kevin's mask off. I've apologized several times on the boat. It was my fault." Bernie looked at Marcus.

"I was close by, and a little below Kevin when it happened. I was able to catch his mask and help him get it back on and cleared. Apparently Kevin has a quick temper."

"I really am sorry about what happened, but, yeah, Kevin does have a temper. And he seems to hold grudges. On the boat ride over here, Saturday morning, Dave was getting seasick."

"Wait, Dave got seasick? A young, fit guy like him?"

"Yeah. Maybe he had too much to drink Friday night. I don't know, but he'd had several drinks at the bar."

"Okay, anyway, back to Kevin." I'd be a little concerned about someone that seemed fit, like Dave, getting seasick on such a calm boat ride but if he'd been drinking the night before then I wasn't too surprised.

"Like I said, on the boat Dave had been near the front of the cabin and he rushed to get to the back of the boat so he could lean over the railing as he threw up. On his way toward the rear of the boat he stepped on Kevin's toes, literally. Kevin gave him an earful, the kind of words I don't like people using around my girls."

"And Kevin pushed Dave off the dock while unloading, right?"

"That's right. And he got mouthy with me last night at the volley-ball game. Then again, a couple of hours later, after he'd had too much One Barrel." One Barrel was the Belizean rum.

"Okay, maybe I need to talk with him. Helene, how was your dive?"

"Oh, it was great. I just loved it. I have no idea what most of the fish that we saw were. I love those rivers of wrasse. They're just beautiful."

"That they are. Do you think Michelle should see them?"

"You don't let up on the sales stuff, do you?" Bernie laughed. "Well, honey, what do you think? Should we let George, Beth and Misty teach her to dive? I think she's ready, but it's your call."

Bernie really put her on the spot, and everyone there waited for her answer.

"Okay, but at least one of us has to be on any dive she makes."

⚜

Not long after Marcus and Dylan had put away all of the dive gear I saw Misty with the two girls, Michelle and Katie, at the end of the dock. Helene and Bernie were upstairs in my office filling out some paperwork. I waited a few minutes, and when they came downstairs, I walked with them down the dock.

As we walked onto the dock I pointed out a baby nurse shark near the shoreline. Annette, our cook, had thrown some food scraps into the water there earlier this afternoon. The shark was scavenging for food. It was a baby, barely three feet long. We get a lot of little nurse sharks and southern stingrays in close to shore, scavenging for food, this time of day.

The two kids were sitting on deck chairs while Misty sat cross-legged on the dock in front of them. She wore a light pair of long pants and a long-sleeved blouse. She's well tanned but that was a good precaution for preventing sunburn. Then again, she might have had a date planned. Gunnar and his parents were in my dining hall, visiting. I walked down to see what the girls were doing and Katie was beaming.

"See my toes? Misty painted them."

"I see that. They're kind of funny-looking."

"No, they aren't!" She put her hands on her hips. "They're pretty. See the dolphin she painted on my big toe?"

"That's cute. What is that on the other big toe?"

"It's a starfish."

"And what is that on your toes, Michelle?"

"She isn't done yet, but this one is going to be a shark, and on the other foot she's going to paint a lobster."

"A shark? Like the one in Misty's tattoo?"

"What tattoo?" Michelle and Katie started looking all over Misty.

Misty looked up. "It's in a place you can't see right now. And I didn't know George knew about it either." She smiled.

What could I say, I liked little bikinis. I was going to miss her when she left. Misty was a beauty but had too many tattoos for my taste. Then again, I thought even one tattoo was like putting graffiti on the Mona Lisa.

"Maybe it's more like the shark over there," I said, pointing to the shoreline end of the dock. They didn't even get up to look: they'd already seen it.

"Those tattoos sure are cool! You know what else is cool?" I asked, looking at Michelle.

"What?" she looked at me, then at her mother and father. Bernie was smiling. These were Daddy's girls, and he couldn't say no to them.

"Learning how to dive, and if you still want to, tomorrow's your turn."

She shrieked in what I had to interpret as happiness. "Can we do it now?"

"No, it's getting late. Besides, I think its dinner time over at Mountain To Sea. I can see people gathering at the dining hall. We'll get started right after breakfast tomorrow."

"What about me? I wanna dive too!" Katie cried.

"I know, but you aren't quite old enough. I have an idea. The classes for older kids like your sister are called bubble-makers and I always go on the bubble-makers dives. Beth usually teaches the class. That means Misty doesn't have to teach the class. So, maybe you and your mother can go snorkeling with Misty. Would you like that?"

"Uh, huh. Can we go out in the deep ocean like Michelle?"

"Maybe. We'll have to see just how well you can swim here first."

"I swim real good. Watch."

Before we could stop her she jumped off the dock into the water and started swimming. That spooked the baby nurse shark. It swam past her, quickly getting away from the splashing and unknown threat.

We got her back on shore. "That's pretty impressive, but if you have something to help you float I think you should wear it."

Helene was drying her off, half-scolding Katie for jumping in so impulsively while trying not to laugh. "She has floaties that wrap around her arms. Katie, I've told you every time you go in the water you need to have them on, haven't I?"

"Yes, ma'am. I just wanted Mr. George to see how well I can swim."

"I know, honey. Just be more careful in the future."

"Yeah, it's not a good idea to scare the sharks like that," I added.

Chapter 16

Sunday, December 24th, 7:00 P.M.

About an hour after dinner I walked down to the Mountain To Sea dining hall. I could hear the guitars and singing well before we walked in. Gator and Gene were entertaining most of the guests with Jimmy Buffett tunes. I was a parrothead myself, but it got a bit boring doing nothing but Buffet's songs for the guests.

"Hey there, boss. Play a song or two," Gator said, handing me his twelve string.

"You play guitar, too?" asked Alicia.

"A little. I'd never make a living at it, but I can pick a little. What would you like to hear?"

"Wow, a dentist, resort owner, and musician. Kim has herself quite the Renaissance man."

"'A Renaissance man.' I like that."

"That's not what she usually calls him."

"Be nice, Gator. They don't need to know all of our secrets." I picked just a few notes, getting familiar with his guitar.

"George, why don't you play that country song you've been practicing?"

"Okay. Here goes…"

The sounds of Spanish guitars out on the shore,
You can hear them from anywhere if you've been there before
But now that postcard panorama's just part of the drama, I'd say
And only dark Spanish eyes can make me feel this way

Dark Spanish eyes? Why was I preoccupied with them? What was Grace trying to tell me?

⌘

"Wow, I've never heard that before. It's really pretty."

"Thanks, Helene. It's called "Dark Spanish Eyes." It was written by a guy who's been here a couple of times: Brian Burns. It's a bit more country than I usually like but I love that song. Are you familiar with XM radio?"

"I am, we have XM in both of our cars."

"On a station called America, Brian Burns was the most requested artist for two years running. I'm not much into country, but I really like some of his tunes."

I played another song, an old Eagles tune that everyone would know, and then handed the guitar back to Gator.

I looked around. "Have a couple of people turned in already?"

"Yeah, boss, Kevin is in his cabana. Dave and Dagan turned in already, too. But we need to talk for a few minutes," Gator said, his guitar on the table. We walked outside while Gene played "Silent Night" and got the two kids to sing along.

"What's up?"

"The five o'clock volleyball got pretty intense."

"Yeah, it usually does. What's new?"

"Kevin had a couple of shots of rum. He got pretty aggressive. Dave was on my side of the net and I set him up for a spike. He hit Kevin pretty hard. Kevin fell to the ground. When he got up he took a couple of swings at Dave. Gene and I had to break them up."

"Anybody hurt?"

"No, Dave can handle himself and just pushed Kevin away each time. They both said some stuff, you know, the usual B.S. Dave walked away."

"Anything else?" I didn't like conflicts. I hated to have to play the heavy around here. I figured people were on vacation and ought to be able to let loose. I also figure people who can afford to come here were able to behave themselves.

"After dinner, Dave and Dagan left pretty quickly. They'd spent a lot of time in the sun today and were tired. Besides, it's their honeymoon. I'm surprised they've been out of the cabana as much as they have."

"I didn't realize they were on their honeymoon. They'd been together a long time, based on what they said at breakfast this morning."

"Yeah, but they just recently got married. Anyway, Kevin had a couple of more drinks and got a little loud and obnoxious. He was using some pretty crude language. Bernie asked him to watch his language around the kids. Kevin's response wasn't very nice. I wound up escorting Kevin back to his cabana."

"Okay, which cabana is he in?"

"Number Seven."

"Okay, I'll go have a talk with him in a few minutes. Who won the volleyball game tonight?"

"The first game my side won, but I had an unfair advantage."

"What was that?"

"Misty played with us. That girl doesn't let up. She seems like this sweet little girl next door, but the competitive fire burns strong in her."

"Yeah, I've seen that a few times. What about the second game?"

"The other team won. That guy Gunnar was here, playing for the other team. He's big, strong, and quick."

"How'd he do against Misty?"

"Misty spiked him, twice. Why? Something there I hadn't noticed?" he asked, grinning.

"Maybe. It could be just my imagination."

"Maybe so, but having been with her a few times myself, I wish him luck. She has that same competitive fire in her then, too. You know, it's almost as if she has to win. It's a power thing. She has to demonstrate that she has the control."

❦

We went back inside. I caught Bernie's attention and we stepped outside.

"Kim and I were wondering about the kids. It's Christmas Eve. Are they expecting Santa to find them tonight?"

"Yeah, at least Katie is. I had to promise Katie that Santa knew where they'd be and would stop by. We've put a couple of bags on the porch for Santa. We have a few things for each of them that Helene will put in the bags after the kids are asleep. Why?"

"Kim does calligraphy, and she paints. She used some of her scrap canvas and made up a treasure map and buried a treasure. How about putting the map into Katie's bag from Santa?"

"George, that's great! You didn't have to do this."

"Oh, this is going to be fun. Besides, it isn't much. We buried a Crown Royal bag, you know, the purple velvet bags that Crown Royal comes in, with some Belizean coins in it." I gave him the map and he slipped it into his pocket.

"So she'll wake up Christmas morning, find Santa's gifts, and one of them will be a treasure map. I love it. Thanks a lot! You know, Helene and I were a little worried about bringing the kids here. You guys are really making them feel welcome."

"It's fun for us, too. We don't get kids here very often. Oh, this is for Michelle. It's one of the disposable dive cameras. I hope she likes it. Well, I'm off. I have to go have a talk with Kevin."

"Good luck with that. I don't envy you. We'll see you in the morning. I think we'll be turning in soon."

As I walked away I could hear Gene and Gator, with the two kids, singing about Rudolph.

⚜

It was past sunset and getting dark. There was a very thin layer of clouds. I saw a few stars blinking through the gaps. A breeze blew from the northeast and forecast an overnight storm.

I could see Kevin's lantern was on. From the base of the stairs I called up, "Kevin, are you up there? It's George."

He stuck his head out the window. "Yeah, c'mon up." He slurred his words some.

I walked in and sat on the wooden bench. "I hear you took a couple of swings at Dave. What's going on?"

"I don't know. He's just been on my nerves, over and over again. It's always something."

"It's not like he's the only one you've had a problem with. What about Bernie?"

"Look, it's not like I went for vacation at Disney World. I wasn't expecting to see kids here. I figure I paid a lot, I ought to be able to be myself."

"They paid a lot to be here too. They have a right to expect you to exercise a little self-control around the kids."

"They shouldn't have brought the kids here then."

"They did, so you need to watch it. I really don't want conflicts around here. There's another boat coming out on Wednesday. If you get into any more fights you'll be going back to the mainland with that boat."

"Okay." He took a swig from a beer and set it down.

"There's something else. Beth and Misty don't think you're paying attention to them during the dives. They're the dive instructors and dive masters. They're responsible for your safety in the water, and their livelihood is on the line as well as your safety. You need to do what they say. As it is, they aren't real sure they want to dive with you."

"I want to dive with Beth and Marcus, but not with Misty."

"Why not Misty?"

"Because she isn't who she said she is."

"What?"

"I don't know who she is, but there wasn't anyone named Misty Lawler in Coal Valley."

"Why would she lie about that?"

"I don't know who she really is, but she isn't Misty Lawler of Coal Valley. Coal Valley High School is really small. My graduating class had thirty-three people. Even if she were a year behind me I'd have known her. I knew everyone in that school. There wasn't a Misty Lawler in that school, or that town. At least, not alive today."

"What do you mean by that?"

"There was a family named Lawler. Jason Lawler graduated the year before me. We played football and basketball together. He had a sister, named Misty or Mindy or something like that, who died when she was five."

"I'm sure you're mistaken."

"No, I'm not. Do you remember me asking about Paul Roberts?"

"Yeah, she said she knew him but not well. Why?"

"There wasn't anyone named Paul Roberts in that school."

Chapter 17

Monday, December 25th, 5:30 A.M.

Kim and I started each morning with a jog around the island. With Kim still on the mainland I invited Beth to join me. Five trips make for two miles and when running in the sand that's a pretty good workout. We passed a little gossip.

"Merry Christmas, by the way," she said.

"And a Merry Christmas to you."

"I looked outside last night around one-thirty and saw Misty coming back from the Mountain To Sea side of the island," Beth said as we started out.

"My guess is she was with Gene, but I didn't think he was all that much to look at."

"George, you're so clueless. It has to be Gator. He's a much better-looking guy, and dresses better too. And he's smart. I'm sure it was Gator."

"I have reason to believe he's—what's the saying—'been there, done that?'"

"George, I repeat, you're clueless. As for having 'been there/done that,' maybe so, but he might want to go back again."

"Could be, I gather he really enjoyed it. I won't repeat everything he's said about her, but I got the feeling she's into some weird stuff. Kinky, domination type stuff."

"I wouldn't know, and don't really want to."

"Maybe it was one of the single guys on the trip? Jerry or Kevin?" *Okay, probably no chance for Kevin, I thought.*

"Kevin? I don't *think* so. He's a jerk. Jerry, hmmm, I don't know. All I've seen him do is kayak and sit in the hammock, reading. I'm not sure he even swings that way, if you get my meaning."

"I suspect he does. I caught him checking out Dagan yesterday."

"Shoot, I've checked out Dagan and I'm straight. She's got super-model looks. No wonder she's on TV."

"He better hope Dave doesn't catch him checking her out. Wait, she's on TV? I didn't know she's on TV."

"I talked with them a little yesterday. She's a business reporter on one of the network affiliates in Boston."

"That's different. Are you sure Misty was coming from Mountain To Sea, and not the docks?"

"The docks? Well, maybe the Mountain To Sea one. Not ours, why?"

"You've forgotten about Gunnar. They seemed interested in each other yesterday."

"Gunnar! Yeah. He's pretty good looking, better than Gene for sure and different than Gator."

⚜

As we finished our run and were walking toward our cabanas I heard something. A thumping sound: thump-thump-thump......thump-thump...thump.....thump-thump...thump "Ow! Damn girl, that hurt!"

We walked around the back side of the cabanas, following the sounds.

"She talked you into holding the heavy bag for her, huh?" I asked, looking at Dylan. Suspended from Misty's cabana hung a homemade heavy bag. It was an old duffle bag, filled with sand. She'd sown some reinforcements and grommets to support the weight. I remember it taking four of us to lift it into place and get it hung securely.

"Yeah, I should have known better." He was leaning over to one side.

Misty was decked out in a tank top, shorts, boxing gloves, and was barefoot. Her clothes were soaked from sweat and clung to her curves. Not necessarily an unpleasant thing for those of us that like tight fitting clothing on such a shapely woman. "Oh, suck it up, you big baby," she said.

"I agreed to hold the bag, thinking you'd just be punching it. I didn't expect you to do all this martial arts stuff." Dylan was trying to stand up straight, massaging his left side.

"I never said that's all I was going to do. Just punching the bag, what kind of exercise is that? Now, get back behind the bag, you big wuss."

"I don't think so. You didn't just kick the bag, you kicked me."

"You should have held the bag steady. George, want to hold the bag for me? Show him how a real man does it."

"Oh no, not me. I've seen you work out. You get lost in it, like you've got a real to the death fight you're trying to win. This 'real man' has enough sense not to hold it."

I walked off, shaking my head. Back in the states, those two dated for a while. They still hooked-up every now and then. I thought Dylan would know better, but if getting the crap kicked out of him is a price he's willing to pay, well, all the luck to him.

Marcus passed me, a quizzical look in his eye, as he headed toward the source of the ruckus. I just smiled, shook my head, and kept going. Then I heard Misty yell out, "Marcus, boy get over here and hold this bag for me."

~◈~

Erin sat by me at breakfast. "George, I had an interesting conversation yesterday with Einar Boxler."

"Oh yeah? What made it interesting?"

"He came over to me and said 'Pardon me, but when we met yesterday I thought I knew you from somewhere. We have met before, yes?'"

"Had you?"

"I told him I'd been a reporter in Bosnia and we'd met a couple of times at press meetings in Sarajevo."

"What'd he say?"

"I told him that I recognized him right away, that in fact I had some notes for my book based on him. I asked him about his biography, the one that said he wasn't married and had no children."

"What'd he say?"

"He asked me if I knew who Linus Walker was. I didn't."

"Okay, who was Linus Walker."

"Is, but that doesn't matter so much as his story. Milosovic was a real bastard. Many of the leaders of the allied forces were afraid of the guy. Linus Walker commanded a British Special Forces unit. His team was often sent out on hunting missions, looking for specific bad guys. They were used on 'bring 'em back, dead-or-alive' type missions with a preference for dead."

"And?"

"According to Einar, Walker's teenaged son was killed by a hit and run driver. The driver actually hit the kid while the kid was riding a bike, went a block and turned around, then ran over him again."

"That doesn't sound like an accident."

"No, it wasn't. The driver ran into another car a block or so down the street. The police arrested him and eventually he was identified as one of the people that the hunting teams were looking for. The belief is that Milosevic sent him to England to kill Walker's family."

"Damn, that's pretty hard." I couldn't think of much to say.

"After that, a lot of the military leaders started trying to hide their personal lives, to protect their families. Einar said that one of the Belgium leaders was married three times, with two ex-wives, and seven kids. His official bio if anyone found it said he was never married and was one of the many openly gay members of the Belgium military."

"So, in his official bio, Einar attempted to hide his family status from Milosovic?"

"Exactly. I found Frida's biography online using her maiden name. She mentions being married and having a son."

"Did you ask him about the rumors about why he left Bosnia?"

"I did, but he said it was a personal matter. He did say that reporters should not believe everything they hear and even where there's truth, it might not be the whole truth. He wouldn't come out and say what he meant."

"Did he say anything at all about it?"

"He said something about remembering the allied forces were there to disarm both sides even though one side didn't have weapons."

"Weren't we there to protect the Muslim population? I seem to remember something about ethnic cleansing."

"Exactly. I've sent a few emails to friends. One said they'd heard a rumor that he got caught turning over some weapons from Milosovic's people to the Bosniaks, the Muslims. It's just a rumor, but it happened shortly after the Srebrenica massacre."

"What's that?" I was on my island, not paying any attention to foreign hostilities a world away that didn't concern me.

"The Serbs, Milosovic's people, murdered over eight-thousand men, women, and children. It was the worst mass-murder since World War Two."

❧❖❦

After my breakfast I walked down to the Mountain To Sea dining hall. The two girls were showing their gifts from Santa to Eric and

Susan White.

"Mr. George, come see what Santa brought us!" Katie shrieked.

"Santa? He found you all the way down here?" I asked, smiling as I sat down. I had to step over Lucky, who was sitting beneath Katie, waiting for a snack. Lucky nudged my feet. I guessed she was getting impatient.

"Uh huh, just like Daddy promised he would."

I looked at Bernie. He had a huge smile on his face. The pride that comes from knowing your child thinks you're perfect.

"Wow! So, what did Santa bring you?"

"He brought me a new doll, and some music, but best of all he brought me this treasure map!" She held it up to show me.

"A treasure map? Really? May I have it?" I reached for it.

"No!" she shouted, pulling the map close to her. "It's mine. Santa gave it to me."

"Maybe so, but the map is of my island. If there's treasure here, it's mine, isn't it?"

"Losers weepers, finders keepers. But, you can help me look for the treasure."

"I'd like that, but you know who'd like to help and is really, really good at finding treasure?"

"Who?"

"Ms. Kim. She loves looking for treasure. She's found some before." *It doesn't hurt that she buried it in the first place.*

"Can we go ask her?"

"Well, not yet, honey. She won't be back from the mainland until about time for lunch. Is that okay?"

She looked dejected. "I don't know. How good is she at reading maps?"

"She's the best, I promise. She'll help you find it."

Of course, Kim made the map so she should have no trouble reading it, I thought.

"Oh, okay. I *guess* I can wait until lunch time."

"How about you, Michelle? What did Santa bring you?"

"An underwater camera! Just like the ones you sell in your gift shop," she said, and smiled to let me know she didn't believe in Santa.

"Hmmm, maybe it was Santa I heard rummaging around in the shop last night." She surprised me by coming over to me, giving me a hug and quietly saying, "Thank you."

Chapter 18

Monday, December 25th, 9:00 A.M.

Beth was certified to teach the Bubblemakers class but I always sat in. I liked to make sure the kids were paying attention, and that their parents weren't manipulating them. I knew it's tough for parents to let their kids learn at their own pace in this class but this was life-and-death stuff. The kids had to understand, not just mimic what Mom or Dad say.

Beth brought with her one of the best teaching tools available: a GI Joe action figure with its own scuba outfit. It was a pretty neat toy, when you thought about it. It was battery-powered and kicked its legs just like we try to teach divers to do. Its arms could be made to do a lot of things, including holding the doll's nose to simulate the process for clearing one's ears.

I used to have one like it. In the doll's, I mean action figure's, scuba tanks you can put in this little pellet, kind of like an aspirin-sized Alka-Seltzer, that fizzes up as water seeps in. The energy released has to go somewhere and they'd engineered a funnel of sorts that caused Joe's legs to move. Somebody crammed several of those tablets into my GI Joe and let it go in the water on the open ocean side of the island. I never did see it again. There's no way of telling how far that little guy swam. It had enough fuel crammed into it that he may have made it to The Wall. Then again, a shark or barracuda might have gotten him.

Bernie was in the dining hall as Beth taught the class. At another table, Erin worked on her computer. I leaned against the railing, alternately watching Beth and Michelle and looking out into the lagoon, waiting for Kim. Instead, I saw the small skiff that Einar Boxler and his family used coming in, and walked out to meet them.

"Merry Christmas! I said as they pulled up to the dock.

"Yah, and Happy Christmas to you. We would like to make a dive this morning, if that is alright." I helped Frida climb out of the skiff and onto our dock.

"Of course it's alright with us. Misty and Marcus are about to take a group out to Victoria's Caye. I'm sure they'd love having you join in. They should be getting their gear ready in a few minutes."

Jeremy pulled away from the dock with a full load of divers. There were enough that, had Juan been back, I would have used two boats. My boats are best suited for six guests, plus two dive masters. In this case we had Larry, Kevin, Dave and Dagan, as well as Mindy and Rich Williams making their first dive this trip, plus the Boxlers.

Naturally, within minutes of that full boat pulling away I saw the *Sensencula* making its way through the coral heads. Another five minutes and I'd have had the second boat captain.

Kim tossed me one of the lines as Juan pulled the boat up to the dock and cut the engines. I tied the bow line while Juan tied the stern. I helped Kim onto the dock, hugged and kissed her, and whispered "Happy Birthday." It's our little secret that Christmas is also Kim's birthday. It's also our wedding anniversary. That coincidence was my brilliant idea. I never miss a birthday or anniversary.

"Merry Christmas, Juan. Was your wife surprised to see you last night?"

"You can say I surprised her, yes. Please, excuse me." He sulked toward his room.

"What was that about?" I asked Kim.

"Seems his wife wasn't expecting him and she had company."

"Oh."

"Yeah, he's pretty upset. Not much we can do about that, I guess."

"No, there isn't. What's the latest on Jack and Sherry?"

"Arthur, that's the doctor we picked up from Southwestern Caye, told me that Jack is going to be okay. His neck and back are fine. He'll have some pain for a week or so but there wasn't any serious damage."

"When will Jack and Sherry be able to fly home?"

"Tomorrow. I've already helped Sherry make travel plans. I held her close, kissed her. "We've done all we can. God, I missed you," I said.

"May I have my present now?" She kissed me.

"It's upstairs." I lead her to our cabana, where I wanted her anyway.

I closed the door and secured it. She pulled the package down from a shelf. "Give me a hint," she said.

"It's old."

"So are you," she said.

"I'm not nearly as old as that."

"You got me something old for Christmas, for our anniversary, and for my birthday? Let me guess, it was cheap too," she said.

I smiled. "It's also used. Well worn, I think you could say, and all I had to do was pay for shipping."

She unwrapped it, treating it far more gingerly than I did when I wrapped it.

She set the wrapping paper aside, and laid it out on the bed.

"Is this, did you get this from Katherine?" she asked.

"Yes. She's letting us have it, just as I gave it to her years ago."

"Does this mean you're ready?"

"Ready, willing, and I hope to show you soon, able."

"The Schroeder Family baby quilt. I love it."

She spread it out. The quilt had been handed down for five generations. The quilt itself measured four feet wide and six feet long. Across the top was a blue field, with a single white star in it. One of the star's points aimed toward the right side. Below the blue field, the right half was white and the left half red. It looked like the Texas state flag. Embroidered on the white half were the names and birthdates of every child that had ever benefited from the quilt's protective warmth. The names formed the family tree.

I pointed to my father's name, then mine and Katherine's beside it. Below my name was Austin's name, and under Katherine's were the names of my two nephews and one niece.

"I want us to add another name to that list," I said.

<hr />

We were otherwise occupied for a while. I hadn't seen the dive boat return. I looked outside and saw Beth and Michelle, suited up, practicing in the lagoon. Bernie was in his wet-suit, taking pictures. Helene and Katie were watching from the dock.

"Honey, the kids were pretty happy with their presents from Santa. I told Katie that after lunch you'd help her look for the buried treasure."

"You want me to keep Katie and her mother busy while you take Michelle out on her first dive, don't you?" Kim had changed into a light dress, kissed me and put her arms around me. She had on a new perfume. It reminded me of strawberries.

"Michelle's bound to be nervous enough without having the whole family watching. Bernie's going with her, of course. I can't imagine any parents, capable of diving, not going with their child on her first." I turned Kim around and I gave her a gentle back-rub.

"You like these kids, don't you?" she asked.

"Yeah, it's been fun having them here."

"I spent last night at the Mountain To Sea guide house in Belize

City. Sticks told me about your conversation. Are you sure you want to sell?"

"Absolutely. I don't know what we'll do next, but yes, it's time. I want us to raise a family."

She leaned in and kissed me. We got distracted again.

Chapter 19
Monday, December 25th, 12:30 P.M.

When I looked out the window the lagoon was devoid of people. All of the boats were in place. We walked down to the dining hall and found most of the Over The Edge guests and staff.

"I'm not very hungry. I'll just have a couple of bites of fruit, I think."

"Kim, are you feeling all right?"

"I'll be okay. My stomach was bothering me this morning. I don't know why. I got sick on the way back from Dangriga."

"That's not like you. Was the water choppy?" I noticed the winds had shifted a bit today, blowing in more from the southwest today.

"No, it was a smooth ride. It's probably just the stress from yesterday. I'll be fine."

❧❖❧

Beth looked up, smiling as if she knew something that was supposed to be a secret.

"So, Beth, how was the rest of the class? Is Michelle ready?" I asked, sitting down across from her and clearing a space for Kim next to me.

"And then some. That little girl is really comfortable in the water. She mastered everything. I even had her get out of the BC and put it back on in the water."

"That isn't a requirement of the Bubblemakers class, that's reserved for the Open Water certification. Is she still looking forward to the dive?"

"She's excited. She and Bernie were ready a while ago, but I went up to get you and realized you were, umm, busy. I suggested we go after lunch."

"Oh, yeah, we'll make hers the first dive after lunch. It'll be just the two of us, Michelle, and Bernie."

"Where to?"

"The aquarium. They've already snorkeled there and it doesn't get too deep." The aquarium is within the atoll and is an area about a hundred yards in diameter ringed by taller coral heads. The Mountain To Sea guests all kayak there on Sunday as part of their orientation and snorkel. It seldom gets more than twenty feet deep but has most of the fun stuff to see.

⚜

Annette and Felicia, the lead cook this week at Mountain To Sea, were working together and had a big holiday dinner planned for this evening. A light lunch of fish tacos, a build-it-yourself salad, and some diced fruit would tide us all over.

⚜

Thirty minutes after lunch was done I rounded up Bernie and Michelle. Beth got Michelle suited up and went through a few minutes of exercises in the lagoon, just to make sure Michelle hadn't forgotten everything she'd learned over lunch.

"Hey, Marcus," I shouted. "Go find Juan and tell him we're ready."

"Yes, your majesty," he said, running off toward the staff's quarters.

Nice to know someone remembers how to properly address the King.

A few minutes later Juan arrived, and we climbed into the boat. Beth and I had decided during lunch that we'd sit on different benches. If Michelle sat next to Beth she'd be the first in the water; if Michelle sat next to me I'd be first in the water. Our theory being the one she sat next to was the one she'd trust the most to help her in the water. She sat next to Beth.

Jeremy, Marcus, and Misty were loading the other dive boat for a trip out to the Sunrise Caye Wall. They had four divers ready. I was happy to see Larry among them. He was making more dives than usual for him.

Good, that means he had more fun and it means more money for me.

As Juan steered our boat toward the aquarium I watched Katie and Helene waving to Michelle. She and Bernie waved back. The island was almost out of sight when I saw Kim spread a blanket at the end of the dock and she sat down with Katie and Helene. I guessed they were getting familiar with the treasure map.

After we each put some air into our vests Beth got in the water, demonstrating to Michelle how to do the backward roll. Bernie took a couple of pictures and caught Michelle in mid-roll. That should make for a great picture. It might be worth sending to SCUBA magazine for their annual photo contest.

The dive itself went pretty well. When Michelle did the backward roll she wasn't holding her mask securely and it came off. Beth grabbed it and handed it to her while I got into the water myself. We waited until she was ready.

"Okay, Michelle, whenever you're ready I want you to raise your left arm and let the air out of the BC. Remember to clear your nose as we descend." Beth said, "Whenever you're ready."

Bernie and I both began our descent. When we got about ten feet down I motioned for Bernie to wait. It was probably was only thirty seconds or so before I saw Michelle come down, cycling her feet, kind of like someone trying to tread water. That's a common newcomer's mistake and delayed her descent. She looked my way and I pointed to my legs, did the cycling motion she was doing, and shook my head. She stopped kicking and her rate of descent improved. Beth gave her the "okay" sign and reminded her to clear her ears.

Once at the bottom, at about eighteen feet, Beth led her through some basic exercises. Beth put a little bit of air in Michelle's BC, helping her to get neutral. Getting the right amount of air in the BC is important. With too much air the diver has to work at staying down, the BC wants to lift them to the surface. With too little air, or conversely too much weight on the dive belt, the diver has to work at not sinking to the bottom.

Once they were through the basic exercises we set off swimming around a coral head. I pointed to a spot on the coral, getting her attention, and pretended to touch it just to have Beth slap my hand. The intent was to show her not to touch any of the coral but especially not this fire coral. It stings, kind of like a fire ant bite.

Beth and I took turns pointing out critters like lobsters and eels. I picked up one lobster and held it a few inches in front of her. She backed away as if afraid of its claws. At almost every turn I saw Bernie, with a proud smile and wide-eyed, taking pictures. Every couple of minutes we'd stop and have Michelle show us how much air she had left. The dive lasted about thirty-five minutes, impressive for a first dive. After a couple of minutes at ten feet for the required safety stop we surfaced. Juan had the boat positioned very close by.

On the boat ride back Michelle couldn't stop talking. "Can we go again?" She gulped down a bottle of ice water.

I looked at Bernie. I couldn't imagine a prouder papa. "What do you say we go back out again in about an hour? Maybe we'll get your mother to go with us to Beth's Garden and make it a family trip."

"We can't make it a family trip without Katie," she replied.

"What if we get Misty and Kim to snorkel with her, above us as we dive?"

"She'd like that. Katie likes them."

The boat ride wasn't but five minutes, if that, but she drank two bottles of ice water. Her gulps of water were the only time she wasn't talking.

Once back at the dock her mother, Katie, and Kim were waiting.

"Honey, how was it?" Helene asked.

"That was so much fun! We saw all kinds of things. We saw lobsters, and eels, and there was that barracuda. Oh my God, I thought it was going to let me touch it!"

"A barracuda?" Helene asked, looking at Bernie.

"Yeah, it was impressive. Maybe thirty inches long, but it just seemed to park itself about two feet in front of her and stayed there for maybe three minutes. That WAS awesome."

I had to ask, "Did you get any pictures of that?"

"I hope so. I'm afraid I took too many and might have filled up the roll before that. I hope not, that was *awesome*," he said as he high-fived Michelle.

I helped Michelle up onto the dock. Katie walked over to her and handed her a chocolate bar. Michelle opened it and took a bite.

"Katie, what have you got there?" I asked.

"Candy! We found a bag of treasure and there was candy in it!"

"Candy? Was there any gold in it?"

"No, there wasn't any gold, but there was money. Ms. Kim said the coins are Belize money. She said its ten whole dollars worth! *And* there was another map." She held up the once buried Crown Royal bag for us to see and another piece of canvas.

"Another map? The treasure had another treasure map in it?" Kim didn't tell me that so I really was surprised.

"Uh-huh. Ms. Kim said she thinks you ought to help me look for this treasure. She said I have to share some of it with you if we find it.

Can we go look for it now?"

"I wish I could, but I've got some work to do and we're going to make another dive in a little while. In fact, Michelle wants your mom to come with us on that dive and we were thinking that you, Ms. Kim, and Misty might come with us and snorkel over us. Would you like that?"

"Yeah! Can't we go now?"

"Not yet. Whenever we go diving we have to spend some time above the water. Let's see, it's three o'clock now. How about we make that dive at four o'clock? That way we'll be back in time for dinner."

Monday, December 25th, 4:00 P.M.

I decided to use the *Sensencula* for this trip. We had all four members of the Stamps family, Eric and Susan White, along with Beth, Misty, Kim and myself. Several others wanted to come with us. It seemed nearly every diver on the island wanted to be part of Michelle's dive but I didn't want a big crowd making Michelle nervous. I sent Larry, Dave and Dagan Cavuto, and Rich and Mindy Williams out on another dive at Sunrise Caye Wall with Marcus and Dylan in another boat.

The *Sensencula* is a larger boat and sits higher.

"Michelle, how did you like doing that backward roll off the boat earlier?" I asked.

"It was kind of scary. I thought it was going to hurt but it didn't." She moved closer to Beth.

"This boat sits higher in the water than the other boat. It's a bigger fall. Does that scare you?"

""It's kind of scary, falling backward." Michelle looked at Beth while answering my question.

"I know. You can also step off the front of the boat so that you can see the water. When you do that, the BC and air tank are not going to go as far into the water as the rest of you will. They'll ride up under your arms. It might hurt a little but it's not as scary."

Michelle looked at Beth. "How do you want to go in?"

"Michelle, I almost never do the forward step. I'd rather do the backward roll. But it's up to you. I know the backward roll is kind of scary."

"I'm afraid I'll flip all the way over from this high."

"You won't do that, honey. The weight of the tank won't let you flip that far. How about I go first and then you can decide?"

"Okay."

Beth smiled and, like a true Texan, said, "Hey, y'all, watch this!" and rolled over the edge. When she was right side up she waved and said, "See how easy that was?"

Michelle checked her own gear and sat on the edge. "I'll go backward. I'm ready."

"Okay, but let's get your parents and Eric and Susan in the water first so they'll be out of your way," I said.

Once the rest of the divers were in I made sure Michelle had her mask on securely and was breathing through the regulator. "Okay, honey, anytime you're ready."

She rolled over, hit the water with an impressive splash, righted herself, and gave the "okay" sign. She looked at Beth and waited while the others descended. Beth pulled her a few feet away from the boat and I joined them in the water.

"Alrighty then, what do you say we go diving?" I asked. Michelle gave me a thumbs-up, held her deflator valve over her head and began letting air out of her vest. Beth did the same.

I watched as Kim, then Katie, and finally Misty jumped into the water on the other side of the boat. Katie had her mask and snorkel plus a floatation vest. She'd be able to swim on the surface and breathe through the snorkel, but not dive down. They swam around the boat where they faced me. I took my regulator out of my mouth, swam up to Katie and stuck my tongue out. She stuck hers out at me. I put my regulator back in and descended, rolling over to wave at Katie as I descended.

Mindful of the depth restriction for kids, we swam to one of the larger coral heads. The adults were deeper. The base of this coral head was about thirty-five feet. Beth and I let Michelle set the pace. We wanted her to really enjoy the dive and get a chance to see things she'd remember. Sensory overload was a real worry.

I got her attention and gave her the signal we'd worked out for hovering. Basically I crossed my arms, each hand grasping the opposite elbow, and pulled my legs into a cross-legged position. The intent was to just hover. Once she'd done the same, and Beth helped adjust the air in her vest to remain neutral, I pointed to the coral head. She focused in and saw what I wanted her to see: a large, approximately fifteen inches in diameter, gray angelfish. The angelfish swam past us, turned, and swam back the other way. Its mate joined it and they swam within inches of Michelle's mask, circling us, before returning to their normal patrol.

A few minutes later the adults below were signaling for us to look their way. Bernie banged an aluminum carabiner against his tank, the sound alerting us. Michelle turned to look at them just as three southern stingrays passed between us. She kicked a few times, trying to follow, but couldn't keep up. When she turned back toward the coral head we looked up to see Katie, Kim and Misty above us. She waved at Katie who pointed down and behind Michelle. Michelle rolled back, face down, just in time to see a loggerhead turtle swim past.

We frequently checked her air pressure. When she was down to eight-hundred pounds of air Beth led her up a few feet to begin the required safety stop. I swam down to join the other adults, hoping we'd get another ten or fifteen minutes of diving in. Bernie and Helene headed up for their safety stop. I motioned for the Whites to come over, and when they reached me I pointed down. I swam to the sandy bottom and pointed. They didn't understand. I reached a finger out and a part of the sand moved. They still didn't get it. What I pointed to was a peacock flounder, a type of flounder that can change its colors to match the surface it lies upon. I showed them a juvenile ribbon fish. At that age the ribbon fish looks like a multi-colored piece of ribbon and its spine wasn't fully formed. It swam in sort of a corkscrew motion. We encountered several parrot fish and a couple of large groupers. Seeing the groupers made me think of the big holiday dinner waiting for us.

Once everyone was back in the boat we headed to the island. There was just enough time for showers before dinner.

Chapter 21

Monday, December 25th, 5:30 P.M.

When Kim and I walked to the Mountain To Sea dining hall I found several people engaged in the nightly volleyball game. This wasn't a game for kids; it got pretty rough. If there's such a thing as full-contact volleyball, these games would qualify. Several guests were watching the game. I saw Kevin sitting on the dining hall steps with a tall drink in his hand.

Gator yelled out, "George, we're a man short. You're on our team now. Get in here, boss!"

I took a spot next to Misty on the back row, thankful to be on her team. I saw the two girls, Michelle and Katie, sitting on the sand near the base of the steps, a safe distance from the action.

The two teams exchanged points a few times until Misty, Beth and I were on the front row. We faced Marcus, Bernie, and Jeremy.

"Alright, Gator, let's finish this. We only need three more points," Misty yelled out.

At that, Gator tossed the ball up high and jumped higher than I'd ever seen him, hitting the ball at a sharp angle. It just cleared the net. Prepared for it, Bernie hit it upward and toward my side of the court. Jeremy jumped up to spike the ball.

Jeremy and I were the same height but I couldn't jump nearly as high as he could. I didn't even try; instead, I got ready for the spike and put it back up toward the opposite side of the court, still on our side of the net. It was just barely going to clear the net. I was trying to set Misty up for the spike.

She and Marcus both went for the ball. They were about the same height. Marcus might weigh, at the most, twenty pounds more than Misty. Skill and strength wise, they're about even. It was just a matter of timing. Marcus got to it a couple of tenths of a second before Misty and went for the spike. Misty's hang-time allowed her to deflect it down over the other side of the net.

"I've got it!" Bernie called out as he dove for the ball. He missed and got scraped up by the coral in the sand. He limped off the court to get cleaned up.

I held up playing for a moment to make sure Bernie was okay. I looked at his scrapes. "There's some ointment in the medicine box sitting on the bookshelves in the dining hall. Why don't you put some of that on, along with a bandage or two?"

"I'll do that. Don't worry, I'll be fine." He limped toward the steps to the dining hall. I turned back to the game.

"Hey, watch it, damn you!" I heard. I turned and saw Kevin rising up, his drink glass on the step, knocked over. I saw Kevin shove Bernie, who toppled over, falling off the steps onto the sand below, where his two girls were playing.

"Leave my Daddy alone!" Katie screamed as Kevin moved toward Bernie, who was struggling to get up. Kevin moved closer to Bernie, shoving Katie aside.

Misty moved faster than anyone else. Bernie still lay on the ground. Misty ran to the steps, jumped off, her right foot out in front. Her foot struck Kevin's right side, shoving him over. He fell on his side and rolled onto his back. By the time he'd shaken it off and started to stand, Misty was standing between Kevin and the girls.

"Get up and I'll kill you. Do you hear me? Come on, get up and move towards the kids. Come on!"

"You're crazy!" he shouted. Kevin stood and staggered in her direction, but I think he was still moving toward Bernie.

I was moving toward them when I saw Misty move: a hard kick to Kevin's groin. He doubled-over and she brought her knee up, striking him in the face. He fell over and she kicked his head.

"Enough, Misty! That's enough," I yelled, getting in front of her. "The kids are okay. That's enough!"

She looked at me. There was fire in her eyes, and yet a sense of darkness. After a few seconds she turned toward the girls and then ran off.

"Gator, come over here and help me with Kevin." Kevin was bleeding from his nose and mouth.

"Marcus, help Bernie and the kids. Beth, check on Misty."

Chapter 22

Monday, December 25th, 6:00 P.M.

After making sure Kevin was okay and escorting him back to his cabana, I checked in on Bernie. Then I went down to Over The Edge and knocked on the door to Misty's cabana.

"I'm sorry," she said as I entered. "If you're going to fire me, I understand."

"I need to understand what happened. Tell me why you lost it."

I sat on a bench. The members of my dive staff each have their own rooms in one of three cabanas. Each room was really small, with just enough room for a twin-sized bed along one wall, and, on the opposite wall a couple of rods for hanging clothes and a couple of low shelves.

"I haven't told you the whole truth about myself and where I grew up. My mother died when I was ten years old, in a car accident. My father was driving." She looked into my eyes. There was no emotion in what she said. No hate, no shame, just a simple statement of fact.

"Alcohol?"

"Yeah, my old man was drunk. Actually, he was a drunk." She laughed. "Sure, he had a job and went to work most days, but afterward he'd go to the only pub in town and get plastered. Unless it was a couple of days before payday, then he'd stop at the package store and pick-up what he wanted because he could write a check and trust that it wouldn't hit the bank until payday."

"I've known a lot of people who survived by floating checks." I didn't really have any idea what to say.

"Getting drunk wasn't all he did, nor the worst. I can remember him coming home, drunk and mean, and taking it out on my mom. I could hear them fighting, but mom usually sent me and Rachel, my kid sister, to our bedroom when he came stumbling in." The same matter-of-fact tone of voice, but now she couldn't look at me. She looked at the floor.

"Just arguing?"

"No. Only once or twice did I actually see him hit her, but I'd see the bruises, the black eyes. Then, every once in a while, he'd decide that instead of beating her he'd want sex, and he'd take it."

There wasn't anything for me to say.

"After Mom's death, he turned to me. We didn't have any family in town, and nobody in that little town would do anything to stop him."

"There wasn't anybody you could turn to for help?"

"I suspect some of the neighbors knew, or at least suspected, but nobody did shit to stop it. But I took it, took whatever crap he did to me, to stop him from going after Rachel."

"How long did this go on?" I wasn't comfortable hearing all this, but I had to hear it.

"Almost seven years. It wasn't until shortly before I graduated from high school that the local cops went after him. I'd gone out of town with friends for a weekend. He went after Rachel, and she fought him. He beat her so bad that when she could get up, after he'd finished and passed out, she went to a neighbor's house. They called an ambulance and she went to the hospital. The hospital called the cops. The next day, Rachel and I moved in with an aunt, my mother's sister."

"Where'd you learn to fight like that?"

"I learned to fight while I was in the Air Force. Not just the stuff they teach in basic training, but I was stationed in Japan for two years and dated a Navy guy, an underwater demolitions guy that washed out of Seal school. He taught martial arts."

Chapter 23

Monday, December 25th,
7:00 P.M.

Dylan, Jeremy, and Marcus helped Gator and Gene move a couple of the picnic tables from the Over The Edge dining hall down the beach to the Mountain To Sea dining hall so that both groups could mingle. I asked Misty to paddle out to the sailboat and invite the Boxlers to join us. Finally, with help from me, Katie blew the dinner horn to announce dinner was ready.

⋆❖⋆

Everyone from both resorts gathered in the dining hall.

"Can I have everyone's attention, please?" I shouted. The group quieted down and the murmur came to a stop.

"Before we dig into this feast I'd like Annette and Felicia to come up next to me."

They each came over.

"Ladies, you've really outdone yourselves with this Christmas dinner. Beyond the ham, you've laid out a spread that includes… what all do we have here? I see grouper and flounder, at least a half-dozen vegetables to choose from, and several loaves of freshly baked bread."

"And, George, we have some freshly made whole grain pasta that Antonio showed us how to make," Felicia said.

"You didn't mention the dessert bar, George. We have lime and lemon meringue pies, coconut cream pie made from our very own coconuts, and your favorite; German chocolate cake."

"Annette, you weren't supposed to mention the dessert bar," I said, laughing. "I was hoping nobody else would notice that and it would be all mine."

I watched as the two single guys from Mountain To Sea, Jerry and Kevin, went through the line first followed by the two sisters from Minnesota. I'd already told Kevin he was to take his food back to his cabana. I'd had enough of his fights.

One couple after another went through the buffet line, with Erin going between Eric and Susan White and then Bernie's family. Once all guests had been served the support staff for both resorts went, then the Mountain To Sea guides, then my dive staff. Finally, Kim and I made our first pass.

Bernie's family sat at a table with Eric and Susan White and the Cavutos. I watched as Bernie said Grace before the family dove in. Kim and I found some room at their table. Gator turned on a stereo and played a CD of Christmas music.

Jingle Bells, hearing about chestnuts roasting on an upon fire, and Bing Crosby croaking out White Christmas, in eighty degree weather, while watching the Caribbean sunset. Now that's Christmas.

"George, this ham is incredible. I've never had anything like it! How did the ladies come up with this?"

"Helene, Belize has turkeys, but the people here don't eat it. I don't really know why, but it's never been a significant part of their diet. Ham though, that's a different story. The people of Belize love a good smoked ham."

"There are a lot of Mennonites in Belize. They don't use pesticides in their gardens and feed their livestock only natural foods. They smoke their pigs naturally, using locally grown trees and herbs," Kim added.

"Kim's right about that. Many of the Mennonite farms, including the one we buy our meats from, have orange and grapefruit orchards as well as mangos. They burn a lot of mahogany and dead fruit trees, and over-ripened fruit, in smoking the meat."

"This is amazing. Oranges, grapefruit and mangoes. I'll have to try that at home."

⁂

When Gator and Gene were done eating they turned off the CD player and broke out their guitars. To my surprise, they'd gone down to my place and gotten mine. They played a few Jimmy Buffett and Eagles tunes, and one or two James Taylor songs. I noticed some of the staff members splitting off, most of the support staff left for their quarters. The Boxlers left for their boat, all three of them.

At some point I noticed most of the women were seated at one table and the men at another. The conversation at the men's table turned to cars.

"George, what was your first car?" Dave Cavuto asked.

"A 1971 Corvette convertible in Classic White. I worked construction for three summers in the El Paso heat to save up for a car. I bought it brand new, and it had all of the extras available."

"Wow, that's a classic. What'd you do with it?"

"I still have it. I worked too damned hard to buy it to let anyone else ever have it. My sister lives near Fort Worth and I keep it in a self-storage unit near her place. We go visit every summer and I get it running nice, clean it up, make sure the inspection sticker and tags are current, and drive it for a week or two."

"What kind of shape is it in? That must be worth a fortune," Dave asked.

"It's in perfect condition. Other than during my freshman year in college, it has always been garage kept. It has all original parts and has fewer than forty-thousand miles on it."

"It's in perfect, original condition? It must be worth a hundred thousand now, especially with so few miles. Ever thought of selling it?"

Dave asked.

"I saw one similar listed recently for fifty-eight thousand with only twenty-five thousand miles. No, I'm not interested in selling it. Dave, how about you? What was your first car?"

"Nothing that nice, I assure you. I worked one summer at a Kmart store and bought a used 1983 Mercury Capris. I wrecked it that fall, trying to race a Plymouth Challenger."

"Larry, what was your first car?" I asked.

"It was 1978 and there was a used car lot across the street from my parent's house when I was in high school. I wanted this 1973 Charger they had on the lot. The owner said that if I washed the cars on his lot all summer, between Memorial Day and Labor Day, he'd give me the car."

"Was it worth it?"

"Yeah, but I didn't even get my license until the following Christmas. Really ticked off my parents too, having that car tying up space in their garage for almost five months before I could drive it legally. On top of that I had to work at a Kmart to pay for my insurance, and the basic insurance was as much as the car cost in the first place. I had to pay my parents for the increase in their car insurance too."

"What happened to it?" Dave asked.

"I sold it to my now ex-wife's younger brother. I'm not the least bit mechanically inclined and he was one of those guys that liked to tinker, and always has to tinker, with a car. He raced it on a local drag strip. He blew the engine and couldn't fix it."

"I didn't know you'd been married," I said.

"I had this girlfriend in my senior year of high school. One of the things I liked about her was that she was really smart, maybe smarter than me."

"You admit that there's a woman smarter than you?"

I'd known him for a few years and, while he's a nice guy, he's got a bit of an ego.

"Sure, I admit at least that it's possible. She believed she was, and I suspected that to be true. I've wondered which the better example of her brilliance was: marrying me, or divorcing me. Our high school graduation came and they paraded the class across the stand in order of class rank. I was ninth in my class. She was tenth."

"So how long were you married?"

"Well, she came to me in late March in our senior year of high school and said 'I think I'm pregnant.' Like I said, I liked her because she was smart. We talked about it and decided to go to the doctor our school track team had. Her family doctor would have called her parents, even though at that point she was eighteen. My family doctor would have called mine."

"And she was right?"

"It was awkward. Dr. Davis saw the two of us in his office and said something like 'I have a bad feeling I know why both of you are here.' What made it really awkward is that I dated his daughter before dating Marie."

"Awkward? Shoot, I'd have been soiling my underwear," Dave said, laughing. A couple of others joined in the laughter.

"Anyway, she was pregnant and we decided to get married. We got married in one of the state parks in Maryland, where my brother worked, on May first. Mayday! Mayday! I moved in with her parents after I graduated from high school. Our baby, my son Jacob, was born on Labor Day."

"Your son's name is Jacob?"

"That was Marie's choice. Her family was Mormon and wanted a biblical name. I wanted to name him Hank."

"Hank? Not Henry? And why, is that a name from your family?"

"No, 'Hank' as in Reardon, one of the heroes from *Atlas Shrugged.*"

"You're an Ayn Rand fan? I didn't know that."

"I loved the ideas in that book. I've never read her others. What I've heard about *The Fountainhead* makes me think I'd hate it. I'm a mercenary though, I like money and think the heroes in *Atlas Shrugged* were motivated less by greed than by a drive to produce."

I wanted to get off that topic. That book divides people into strong groups. I happen to agree with Larry but I've seen way too many arguments over it.

"How long did the marriage last?" I asked.

"The only really smart thing we did was keep Marie in school. She had a combination of athletic scholarships for track and gymnastics, along with some academic ones, for Virginia Tech in Blacksburg, Virginia. She and the baby moved into one of my aunt's homes. My aunt ran a daycare center out of her home in Roanoke, about fifty miles away, and her own kids were grown and on their own. She had an empty room. Instead of rent, Marie had to help with the kids in the center between classes."

"Larry, you aren't answering my question."

"I know. Teenagers, married at eighteen, seventeen for me because she was two weeks short of a year older than me, and having a baby. That's bad enough. Then for them to live several hundred miles apart and only see each other every few weeks and holidays, that doesn't help. She found someone else, my best friend at the time. Officially, the marriage lasted four years but Maryland had a two-year waiting period for a divorce back then. We were together for less than two years."

"Do you see your son?" I was floored. I'd never heard this story.

"Not often. I was working in Georgia and Florida for a while. I had the state forward my child support to her. She finished school and became a veterinarian. I told myself I didn't want to cause problems for Elvis, Marie's husband, with the kid playing us off each other. I've realized since thaen that the truth was it hurt me too much. I didn't have much to do with raising him."

"How'd he turn out?"

"He's a good man. His mother and stepfather deserve all the credit for that. They're still together. Jacob turned thirty a few months ago. He was lazy in school and barely graduated, but he'd always been physically fit. In that, he took after his mother more than me. I was healthy and played football my senior year and ran cross country my junior year, but Marie was definitely the more fit member of our household. After high school he went into the Navy and became a rescue swimmer. He got out recently and is going to school to become a physical therapist and does some personal training."

"And you didn't have anything to do with raising him?" It just didn't fit with my image of Larry.

"Not much. I fulfilled the financial commitment, paid the child support regularly and even paid the alimony I was ordered to pay for two years. Marie's parents were very rich, mostly in real estate holdings, and died when Jacob was three or four. They left him millions and Marie a lot more. She really didn't need my child support payments."

"How often did you see him?" I didn't have a problem believing he'd met the financial commitment. He's big on personal integrity and honor. I was just surprised he had so little involvement in raising his son.

"Not often, once or twice a year and even then it was usually a matter of a couple of hours. When he was fifteen I lived in Richmond, Virginia, and they lived in western Maryland. He ran away from home. He was the luckiest kid you'd ever heard of."

"How so?"

"He walked about half a mile, if that, to the highway and stuck out his thumb. A trucker from Overland Freight picked him up and took him almost to Washington, DC. The trucker was going to drop him off near I-95 and he'd have to make his way from there. Jacob said 'I noticed on your truck that the company you work for is based in Richmond. Is there any chance another Overland Freight truck is heading that way?' The trucker used his radio and found another Overland Freight truck heading toward the base in Richmond and handed Jacob over at a truck stop."

"Lucky, indeed," I said.

"Oh, it gets better. When they got to the trucking company headquarters, about six miles down the road from my place, Jacob told the driver he wasn't sure where my place was but he had the address. The driver said 'that's right on my way home. I'll drop you off at the stoplight.' Jacob wound up walking about three hundred yards to get to my place. He walked well under a mile of that two hundred and seventy mile trip."

"What'd you do?"

"I was working graveyards then. I slept during the afternoons and evenings. He woke me up. When I saw him I looked for his mother or stepfather. He told me he ran away."

"Then what?"

"I let him in, and asked him why he'd come to me. 'I wanted to use some of my inheritance money to buy a motorcycle and Mom won't let me.' I agreed with them. He got mad. 'Mom said you had a motorcycle when you were my age. It's not right that you'd say I can't have one.'"

"What'd you say then?"

"I told him that I didn't say he can't have one. If he got a job and earned the money to buy it, then I'd argue with his mother and stepfather on his behalf. I'd done that myself. I mowed lawns and had the afternoon paper route for two years to save up for that bike."

"How'd he take that?"

"Not well, but he couldn't say a lot. I called his mother next. That was fun. 'Hey there, Marie, do you know where Jacob is?' I asked when she answered the phone. I let him sleep in a guest room and took him most of the way home the next morning and had Marie meet us at a restaurant we used to like. It felt good knowing that she'd bitched about me off and on for years and here he took off and ran to me."

"Was that the last time he ran away?" I asked.

"Yeah, but she called me the following January. 'You need to talk with your son,' she said."

"What did he do that made her mad enough to call you?"

"He played trombone in his high school marching band. The band went to Las Vegas for a New Year's Day parade. He got caught climbing up the side of their hotel, climbing from one patio to another, to get to his girlfriend's room."

"That must have been a fun talk," Dave said, trying not to laugh too hard.

"Yeah, I drove about six hours to get to their place. Marie was in the kitchen, listening in. He said 'But Dad, I had condoms. We know to practice safe sex.'"

"Smart kid, I guess." I was trying to picture having that conversation with my son, someday. Would it be as funny as Larry was making this out to be?

"Maybe so, but I laughed at him. 'Jacob, you're working at the ski resort up the road a couple of miles, right? You're saving money for that motorcycle, or a car, right?' Well, I can tell you within a four hour window when you were conceived. Your mother and I, and Elvis and his girlfriend at the time, were at that same ski resort for the week. Your mother and I ran out of condoms at about two in the morning and the gift shop didn't open until six. By the way, that morning was my seventeenth birthday."

"And Marie was listening in?" I was trying to hold back the laughter. Dave Cavuto was nearly doubled over from laughing.

"She came running in and shouted 'You can't tell him that story!'"

"I bet she never asked you to talk with him again."

"Nope, never again. But, you know, he's thirty, filthy rich, and single with no kids so I guess it worked. He bought a modest two bedroom condo when he left the Navy and paid cash for it but he doesn't let anyone know he's got money. He even has a roommate that thinks he's paying half the rent on the place."

I saw Larry differently now. I'd always thought he was just shy around women. Now, I suspected, he'd been hurt enough to not pursue any of them. Then again, the only woman I know he's been interested in is Beth and she's married. Having had his wife cheat on him I suspect he wasn't going to try to come between any other couple. Not that he had a chance with Beth anyway.

✦

During a break in the conversation at the men's table I heard Dagan ask Kim, "What has been your favorite dive?"

"Oh, there have been so many. I've made dives with several types of sharks, dolphins, rays—you name it. If it swims around here, I've been in the water with it."

"Yeah, but isn't there one dive that stands out?"

"There was one dive just last year. We had a couple here. They kind of remind me of you and Dave."

"What made that dive special?" I couldn't tell if Dagan was asking from a professional vantage, you know, the reporter wanting to know, or if it was something else, something more personal.

"We were going to The Crack. As the boat went through the break in the reef we encountered a pod of dolphins. That's always fun for the guests, but it's often enough that it isn't special. They usually swim ahead of the boat and when we stop they keep going."

"And... what happened? Did they stop too?"

"We all got in and began our descent. I could see the whole pod, a hundred feet away. We got to the entry point of The Crack and started down, one at a time. If you haven't been there yet, The Crack is a swim-through on The Wall. The entry point is at about fifty-five feet. You drop down, there's only room for one person at a time, and get to the bottom at about ninety feet. Then you swim out horizontally."

"So, what was special about this? What about the dolphins?"

"One at a time, we dropped down and swam out. There were seven divers on that trip. Beth, you were there. I think you went first."

"I remember, I went first to show the way and make sure the point at the bottom didn't hold anything scary. Sometimes we find sharks in there."

"As each of the divers went down, the pod of dolphins came closer. At the end, there were just two of us."

"Two of us? You and one other?"

"Right, her name was Teri. The dolphins came nearer, circling her. It was strange, having them circle like that, slowly but cautiously. Teri was as surprised as I was but she took her turn and went down into The Crack."

"And what happened? Did the dolphins follow her?"

"I followed her, so I couldn't see it at first. When she came out of the swim-through the dolphins surrounded her. If she moved toward the others the dolphins would swim between her and the others. More accurately, they'd swim between her and any man in the group. They didn't seem to care about the women."

"Why would they do that?" Dagan and the other women were listening closely, leaning in to hear her.

"I'd always thought it was an old wives' tale. Now I believe it."

"What? What old wives tale?"

"They say the dolphin's sonar can detect a baby's heart-beat. Teri found out a few days after she got home that she was pregnant. The dolphins knew, and swam between her and the men to protect her, to protect the baby, just like they'd do for one of their own."

"That's…that's so beautiful."

Chapter 24

Monday, December 25th, 9:00 P.M.

G ator walked over to the men's table, carrying my guitar. "Your highness, your instrument waits. Won't you please join us?"

"Sure," I took my guitar. "This is for Kim. It's our song. There have been several versions of it but we like the Gary Morris version the most. It's called <u>The Love She Found In Me</u>."

Gator and Gene each played another song. My next turn came. I'm a huge Beatles fan, and I think John Lennon wrote some of the most beautiful songs. I looked at Kim, and she watched as I sang my favorite John Lennon song: "Grow Old With Me."

God bless our love

The gathering started to break up. I saw Misty in the kitchen, getting something to take back to her cabana I guessed. It was past the kids' bedtimes. They each came over to me and kissed me good-night, then went and did the same to Kim, Beth, and Misty. Dylan and Marcus carried our tables back to the Over The Edge dining hall, a full moon lighting the way. The Over The Edge guests, Dylan and my three dive masters all gathered round our patio area. We had a round table under the palm trees, covered in a tile mosaic that Kim made, near the kitchen. A couple of torches light the area. The flickering light, bouncing off the tile mosaic, created a calm, almost mystic environment.

"Drinks tonight are on the house," I said to hushed cheers.

❦

A Jimmy Buffett CD played softly in the background, the wine soothed us all, and the small talk continued. As "Why don't we get drunk, and screw" played Dylan got Misty's attention as if to suggest they go off and follow Jimmy's advice. She didn't seem interested and was the first to turn in. Dylan followed her, only to return a few minutes later.

"No joy in Mudville?" I asked.

He grinned as he took a seat. "There's always tomorrow. You never know when you take your swing if it's going to be a homerun, a triple, or a strike. You know, I thought it was over after the plane crash last year."

"What plane crash?" I asked.

"You didn't know about the crash? Yeah, she worked for a small commuter and charter air service in Arizona. That's how we first met. She had to call the Park Service and clear their flights with us—they did aerial tours of the Grand Canyon —so that we didn't have multiple tour flights in the same area at the same time."

I tried to remember hearing about that before but couldn't.

"The company had two planes. The owner of the company flew all of the charter flights. He and his son took turns on the Grand Canyon tours. Anyway, the owner crashed their larger plane on a charter flight. Everyone died. Not long after that the man's widow closed the company."

"What happened to Misty after that?" I asked.

"She didn't do much of anything for a while. I guess that was maybe three or four months before she came here."

I thought about it for a minute or so and turned to Beth. "You referred each of them to me. Did you know they were a couple back then?"

"I knew they knew each other. Calling them a couple is, and always was, I think, a bit of a stretch." Beth looked at Dylan, who just shrugged.

"I knew that Misty was working here before I approached you for a job. I didn't think anything, one way or the other, about telling you I knew her. George, is that a problem?"

"No, no, I guess not. How'd she get by between jobs?"

"I don't know. I've never gotten a sense that money was an issue for her, but I don't know why. She lived pretty frugally there, so maybe she just saved for a rainy day."

"Maybe."

"Well, I'm off to bed. See you folks in the morning," he said, heading off toward his place.

Chapter 25

Tuesday, December 26th,
5:30 A.M.

Kim and I were out for our morning run; in my case working through a bit of a hangover.

"You woke up a couple of times again last night. Did you have the same dreams?"

"Yeah, I guess. Grace was playing with Austin. He was maybe two or three, it was Christmas time, his first Christmas to be old enough to enjoy."

"What do think this means?"

"I still don't know. I think she's trying to tell me something, I just can't figure out what."

❧❖❧

The wind this morning was stronger than we'd experienced the past few days. The diver-down flag on my dock, now pointing toward the southwest, snapped in the wind. On our fourth circle, we were passing by the Mountain To Sea showers when we heard a scream coming from Cabana Eleven: Bernie and Helene Stamps.

We ran to the cabana at the same pace we'd been at, half-expecting the scream to be from the surprise of finding a lizard or hermit crab in the screamer's bed or clothing. No such luck.

Helene stood motionless, pointing at Bernie's body. He was lying on his back on the bed, naked except for a pair of shorts.

I checked for a pulse and, not finding one, turned to Kim. "Honey, take Helene and the girls downstairs. Don't let anyone else come up except Gator. Send him right up."

Gator came in. "Hey, boss, what happened?"

"Bernie's dead. You'll need to call the Maritime Police."

"He's dead? How?"

"I don't see any blood. Maybe a heart attack, I don't know. I think he's been dead several hours." He was already cold to the touch.

"Gator, get Susan White for me." I thought Helene would respond better with her friend there.

"Yes, boss."

When Susan and Eric arrived I met them at the bottom of the stairs. "Susan, Bernie's dead. It looks like he died from a heart attack in his sleep. Would you and Kim please take Helene and the girls down to our house?"

Eric was shaken. "Bernie's dead? You think it was a heart attack? Really? He's pretty young for that, and he's physically fit."

"How old was he, anyway?" I asked.

"Two years older than me: forty-four. He's always been an avid runner. He ran the Boston Marathon last year, and the Chicago Marathon the year before."

"Running can be good exercise but it's no guarantee of overall fitness. Do you remember who Jim Fixx was?"

"Vaguely, a runner, I think."

"Yeah, he wrote the book, actually a couple of books, on running. The first was kind of a Bible for distance runners. Anyway, he died of a heart attack after one of his daily runs. He was fifty-two."

"Eight years older than Bernie."

I figured they could sit with Helene awhile and calm her down. Beth and Misty could distract the kids by playing along the beach and watching the fish swimming near the dock.

I checked Bernie's body closely. There was a very small amount of dried blood in the center of his chest, so little I almost mistook it for a mole or birthmark. It covered a small puncture mark. The puncture mark was too small to have been a knife. I don't know much about weapons but I think even the slimmest stiletto would make a larger hole than this. It was too big for a needle.

"Hey, boss, are you up there?" I heard someone shout.

I looked out and saw Gene at the foot of the steps. I also saw several guests were gathered around outside. I could hear them talking, just a murmur, speculating about what had happened. I decided I'd better talk with them.

"Folks, obviously you know something's happened. Helene woke this morning and tried to wake Bernie. She couldn't."

"He's dead?"

"Yes, Dave, I'm sorry to say he is."

"How?"

"There's no sign of foul play. Until the Maritime Police come and say otherwise, my guess is that he had a heart attack."

Slowly they moved away. A few glared at Kevin, as if suspecting he'd done something to their new friend. He just shrugged and walked to the dining hall.

It was time for breakfast.

Chapter 26

Tuesday, December 26th, 8:00 A.M.

"Hey, boss, the Maritime Police will be here in a couple of hours."

"Okay, Gator. What's on your schedule this morning?"

"I've got a windsurfing orientation. The winds are nearly perfect this morning. Some of the guests are planning to kayak over to the Marine Research facility on Victoria's Caye. Marlene is going to lead that trip."

"Okay, but I want someone to stand guard for the Stamps' cabana. Who's available?"

"Everybody has something to do, but I guess we could spare Gene for a while."

"Alright, have him stay at the base of the cabana. Nobody goes up there except me until Charlie—at least I'm assuming it will be Charlie—arrives."

I didn't want the other guests to interfere with what I suspected was a crime scene. I didn't expect it to matter. The Maritime Police would do little to collect evidence. Still, I had to do what I could to assist local law enforcement.

⋘❖⋙

I was tinkering with the motor on my larger boat when Larry started gathering his gear. Erin was lying in a hammock under a palm tree near the end of the dock, reading something I guessed were notes for her book. Larry started to put his wet-suit on and asked, "What was the excitement down at Mountain To Sea this morning?"

I looked up and sighed. "Bernie Stamps died sometime during the night. It looks like he had a heart attack. We're making arrangements to get the family home, along with his friends."

"I'm sorry to hear that. He seemed like a nice guy and he had a cute family."

"Yeah, they've been the picture-perfect postcard family. I'm expecting the Maritime Police out in a couple of hours."

"Until then, I'm guessing it's business as usual, otherwise?"

"Yeah. Marcus and Beth will lead this dive. I think it's you and Kevin plus Alicia and Carolyn. I haven't seen Gunnar, or his parents, so I guess they won't make this dive."

"Me too, especially since their boat pulled out of here a couple of hours ago." He had his wet-suit on but not zipped up. He sat down and started putting on his dive boots.

"Huh." I looked at where their boat had been moored last night. I hadn't noticed they'd left. "When did they leave?"

"Well, after breakfast I went to the bathroom, and when I came out I saw the sail being raised. I guess that was about two, maybe two-and-a-half hours ago." He put the second boot on and stood up again.

"Damn, I hadn't noticed. Did you notice which way they went?"

"South, I think. That way…" he pointed as he waded into the water. There are a couple of cayes to the south of us, then a few hours of open-water sailing into the waters of Honduras.

❧❖❧

While everyone from Mountain To Sea was busy I searched Kevin's cabana. He hadn't brought a lot of clothing, just two pair of swim trunks—well, three with the pair he was wearing, three t-shirts, sandals and a couple of pair of underwear. Kevin had several bottles of prescription medication, some I recognized as diabetes medications. They were taken orally; nothing required needles and I didn't find any syringes. I made a note to check his paperwork for diving. He hadn't indicated on his release form that he was a diabetic and we require a medical release for diabetics.

I found a bag of marijuana which I dumped into the surf. Marijuana is common in Belize but it's illegal. I've even had taxi drivers in Belize offer to sell me some.

The cabana was messy. Kevin hadn't made his bed and his clothes were scattered around the room. There were a couple of paperbacks on the floor including two Harold Robbins novels, and one of Don Pendleton's *The Executioner* series. The Harold Robbins novels I didn't recognize but there are a couple of old Executioners in the dining hall library.

<hr />

When the Maritime Police came, right at lunchtime, naturally, I showed Charlie the Stamps' cabana. "No one's been in the room but me since Mrs. Stamps woke-up."

"Kind of messy in here, isn't it, George?"

"No, not really. They've got two kids. It was actually better this morning, but I left everything the way I found it and that includes the windows being open. The wind's getting pretty strong and has blown some stuff around."

He shrugged. "George, there is no blood and I see no signs of a fight."

He didn't look closely. He didn't seem to even want to be in the room. A lot of Belizeans, especially those living in the outer cayes, are easily spooked by dead bodies. It's a pretty superstitious society; just being in the cabana with the body made Charlie uncomfortable.

"I agree. There was no struggle in here, Charlie."

Charlie pointed to Bernie's legs. "He has a lot of scrapes and bruises."

"Yeah, he was playing volleyball yesterday and dove for a spiked ball. He got pretty scraped up. After that, he got into a little scuffle with another guest."

"A scuffle?"

"Yeah, with Kevin. He's a hot-head, and had been drinking. Kevin shoved Bernie and picked a fight."

"I should talk with that guest, Kevin, and search his room."

"Sure, he's in the dining hall right now. He was out on a dive earlier this morning."

Charlie searched Kevin's room but found nothing I hadn't found. The drugs, of course, were long gone—I didn't need a guest getting arrested for drug possession here.

⁂

Charlie first talked with Helene Stamps in my office. I was present but no one else was.

"Helene, this is Officer Charlie Johnson from the Belize Maritime Police. He needs to ask you a few questions. Charlie, go ahead."

"I am sorry about your husband. Was he a good man?"

"Yes, he was. He loved people almost as much as he loved his work."

"What kind of work did he do?"

"He was a lawyer. He specialized in environmental law and fought corporations he felt were raping the land and sea."

"Did he have any enemies?"

"I don't know of any enemies. Maybe some of the companies he sued and fought, but I don't think there was anybody who would hurt him. Why?"

"I'm just checking, ma'am. What time did he go to bed last night?"

"About nine-thirty."

"Did you come to bed at the same time?"

"Yes. We'd had a big Christmas dinner. After dinner, there was a bit of a party. We let the kids stay up late but they'd had a busy day. Katie, she's our four year-old, fell asleep in my lap and Michelle, our eleven year-old, fell asleep on one of the benches. We carried them up to the cabana and then went to sleep ourselves."

"So you went to bed, the whole family, at the same time?"

"Right. Around three o'clock I asked him to close the door and windows. You know, the wind and surf were getting pretty loud and it started to get cool. I thought we had used a piece of line round the door handle to secure it shut but the door was open. I asked him again a few minutes later and then got up and did it myself. Oh God, no..." She started to cry again as she realized Bernie was already dead by then.

"Girl, it isn't your fault and you could not have done anything for him. It looks to me like his heart attacked him while he was sleeping. Take comfort in that he did not suffer."

I went to the dining hall to get Kevin. On the way to my office, I talked with him.

"Kevin, you know that after your arguments with Bernie, and your fight last night, you'd be a suspect in any violence, right?"

"I haven't done anything wrong. I damned sure didn't kill him. Besides, you said it was a heart attack."

"The Maritime Police have searched your cabana."

"They can't do that, not without a warrant, right?" He was obviously worried.

"This isn't America. The Constitution as you know it doesn't apply, and so yes, they can. Besides, as the owner, I gave them permission."

"Oh no, I'm going to spend the rest of my life in some little shithole in Belize."

"Maybe so, but I searched it first. They didn't find the pot. I dumped that stuff into the sea while you were diving."

"Oh God. Thank you." Kevin was genuinely relieved.

"What the hell were you thinking, bringing marijuana here?"

"It's the Caribbean. I'd have thought it was okay. Besides, I bought it here, I didn't bring it here."

"Here as in Belize or here as in this island?" I asked.

"Here as in this island."

"Who did you buy it from?"

"What difference does it make?"

"It makes a lot of difference to me. Whoever it was might get caught if the Maritime Police decide to search other cabanas. Besides, you're in a heap of trouble already and you don't strike me as the kind to stand up to the authorities and cover for someone else."

"It was Gene."

Chapter 27

Tuesday, December 26th, 11:00 A.M.

I listened for a few minutes as Charlie asked Kevin some harmless questions. Charlie hadn't noticed the puncture wound in Bernie's chest and didn't suspect foul play. He wanted to believe it was a heart attack.

❦

I left Charlie alone with Kevin and went to the dining hall. The wind buffeted Charlie's boat against the dock. All of my boats were on the other side, straining against the ropes binding them to the dock. In the dining hall I found Gator and Gene.

"You guys, come with me."

"What's up, boss?"

"Before Charlie searched Kevin's cabin, I did too. I found a bag of weed. I got rid of it but chewed him out. Gene, he says you sold it to him."

"He's full of shit!"

"I want to believe that, but Gator and I are going to go through your cabin. You'll be at the base of the stairs. Got anything you want to say before we get started?"

Gene shifted his weight, shuffled his feet. "You can't just search my cabana without cause."

"I've got the statement of a guest saying you sold him marijuana, so I've got all the damned cause I need. Besides, as I reminded Kevin, you aren't in the United States. On this island, I'm the only authority figure around and there's no Constitution. I'm the King, remember? Now, am I about to find something?"

"If you have drugs, tell us where they are. You know we'll find them," Gator added.

"It's in the nightstand, the second drawer from the top."

We found some marijuana in that drawer, and some Ecstasy in his foot locker.

"You'll be going home on Wednesday's boat. There won't be any severance. Four seasons you've been here and now you won't even be able to list us as a reference. We'll also notify the river rafting company you work for in the off-season." A professional courtesy I'd only hoped would be reciprocated. No business in this industry can allow staff to be selling drugs to clients.

He started to say something but I cut him off. I didn't want to hear it.

"Gator, dump all of this stuff in the ocean before Charlie gets a chance to see it. Gene, until the boat arrives tomorrow, you're confined to your cabana. Don't even think of going near any of the guests."

I hated having to play the stern boss but we could lose our operating licenses for the two resorts if our staff members got caught selling drugs. I'm all for legalization of some of this stuff. Heck, when I was younger I did some of that stuff, and I even tried peyote a couple of times. But I won't lose my business over it.

❦

Charlie finished interrogating Kevin. He and his boat driver sat down with us for a plate of our Christmas leftovers. About one-thirty that afternoon Charlie got up to leave.

"George, I don't see any crime. I'll get back to you about shipping the body back to the states."

"Charlie, there's something else. It's probably nothing, but there was a boat moored here overnight."

"A boat? Who was it?"

"It was a sailboat, flying a Swiss flag. They were an older couple and their son. The son just finished his military training and will be in college soon. They made a couple of dives with us yesterday and the day before. I thought they'd be here for a few days but they set sail at breakfast this morning."

"Did they have any problem with Mr. Stamps?"

"No, Gunnar, their son, dove with him but they had no problems. They might have just decided to get going and make some dives near Roatan. I don't think they were even on the island this morning."

"If they were heading south they'd be in Honduras by now. Well, I'll see you later this week. I hope you have a Merry Christmas, even with all of this." He and his boat driver waved as the boat pulled out.

I went up to my work out room for a light workout. Kim came up. "Honey, are you okay?" she asked.

"No, yeah, hell…I don't know. I'm tired and angry."

"I'll be on the phone and internet for a while longer, making arrangements. I've got the *Tropical Breeze* coming in tomorrow with some supplies. They'll take Helene, the kids, and the Whites back to Belize City with them."

"Good, where's the boat leaving from?"

"I don't know. Why?"

"If I can get hold of him, I'd like to get Sticks back out here."

"Is there something else?" Kim placed her hand on my shoulder.

"Yeah, drugs. Nothing serious, just dope. But Gene's been selling it. At least, he sold some to Kevin. I don't know about anyone else."

"Gene? What are you going to do about it?"

"I fired him. He goes back to Belize on the boat tomorrow and is confined to his cabana until then. I've got to check all of the other guides and dive masters now too."

"Well, if that's what you think is best. You know, Helene and the kids will be here overnight. There's still some time to play with the girls, if you want."

"I don't think Helene or Michelle is going to be in the right frame of mind for diving. I still have a treasure hunt to go on though, don't I?"

"Yeah, and I think that might help. Invite both girls, not just Katie."

"Are you sure you don't want to tell me what's in this treasure?"

"Oh no, it's a surprise!" She kissed my forehead and went back into the office.

Chapter 28

Tuesday, December 26th, 2:00 P.M.

The two girls were in our dining hall, playing a card game with Beth. Someone had lowered the tarps on the windward side, blocking most of the wind. Without the breeze it was getting a little stuffy. The lights weren't very bright either.

"Hey, girls, how are you?" I asked.

They looked up but neither said anything. I sat down at the dining table. "Katie, are you okay?"

She stood on the bench and shrugged her shoulders.

"I bet you're scared, huh?"

"Uh-huh."

"I understand. I'm a little scared too. Can I give you a hug?"

She climbed up into my lap and hugged my neck, almost choking me. "Michelle, how about you?"

She came over and put her arms around me. Together, I think we held each other and they sobbed for almost five minutes.

"You know what? We haven't looked for that other treasure yet. Do you still have the map?"

"It's in the cabana," Katie said. "I don't want to go there."

"I understand. We'll move all of your stuff to one of the cabanas down here on this end of the island later. They're a little bit nicer and, in case you get scared, closer to me. Where's the map?"

"On the table, next to the door, in my backpack."

"She means the pink one. Mine's blue," Michelle added.

"Okay, I'm going to go get it. I'll be right back, okay?"

They slowly let go of me.

✦

As I walked down to their cabana I couldn't help but think about losing my parents. I was almost thirty. I couldn't imagine what it would have been like to grow up without my dad. We weren't real close, even if we did work together for the last couple of years. When I got my license to practice dentistry he brought me into the family business, as if that had ever been in doubt. My grandfather did the same with him.

Then came that week.

I worked late at the dental office, trying to do some paperwork and get caught up on insurance filings, and heard glass shatter: someone breaking in. I grabbed a gun, an old revolver we kept in my dad's office, called El Paso's new 9-1-1 number to report the break-in, and waited. The guy came through a window in one of the patient rooms. There wasn't any conversation, it was just one guy.

I stepped into the hallway, my gun pointed at him. "That's far enough. Put your hands up. The cops are on their way."

"Hey, man, chill out. Nobody has to get hurt here. Put your gun down."

He was dressed in jeans, torn at the right knee. Grease stained both pant legs. He wore a camouflage t-shirt with a black vest over it. A bandanna around his neck was nearly covered by his beard and he had long, dirty hair. A biker. El Paso had its share of bike gangs, and wannabes.

"I don't think so, not until the cops get here. Keep your hands where I can see them." I took a couple of steps closer to him, stopping a good six feet away, by an opening to the lobby.

"Man, you don't want the cops. They bust me, my friends will be all over you. Just let me go and nobody has to know I was here."

"If you wanted to be free you shouldn't have broken in here. You made that choice, not me. Now, take a step, just the one, toward me. I want you in front of that opening to the lobby." I pointed my gun toward the opening.

"Sure, man, sure. Whatever you say, but you really don't want to do this."

"You're right, but here we are. Okay, now take two slow, and I mean slow, steps to your right, into the lobby." I used my left hand to turn on the light switch for the lobby.

He moved, just as I instructed him to. He seemed to accept that the cops were going to arrest him. It seemed like he thought it wouldn't matter in the long run.

"Okay, now stay where you are. I'm going to unlock and open the office door and make this easy for the cops." I shuffled to the door, unlocked it, opened it, and stepped back against another wall.

"Alright, now, get down on your knees. Do it slowly. Just bend at the knees, keep your hands up."

He did as I said; still talking, trying to persuade me that I was the one in real trouble.

I heard the sirens a block away. I saw the headlights as the police car came to a stop in front of my office. Two cops approached, one taking a stand on either side of the open doorway. One shouted in, "Police."

I shouted back, "I'm Doctor Schroeder. I have a gun pointed at the guy who broke in."

"George, is that you?" A familiar voice.

"Yeah, who's that out there?"

"George, it's me, Karl Sparks. Is it safe for me to come in?"

"Yeah, Karl. Come on in. Once you're in I'll set my gun down." Karl and I went to high school together. We played baseball and basketball together. I hadn't seen in five or six years.

They arrested the guy and took him in.

That was just the beginning of my trouble....

⚜

When I got back, carrying Katie's pink backpack, she pulled the map out. "Wait, that's the wrong one. We found that treasure already." She dug around a little more and pulled out another torn piece of canvas.

I used a couple of paper napkins to wipe down the dining table before spreading the map.

"Well, let's see. Where are we on this map?"

Katie pointed to a spot marked 'OTEDH' and said, "We're right here, at the Over The Edge Dining Hall. See?"

"Do you mean the pirates knew where the dining hall is?"

"I guess 'the pirates' know where all of your buildings are," Michelle said with a giggle. "And the x is between Cabanas Five and Six, but behind them."

"Good, Michelle. Should we see if we can find a shovel?"

"Ms. Kim said to use a rake," Katie said.

"A rake? She doesn't think it was buried very deep, I guess."

"The other one wasn't buried deep. I could have found it with my fingers," Katie said.

"Well then, shall we go find the rake and get started? Would you girls like Miss Beth to come with us?"

They nodded yes and the four of us headed off in search of treasure.

We walked to the guest cabanas, stood between Cabanas Five and Six, and looked around. The area between the cabanas and the shoreline was open sand. The cabanas' porches stretch out to within five feet of the shoreline. Between the cabanas lay a stretch of hard packed sand roughly fifty feet across. Behind the cabanas native ground covers grew between palm trees. Kim buried the treasure on Saturday evening, before Jack's accident. It had to just be a coincidence that the treasure was buried next to Cabana Five: Jack and Sherry's cabana. My eyes were drawn to the newly repaired railing and then to the spot where Jack had lay. I still couldn't see how we'd have botched the job of replacing the railing a couple of weeks ago.

Michelle had the map, spread out on the sand.

"Michelle, where do you think we should start?"

"The x is behind the two cabanas, but halfway between them. So... here!" She walked to a spot, and pointed down, between her feet. "Dig here!"

I started to hand her the rake. "No, you dig!"

"Me? Why me?"

She smiled. "Because you're bigger, and stronger than us."

How is it that even girls that young know that if they smile they can get men to do things they don't want to do?

"Okay, but if we find the treasure I get to pick my part first. Is that a deal?"

Both girls nodded yes.

I extended the rake toward the ground cover around the base of a palm tree, and pulled it lightly toward me. Nothing.

"Are you sure about this?" I asked the girls.

"Dig, George." Michelle was getting bossy.

I'm going to have to talk with Beth about laughing at me.

"Okay, Michelle, okay." I extended the rake out again, overlapping just a few inches over the previous pass. On the third pass I snagged something. "I think I found something."

Katie jumped over to where I stopped the rake, bent down, and ran her fingers through the sand. "I got something!"

She stood up, holding my missing ratchet wrench.

"Oh, I don't think this is our treasure," she said, and she tossed it down on a previously raked section of sand.

I reached over and picked it up. It hadn't been there long, it hadn't started to rust.

"Mr. George, you need to rake some more. That isn't our treasure!" Katie insisted.

"Okay, but I need to take this back with me. I think maybe one of the guys dropped it when we were working on the railings a couple of weeks ago."

I didn't believe that. We'd had rain a few times since then and the wrench would have started to rust, or at least have had sand stuck in the mechanism, and it seemed to turn smoothly. It couldn't have been there more than a few days. I put the wrench in my back pocket. I'd read once, years ago when I had a reason to think about murderers, that professionals usually throw their weapon down at the murder scene. They're professionals, and don't leave prints anyway but they don't want to risk getting caught in some unrelated stop with a weapon. Could someone have removed and then reset the railing and then just tossed the wrench in the brush behind the cabana?

I extended the rake again and again. Finally, on the eighth pass, I snagged something else. "I've got something."

This time it was Michelle who knelt down, scratched through the sand, and pulled up a plastic box. It was one of the storage containers I use in my shop to store small stuff I want protected from the wind and rain.

"Should I open it?" Michelle asked, looking at Katie.

"Let's see what's inside. I can see another bag, like the one I found yesterday. There's something else."

Michelle opened the lid and retrieved the Crown Royal bag. She opened the bag and spilled the contents out on the map.

Katie shrieked. "More money! Even more than yesterday! There must be a zillion dollars in here!"

"I don't think it's that much, Katie." Michelle took the Belize currency. See, this one's a dollar in Belize. That's only worth fifty cents in America."

I was only a little surprised that Michelle knew that. Belize currency is tied, permanently, to the U.S. dollar at exactly half. One dollar in Belize is fifty cents in the U.S.

Beth walked over to Katie. "May I count it? I like Belize coins. They have all these pretty figures on them. See, this one is Queen Elizabeth," she said, holding a Belizean dollar.

She counted the coins and said, "Most of these are dimes. It adds up to seventeen dollars and thirty cents, in American money."

"I'm rich," screamed Katie.

"Well, maybe," I said. "Remember, you agreed I get to pick what I want to keep from the treasure since I had to do the digging."

"Oh, yeah," she said, dejected.

"What else was in the treasure chest?" I asked.

Michelle pulled out something wrapped in felt. She unwrapped it. "Silver picture frames."

"Wow, I wonder what the pirates were doing with these. I wonder how the pirates got these," I said.

"Do you know who the pictures are of?" Michelle asked.

"Yes, I do. This pretty little girl is Miss Kim when she was about your age." A black and white picture, taken when she was about nine. She wore a Catholic school uniform. She was an angel, even then.

"Who's the goofy-looking boy in that picture?"

Beth laughed at Michelle's question.

"Hey, I think I looked really cool back then. That's me." A color photo with me standing in front of our family's Christmas tree. I was holding my new pet spider monkey.

"Nobody with that long hair and geeky-looking shirt could look cool, Mr. George. It was Christmas morning, you were at home, and you had a pocket protector," Michelle laughed. Beth and Katie did too.

"Is that a monkey? Did you have a pet monkey?" Katie asked.

"I did. That's the year I got him."

"That's a funny pet. I asked Daddy for a puppy but he didn't bring me one." Katie got quiet for a moment.

"Well, Spidey, that's what I named him, was a lot of fun. He was smart."

"Could he do any tricks?" Katie asked.

"Well, I have a younger sister. Her name is Katherine. Do you know what I taught Spidey to do?"

She shook her head from side to side. "Unh huh. What?"

"I taught him to go into Katherine's room and pee on her clothes."

"That's mean!" Katie said.

"Maybe, but I thought it was funny."

"What about this picture? They look more like Indians than pirates."

I took the picture frame from Michelle. Written on the back of the frame was a date, and even after twenty-three years I recognized the handwriting. A rush of memories hit me and left me light-headed.

"Mr. George, are you okay?"

I looked up at Michelle and wiped my eyes. "Yes, I'm okay. I will be in a minute, anyway."

"Who are they?" Michelle put her hand on my shoulder. I didn't remember sitting down.

"Many years ago, long before I met Miss Kim, I was married. That is my wife, Grace, and our son, Austin. The picture was taken on Austin's sixth birthday, at Grace's brother's ranch. They'd just had a new colt born and were giving it to Austin."

Beth came over and gently took the picture from me. "George, you've never told me about them. Where are they now?"

I looked at the kids, then skyward. "Heaven, if there's really such a place."

And if there is, then I hope the guys that took them from me are still rotting in Hell.

❧❖❧

"Hey, there's more candy in this other bag," said Michelle.

"Now, you agreed I get to choose what I keep from the treasure, right?"

They each nodded.

"Well, I want to keep the pictures." I wrapped them up in the felt. "Now, how do we split up the money and candy?"

"I want the money," Katie said.

"That's okay with me, Katie. I'd rather have the candy," Michelle said.

"Well, what about Miss Beth? Doesn't she get something?" I asked.

"She should, shouldn't she?" asked Michelle, looking at Katie.

"I guess so. Beth, what do you want?"

"How about I get a couple of the coins that Katie wants and a couple of pieces of the candy that Michelle wants? Isn't that fair?"

Michelle handed her the candy to choose from. She took one candy bar and some M&Ms. Then she looked at Katie's bag of money. "I like the quarters. Can I have two of them, and one dime?"

Katie said that would be okay.

I picked up the rake, the plastic container, and my pictures and the four of us walked back to my dining hall. When we got back the two girls went up the stairs to show their mother, and Kim, what they'd found. Beth and I went into the dining hall. I set the stuff down on a dining table and walked over to a counter on which we keep fruit, next to a squeezer.

Beth gave me a hug. "You know, they wouldn't talk much with me, or anyone else."

"Well, I'm just a big kid to them," I said as I squeezed a couple of oranges for some juice.

"I don't think that's it, George. They really like you. You're better with kids than you know. But…you know I've got to ask…"

"Not now, maybe not ever. I'm sorry, but I can't talk about what happened to them."

❧❀❧

A few minutes later Michelle came into the dining hall and sat at the table next to me. "Mommy and Miss Susan are on the computer. They're making plans for us to go home tomorrow."

I gave Michelle a hug. "I know. We're going to miss you. You and Katie have made this a lot of fun for me and Ms. Kim."

Katie walked into the dining hall and sat next to me. She opened her pink backpack and pulled out another sheet of paper.

"Mr. George, before dinner last night Daddy said I should give you and Ms. Kim something to let you know how much I like being here. I made this for you," Katie said and she handed me the paper.

"You made this for me and Ms. Kim? You didn't have to do that," I said.

"I did too! Daddy told me so," she said. I thought she was going to start crying.

"Well, I love it. That is a really nice picture of your cabana. You know, I've always thought that cabana had the prettiest view of the ocean of the places here. We'll put this in a frame and hang it where we see it every day."

She gave me another hug. I was really going to miss her.

"Hey, if Ms. Susan is upstairs with your mother and Ms. Kim, where is Eric?" I asked.

"I think he went out on a kayak. I don't think that he likes us. That's okay though, I don't really like him either," Michelle said.

"What? Why? Isn't he your father's friend?"

"They worked together, but I don't think Daddy really liked him that much." She ate a piece of her candy, and sold another piece to Katie.

"What makes you think your father didn't like him?"

"They argued a lot. Daddy said the man that wants to build that big resort is a bad man. Mr. White said he isn't, but that he's dangerous and they should be afraid of him."

"Did they ever get into a real fight?"

"I don't think so. I don't think Daddy ever hit anyone. They argued a lot. They shouted at each other sometimes."

"Did you ever hear what they were saying, when they shouted?"

"Once, Daddy said he thought Mr. White was getting money from the man building the resort. He said something, called him 'unethical' or something like that. I don't know what that means."

Chapter 29

Tuesday, December 26th, 2:30 P.M.

"Beth, other than Larry, we've got a few of the younger divers on this next trip. Why don't we go to The Crack?"

"That sounds good to me. We haven't heard jokes about looking for crabs in your crack yet this week. So, you're coming with us?"

"Yeah, I need to get some exercise, you know, clear the cobwebs."

"Are you okay to dive? Those photos, the one of your first wife and son, they really shook you up."

"I'm fine. We'll let the younger divers lead the pace, make it a bit more of a workout." *Maybe I can drown the ghosts.*

"Larry isn't going to like that. He likes taking it slow. He says he's conserving his energy and that helps conserve his air. I think he's lazy."

"He's right, and so are you. He'll sit on the sand near a coral head and see what swims up to him, if we let him."

She laughed. "I know, I've let him do that before. One of his favorite dives was like that. A couple of angelfish swam around him, and then a huge barracuda came up to him and stared for a while."

"Yeah, I remember that trip. He even stayed still when a nurse shark swam around him. At least, he stayed still for its first two passes. Then he stood up, extended his arms and legs to let the shark know how big he was, and it swam away. I'll make up for pushing the pace to him later."

❧❦☙

When I got back from the dive and changed into my shorts and t-shirt I walked down the beach to Mountain To Sea. I gathered the staff for a meeting and read them the riot act about drugs. Then I had all of the guides accompany me and Gator to each guide's cabana and stand together outside.

"Gator and I are going to search your rooms. If I find drugs, you're history. Anybody want to speak up now?"

No one volunteered the location of any drugs. A couple griped about warrantless searches and Constitutional rights. For some reason, they just didn't get it.

Marlene, a first-time guide for Mountain To Sea, was the first guide whose cabana was searched. Her place was clean. Then it was Joanne's turn. It was her second season with Mountain To Sea. I found a small amount of grass in her drawer. I tossed it out; she'd get a warning. That small amount was clearly for personal use. She wasn't selling the stuff. As I searched each guide's cabana I kept them all together. I didn't want one to go hide their drugs somewhere else. No other guides were caught with any drugs at all. I had the same discussion, and searched the cabanas, of my own staff. Fortunately my staff all know drugs and diving don't mix and I found nothing.

❧❦❧

I retrieved the photos, still wrapped in felt, and retreated to my gym. No one ever comes up there except, sometimes, Kim. It was the photo of Grace and Austin I needed to inspect. The writing on the back wasn't mine, or Grace's. It was her older brother's. Andrew was two years older than me. Their family, a mix of Spanish and Pueblo Indian, lived within the Tiqua Indian reservation. It's entirely within the city limits of El Paso. He went to school with me, and we grew up as friends, even with the racial tensions of the time. The reservation wasn't even an officially recognized reservation until the late Sixties.

After high school he went to college through the Army's ROTC program. In his first stint he was a soldier, part of the Rangers. After his first tour he was accepted into a flight program. If he re-enlisted they'd make him a pilot. He did, and the Army lived up to its promise. He became a pilot, flying small observation planes. In Vietnam he flew rescue missions, providing communication with downed aircrews and directing rescue helicopters to the men on the ground. He complained to me once that they'd given him the call sign "Red Cloud," completely unaware that Red Cloud was from a different tribe, the Souix, and a different part of the country. Cochise or Geronimo might have been closer, at least geographically. After his tour was up he couldn't find a job with an airline. He scraped together some money and bought a small puddle-jumper and suddenly seemed to have money. I know he made a lot of short flights across the border.

As kids, Andrew and I had this fort we'd made out of scrap pieces of lumber, plywood, and whatever else we could scrounge up. In it we had a small table and some stools. We also had a picture on that table of the two of us on a camping trip. We'd leave a note to each other by hiding a single page of paper, very neatly folded, behind the picture. You'd have to look pretty close to notice a slight bulge near the bottom of the picture.

I thought I felt a slight bulge behind the picture, as if there was something between the photo and the back of the frame. I loosened the staples holding the cardboard backing in place and pulled the photo out of the frame. I unfolded the letter Andrew hid behind the photo and read it.

George,
Your sister, Katherine, called. A welcome voice from my past, not heard from in almost 20 years. She tells me you are married, and have been for a long time. That lifts my heart. I know that you have grieved enough for many men.

She tells me that you and your new wife are thinking of having children but you are having visions of Grace and Austin, and these visions worry you.

I have given Katherine a letter from me to you that I trust you'll share with your new wife. This is not that letter.

Let me tell you, my brother, that it does not dishonor Grace, or Austin, for you to re-marry and will not dishonor them for you to have another family. If God deems to give an old man like you another family then I know that they would want you to be as happy with this new family as you were with them.

The Tiqua tribe, under new tribal leadership that does not revere our heritage, is working to build a casino on land ten miles outside of town that the tribe acquired a few years ago. These new tribal leaders don't care about an unrecorded burial site, holding three bodies, workers at the site found nearly a year ago. They only care about the money the casino can bring. So far, no effort has been made to identify the remains.

Know that you and your new family are always welcome to regain your place with mine. Our families will always be joined. I hope someday to introduce you to my wife and our children.

I folded the letter, put it in my pocket to be destroyed later, and placed the photo securely in the frame.

They found the bodies, and so far nobody cares. Is that good news, or bad?

Chapter 30

Wednesday, December 27th, 5:45 A.M.

Wednesday morning Kim and I made our morning run around the island alone. Beth slept in.

"I'm going to Belize City with the others. I'm not sure when I'll get back, or how, yet." Kim was pushing our pace today.

"When you're done, just take a commuter flight to Dangriga and I'll send Jeremy over with the *Sensencula* to pick you up."

"Do you think Charlie will be back out?"

"No, I don't think so. He thinks it was just a heart attack. He barely even looked at the body."

She stopped running, put both hands on my arm, and stared up at me. "Does that mean you don't?"

"Babe, I know that it wasn't a heart-attack." I told her about the puncture wound.

"So, if it wasn't a heart attack, then who killed him?"

"I don't know. Kevin is the obvious answer, but I don't think it was him. He's got an attitude and has probably been in more than his share of fights but he's too stupid for something like this. He'd probably use a knife, or some blunt instrument."

"But you don't know what Bernie was stabbed with?"

"No. Not yet. I want to take a look around in the kitchens, see if there is something in them that might fit."

"What makes you think there is?"

"Nothing really. I don't think anyone in our staff would have a reason to kill Bernie. That suggests a guest. Other than Kevin, everyone's gotten along pretty well. The only person I've seen with knives of any kind is Antonio Terrazzo."

"You suspect Antonio?"

"I don't know who to suspect, or who to trust. He's pretty fit for a chef. What's that saying, 'never trust a skinny cook'?"

"Is there anybody else you suspect?"

"Well, Bernie and Eric work together and they're on this vacation together. They didn't see eye-to-eye on the new resort. Michelle said that Bernie and Eric argued a lot."

"So, you suspect Eric?"

"I don't know. He seemed really shocked, frightened even, that Bernie was dead. I think he might suspect something but doesn't seem to have the balls to do something himself."

"Do you think figuring out what was used to kill him will help you find out who did it?"

"Yeah, and I have no idea what could make that size puncture wound," I said. I was thinking about an ice pick as a possibility. Probably too thin, I thought. Besides, I don't think we have one.

Kim held my hand a little tighter. "George, there's something about the boat trip to Dangriga I didn't mention."

"What, did the nice doctor hit on you?" I asked, not blaming him if he did.

"He's a young guy, and attractive enough that I wish he had, but no. Jack was in and out of consciousness during the trip. At one point he was somewhat lucid, and trying to talk. He said something that didn't make much sense."

"He was trying to talk here, before the boat left, but didn't have enough strength. Could you make it out?"

"I think he said there was somebody on their porch during the height of the storm. I chalked it up to the injury."

"As a soldier, recently in the battlefield, his senses would all be on alert. If anyone had been there, he'd know. But if he'd heard anything at all I'm sure he'd have gotten up to check it out. If he didn't do that then I suspect he imagined it after the accident."

Could someone have been on the porch? Did they reverse the railing during the storm and remove the bolts? Who would want to hurt either Jack or Sherry? It would be a gamble that either one would lean against the railing and impossible to expect Jack to do so. I had no answers.

"The storm was pretty fierce, with a lot of thunder and lightning," Kim said. "There'd have been lots of strange noises to deal with. Even if he thought he'd heard someone he might have thought it was just another storm related noise."

"Maybe. There's no way to tell."

"By the way, did you sleep through the night? I didn't sense you waking," she asked.

"I slept most of the night. Andrew's letter helped. I had a dream. This one was different."

"What was different about it?" she asked.

"Grace was standing next to you. Both of you were smiling and watching Austin. Austin was about ten. The age he was when he died. He was walking a pony around, leading the pony by his reins."

"I was there, with Grace and Austin?"

"Yeah, and someone else," I said with a grin. "There was a little red-haired, freckled-faced boy seated on the pony, laughing."

"A red-haired boy? Our son?" she said, smiling, almost glowing.

"I think so. I think this dream was Grace and Austin's way of telling me they're okay with us having a family."

Kim hugged me, gave me a light kiss on the cheek. "I'm glad. I only wish I could have known them."

I didn't tell her about the rest of the dream, the reason I woke up. In the dream a snake coiled, its rattle spooked the pony. The pony reared up on its hind legs. I woke before I could see the little boy fall to the ground. Worse still, both Grace and Austin were ghosts yet they were as clear to me as were Kim and the little boy. Could they have been ghosts too? I couldn't help but think it was another warning that I can't protect my new family any better than I did the first one.

"May I read Andrew's letter?" Kim asked.

"Sure, I assumed you read it when Katherine sent it." I wasn't going to tell her about the hidden one. I've never lied to her, but that doesn't mean I tell her everything.

❧❀❧

"George, we've got a few people ready to dive."

I was tinkering with the motor on one of my dive boats, doing some thinking, when Kim walked up. "George, did you hear me? I said we've got a couple of people ready to dive."

"Alicia and Carolyn, plus Dave and Dagan, right?" They'd all said they wanted to make a dive this morning. Bernie's death was a heart-attack, natural causes. No reason for them to panic.

"Right. Larry wants to go too. So, where are they going, and who's leading this trip?"

"Let Beth and Marcus lead this one. We haven't sent them to Victoria's Caye Wall yet."

"Yeah, Marcus knows where a moray eel lives on that wall. That should get everyone excited."

It's an easy, mostly shallow dive but if they want they can go over The Wall and drop down as deep as they'd like—within recreational dive limits anyway. Most of the fun stuff is between fifty and sixty feet. I covered up the motor cowling and put my tools away.

"Wait, did you say Larry was going?" I asked.

"Yeah, he's been making a lot of dives this week, at least in comparison to past trips," Kim answered.

"Do you want to talk him into the twelve-dive package? I'm sure Beth can get him to sign-up for more dives."

"Maybe, but he'd have to do at least one night dive. You know, Beth and I were talking with him last night. Beth said that he looks like he's lost weight since his trip last year."

"He does look a little lighter. He's been more active this week."

"George, I saw him swimming in the lagoon out here earlier today. Not just floating, actually swimming between the two docks, doing laps."

"Good. He's keeping busy and making more dives and that means spending more money."

✦

The *Tropical Breeze* crew arrived at about nine-thirty. I greeted Sticks and asked him to stow his gear and meet me back at the boat in twenty minutes. I had Gator help Gene gather his stuff.

I helped Helene and the girls get their bags on the boat and went to help the Whites.

"Eric, how big was the team working with Bernie to stop the new resort?"

"What team? It was just the two of us. He had a local law firm involved, but as far as our firm was concerned it was the two of us."

"You and Bernie weren't on the same page about the resort. That was obvious from the conversation that first night you were here."

"Bernie was too much of an idealist. He loved this place, and it is a great place, but it can only serve a small number of people. The resort that Martinez is planning can serve a lot of people, and bring a lot of jobs to the area."

"Is your firm going to keep fighting Martinez?"

"I don't think so. I've recommended to the rest of the partners that we drop out."

"I've heard that you and Bernie had some pretty intense arguments about the resort."

Eric stared out toward the ocean. "Bernie was a dreamer. He lived in some fantasy world, where lawyers stop bad guys from doing things. The truth is, we might try to make a bad guy pay for damage if something goes wrong, but we don't get to decide whether they do whatever it is first."

"If you thought the resort was a good idea, why'd you work with Bernie on it at all? Isn't that a conflict of interest of some kind?"

"What's with all the questions?"

"I just see it as kind of strange, that you'd be partnered with Bernie, a dreamer as you put it, on something you disagreed with him on. Why invest your time in something you didn't believe in?"

"I'm just an associate at the firm. Bernie was a full partner. I worked on what the partners assigned me to, and in this case it was Bernie's pet project."

"Did he ever accuse you of a conflict of interest? Did he ever accuse you of taking money from Martinez?"

"Where'd you get an idea like that?"

He was getting more defensive. I couldn't tell if I'd hit home, or if he was just ticked that I'd question his integrity.

"That doesn't matter. Did he accuse you of a conflict of interest?"

"I don't know where you heard that, or what good it does for you to suggest it, but, yeah, he did."

"Did he tell his partners at the firm?"

"No. He had no evidence. His sense of fair-play wouldn't allow that."

"Does his lack of evidence mean it wasn't true?"

He glared at me but said nothing.

"So, Martinez wins."

"I don't see it as Martinez wins. I see it as Belize wins by adding hundreds of jobs. The firm wins because it cuts its losses on this. I win because I've got a shot at replacing Bernie as a partner."

Chapter 31

Wednesday, December 27th, 10:30 A.M.

I saw smoke coming from the south end of the island. It was the middle of the week and the maintenance guys were burning a debris pile. Some of what they burned was trash that washed up on the beach. Some was waste building material. Some of it was saplings and other brush we'd cut down to make room for a couple of more guest cabanas. I walked to the pit and threw Andrew's secret letter to me into the fire. I hoped it would burn away some of the memories he'd dredged up.

⚞◆⚟

The day after the break-in at my dental office, around lunch time, I heard a lot of noise outside the office. I walked out to the front of the building to find a group of about a dozen bikers. They were driving in circles, harassing my patients, scaring them away.

One of them stopped his bike in front of me. He looked me up and down, trying to intimidate me. "You Dr. Schroeder?" he growled.

"Yeah, who are you?"

"It doesn't really matter what my name is. What matters is that you have to drop the charges against my friend." He flexed his biceps causing a tattoo of a knife through a skull to move.

"Your friend? Is that the guy the cops arrested last night trying to break in here?"

"Yeah. You should have just run him off." He revved the engine on his Harley. His friends all stopped their bikes in front of me too.

"Well, he shouldn't have tried to break in here. Look, he didn't get anything, and nobody got hurt. I'm sure he'll get off with a slap on the wrist." I watched as a woman and her kid got back in their car. My twelve-thirty appointment just got canceled.

"I don't know, Texas has one of those 'three-strikes and you're out' laws and he's been inside a couple of times. You need to drop the charges."

"Why should I do that?"

"Someone might get hurt if you don't."

"I can take care of myself."

"Maybe so, but I didn't say you might get hurt. Just that someone might. It could be someone else. It could be someone you care about. Call the cops and drop the charges."

"I don't think so. Speaking of the cops, they're on their way here now." My receptionist was calling them as I came outside.

"You've been warned. I only warn people once." He revved his engine, waved one arm in circles above his head, and the rest of his crew revved up their engines. They rode off.

Chapter 32

Wednesday, December 27th, 1:30 P.M.

"Beth, we've got Larry, Alicia, and Carolyn wanting to make another dive this afternoon," I said as the staff at Over The Edge finished lunch.

"Have you noticed Larry's been making more dives than usual this trip?"

"I have. What do you think, is it because you're here?"

She blushed a bit. "No, Kim and I were talking earlier today. We've both noticed, he's lost some weight since his last trip. Not a ton, mind you, but maybe twenty or thirty pounds. Maybe he has more energy?"

"He told me the day he arrived that he lost fifty pounds this past year. He still has a long way to go. He's been more active, not just in diving but he took one of the kayaks out for a paddle Sunday, and was playing with the kids a little on Monday. He even played in one of the volleyball games."

"Well, he's diving pretty well too. He's got his buoyancy down. He still carries a lot of weight but he doesn't have to waste as much time or air getting himself neutral during dives. Anyway, where do you want me to take them?"

"Larry wanted to go on the late afternoon dive. I've got Misty taking him and the Cavutos to The Crack. Since that's a deep dive, let's keep this one shallow. Take them to your garden."

"Will do."

"George, may I go on the later dive?" Dylan asked.

"Sure, Dylan. You want to dive The Crack? Still trying to impress Misty?"

"Yeah, another turn at the bat, so to speak."

"It's your life."

I watched from my office. "We'll be going to The Crack this dive. Everyone, pay attention." Misty gave them the usual pre-dive review.

Larry had been floating in the lagoon, next to the dive boat, getting the air bubbles out of his suit. He stood and faced Misty.

"We'll get in the water, one at a time. Dylan will get in first and go down a few feet, then Larry. Larry, its okay to start your descent with Dylan. You don't need to wait on the rest of us."

"Thanks."

"For the rest of you, it's a deep dive, the deepest any of you have done here this week. You'll follow Dylan and Larry down to the entrance. Then I'll go in first, followed by Larry, Dagan, and then Dave. Dylan will go through last."

"Then what?" asked Dave.

"We'll come back up along The Wall and swim at a depth of about thirty feet for a while. When whoever the first person to get to seven-hundred pounds of air left is, let me know. That's when we'll start the safety stop."

Dylan helped get all of their gear in the boat.

I watched them leave from one of the chairs at the end of the dock, enjoying the breeze and appreciating the shade from the thatched roof overhead. I closed my eyes. I'd almost drifted off when I heard the rubbing of something heavy being dragged across the deck. Sticks had walked, barefoot, down the dock and moved another chair into the shade.

"Welcome back," I said.

"From what I've been hearing, it sounds like it's been a rough week so far. Why'd you want me to come back early?"

"I sent Gene home this morning. With Bernie's death and Jack's accident, well, I wanted someone else around I can trust. Gator is a good man, but he's still young. I wanted someone a little wiser around."

"I heard about Gene and the drugs and I can't blame you for firing him. You can count on me for whatever you need. Hey, did you talk with Beth about buying Over The Edge?"

"I have. She and Mike are interested. Mike's talking with their bank back in the States to see what they can come up with."

"I went to an office of Bank of the Caribbean yesterday and talked with a loan officer."

"Yeah, how'd that go?"

"It went pretty well. I've got about a third of what I think we'll wind up settling on. They'll finance the rest for me, provided we come to terms on the price."

"Well, you know what I think Mountain To Sea is worth. What's your offer?"

"I think your numbers are about right. I was thinking….hey, look, the boat's coming back pretty quickly, isn't it?"

"I bet Larry got nervous and wanted to come back in. He's done that a few times in the past, but it'd be the first time this week."

"I know that he's been here before, but I've never made a dive with him." Sticks stood, adjusting the brim on his cap and putting his sunglasses on.

"Sometimes he gets into the water and if there's any surface chop he gets nervous. He'll start to hyperventilate and when that starts he gets back in the boat. Once Larry gets down a few feet from the surface he's fine. The trick is getting him below the surface quickly."

But as I saw the boat rounding the point I could count heads. I could make out that Larry was on his knees, holding something on the deck. My headcount showed one missing.

"Something ain't right, George. Misty's waving wildly and shouting something."

"Yeah, something bad has happened."

Jeremy quickly pulled the boat up to the dock, sending strong waves against the shore, and threw me a line. He was jabbering in that Creole mix the native Belizeans speak. I looked and saw Dylan, unconscious and bleeding from the nose and mouth. Misty and Larry had taken his BCV off. I could see it was fully inflated.

"Marcus!" I yelled as loud as I could to get his attention. He was in his cabana. He looked outside.

"Marcus, get on the radio and call for the rescue helicopter. We've got a case of A-G-E!"

"Misty, what happened?"

Sticks jumped down on the boat. He, Jeremy and I lifted Dylan off the boat and onto the dock.

"Sticks, go get my medical kit from the office. Make sure you bring the pure oxygen tank." The scuba tanks aren't pure oxygen. They're basically same mix as the air we breathe, roughly twenty-one percent oxygen and seventy-nine percent nitrogen. For emergencies I have a small tank of one-hundred percent oxygen.

Larry and the other two divers stood in the boat, looking on.

Misty looked frightened. "I'm not sure what happened. We were all in the water and descended to the top of The Crack. It started the way we'd planned. Dylan and Larry went down first, then Dagan and Dave, and then me. Once we were all at the entrance I went through The Crack first, just the way we'd planned. Dylan was coming down as I led the others out of The Crack. When the four of us were clear I looked back and saw Dylan in The Crack. He was upright, fumbling with his inflator valve. I couldn't tell what was happening so I swam back into the hole. Just as I got to him I could see his vest was full of air, like he'd been constantly putting air into it. Then he did something really crazy: he unbuckled his weight belt and dropped it."

"He dropped his weight belt while in The Crack? That's crazy, he was at ninety feet. With a full vest he'd pop up to the surface."

"And that's what happened. He popped up to the surface," Misty said, shooting her left arm up high, quickly.

"What'd you do then?" I listened while trying to control Dylan's convulsions.

"The only thing I could do. I called off the dive, and led the other three up as quickly as my dive computer would allow. When we surfaced Jeremy was pulling Dylan up into the boat."

"Yah, mon, he was barely conscious and he was talking nonsense. When you say he 'popped up,' you aren't kidding. He actually came out of the water! He started having convulsions and passed out. I got him into the boat and was about to head in when I saw Misty and the others coming up, so I picked them out of the water and high-tailed it over here."

I could barely understand Jeremy, he was talking so fast.

"It's an Arterial Gas Embolism. The air in his lungs expanded and may have burst a lung. Worse, the air in his bloodstream would also have expanded with such a rapid ascent. Most of the air's taken from the lungs to the brain and he likely burst several arteries in his brain."

"How much would his lungs have expanded? I don't quite understand," Dagan said.

The science behind this is usually covered in a diving certification course and is part of the certification exam. I wasn't surprised that that she didn't understand. I think most divers forget all of that after getting certified, especially if they dive infrequently and only with certified dive masters.

"For every thirty-three foot descent, your lungs get compressed by the water pressure to half their previous size. So to get to ninety feet deep your lungs would be compressed to about fifteen percent of their normal size. When you come back up they expand again. Your body can't handle that expansion too quickly. That's the reason for the safety stop. That, and to let your body expend some of the nitrogen that builds up in your bloodstream while diving."

"The bends?" Dave asked.

"Yeah, the bends are one of the problems that can come about. The body doesn't expel the nitrogen and the nitrogen gets caught in your fat cells."

I put the oxygen mask on Dylan and tried to stop him from hurting himself further during the convulsions. It took twenty minutes for the rescue helicopter from the British Royal Air Force Base on St. George's Island to get to our island and land on the beach. It only took a couple of minutes to get him onto the helicopter.

Before I climbed aboard I grabbed Marcus. "Marcus, I want you to get Dylan's gear from the boat and put it into the compressor building. Then lock the building. Don't let anyone else get to his gear, or into the compressor buildin until I get back. Don't let anyone else into the compressor building before I get back. That probably won't be until late tomorrow. Call Kim for me, tell her what happened, and have her meet me in San Pedro. We have to be going there since they have the only recompression chamber in the country. One more thing: no more dives for anyone until I get back."

As the RAF helicopter lifted off from Sunrise Caye I saw every guest, and most of the staff members, watching from their respective dining halls. With now two accidents and one death, as far as they knew from natural causes, they must have been getting pretty nervous. There wasn't much I could do right then to calm them. Dylan was my immediate focus.

❧❖❧

The helicopter landed in San Pedro Town, at Ambergris Caye, near the building that houses the only recompression chamber in Belize. The copter's engines had just wound down when my cell phone rang.

"George, how is he?" Kim asked.

"He didn't make it. He died in the helicopter. We're at the hospital now."

"How did this happen?"

"I don't know, honey. First, we had the accident with Jack Bunton, then Bernie Stamps, and now Dylan." My mind was racing, going in a thousand different directions.

"They aren't related."

"I think they are. I just don't know how. Where are you now?"

"Belize City. I can be in San Pedro in about an hour and a half."

"No, don't do that. I think this is going to take all night. What I need is for you to go back to the island and get the emergency contact information we had for Dylan. I'll need to contact his family and make arrangements."

"Okay, but what do you mean you think Dylan's accident and what happened to Bernie and Jack are related?"

"I'll explain when I get home. In the meantime, don't say anything to anybody about my suspicions. So far everyone else thinks Jack's injury was an accidental fall and Bernie had a heart attack."

"Alright, but you're scaring me. If I'm heading home, I have to go. I can see Tropic Air is starting to load their plane to Dangriga."

"Kim, I love you. Be safe."

⊱⋆⊰

I made the painful call to Dylan's parents that evening. The doctors didn't perform an autopsy, but confirmed the cause of death was an embolism resulting from making a rapid ascent. I spent most of that evening talking with an officer from the Belize National Police. They would have the Maritime Police come out to Sunrise Caye to take statements from Misty and Jeremy and the other three divers, but as long as they all told the same story the case would be considered an accident.

The hospital released the body the next morning, and I made arrangements to get it on the last flight out of Belize City that afternoon.

Chapter 33

Thursday, December 28th, 6:00 A.M.

I spent the night at a local rooming house, essentially a bed and breakfast but not nearly as cozy as you'd find in the States. I had a fitful night as a nightmare played over and over. It was a memory of a weekend visit with Grace's parents.

We let Austin, then not much more than two years old, play in their yard with a slightly older cousin. The courtyard itself was bordered by a five-foot tall adobe wall to keep out small animals. There was, however, a sidewalk leading from the driveway to the front door. Their sidewalk had a cast-iron gate with a thin mesh. It would keep out animals like coyotes and armadillos. The adults sat around a table, under the patio awning, and only looked in on the kids every few minutes.

We heard a shriek from the older cousin, then Austin crying. I walked out to see what was wrong. I expected it to be something small, one of the kids taking a toy away from the other. As I approached I saw the cousin pointing at a rattlesnake.

We called an ambulance and took Austin to the local hospital. They gave him a shot of anti-venom and kept him overnight, with Grace and me alongside his bed all night, for observation. Grace and I were both scared, and it led to bickering about not doing enough to protect our son.

Is Grace accusing me with this dream, or warning me?

Early Thursday morning I boarded a commuter flight from San Pedro to Dangriga. I took a taxi to a private dock area I use and waited for Jeremy and *The Sensencula*. The boat's name was fitting today. It roughly translates as "a little bit crazy."

I tried to take a nap on the way across only to be awakened by Jeremy as we approached the island. "Mr. George, it looks like Charlie's waiting for us."

I looked toward the island. My dive boats were all in place and, sure enough, a Maritime Police boat was tied to the end of the dock. Jeremy pulled up to the dock, letting the waves rock the boat against the buffers. I tied the bow of the boat to a piling and walked down the dock toward the dining hall.

"Good morning, George," I heard Charlie say. He didn't get up. He was quite content with a sandwich that Annette had prepared for him and a soda.

"Good morning to you, too, Charlie. How long have you been here?"

"Oh, I guess it's been about an hour. I've already talked with Misty, and the other guests that were on this dive. It is unfortunate, what happened to Dylan. I liked him."

"Yeah, he was a good man." I squeezed some orange juice and sat down across the table from him. "So, who else do you need to talk with?"

"I need to talk with Jeremy. And with you too, I suppose. I understand you've already given a statement in San Pedro. I will keep it brief, but I should talk with Jeremy first."

He went off to find Jeremy, taking his sandwich and soda with him.

⚜

In fewer than ten minutes Charlie found me in my office. "This has not been a good week, George. I've been out here three times for three tragic accidents."

"I know. We've been here for twenty years and have never had a serious injury. This week we've had two deaths and a serious injury. I don't know what to think."

"It seemed like everyone had the same story to tell. It sounded like an accident to me, just one of the risks with diving. That is what my co-workers in San Pedro believe as well."

"We're going to go through all our dive gear very thoroughly this morning. We need to figure out why Dylan's buoyancy compensator got stuck."

"I'll leave in a few minutes so that you can get started."

"Great. Well, I hope you don't take this wrong, but I hope not to see you for a while."

"There is something else, George." He almost seemed apologetic.

"Oh? What's that?"

"Today is my normal day to visit here. You know, to collect the guest taxes."

Chapter 34

Thursday, December 28th, 10:00 A.M.

"Marcus, I want us to do a thorough inspection of the rental gear," I said.

"I don't think the Mountain To Sea guests want to dive with us anymore this week. I think they're all spooked. I can't blame them."

"Marcus, I can't blame them, either. If I were one of them I'd be demanding that the Mountain To Sea boat come fetch me and take me back to Belize City."

"Larry's still here, and wanting to dive. Joe and Terri Wright are still here as well. They've only made two dives this week. They said they'd like to make another."

"Beth, do you want to take Larry on a dive?"

"Sure. He has his own gear and knows how to use it. He told me the other day that he took an equipment maintenance course from his local dive shop."

"He did?"

"He said he learned a little, but he also said he wouldn't do anything on his own without someone more experienced checking it out. He said he applies the rules that skydivers have. Skydivers pack their own main chutes after each jump but a certified packer has to pack the reserve chutes," Beth said.

"Okay, check out your equipment real carefully and check out his gear too. Have Misty check with Joe and Terri, to see if they want to make a dive. Let them know that this dive is free for Over The Edge guests, if they're interested. I want the two of you to check all of their gear very closely. If it all looks good, take them out somewhere this afternoon."

Beth left, and half an hour later I heard the boat pulling out with all three Over The Edge guests aboard.

✄⬧✄

"Marcus, we need to inspect Dylan's gear."

We retrieved Dylan's gear from the compressor room. Marcus placed Dylan's vest and other equipment, still attached to the air tank, on a dining table. The dining room was the best workspace I had, but not very private. Fortunately, Erin was in her cabana, proof-reading her book.

Marcus disconnected the air tank from the breathing regulator. "The O-ring on his air tank looks okay. It has a small crack but not something we'd be worried about yet."

I looked at it. My eyes weren't as good as Marcus's, and I needed to shine a dive light on the O-ring to see the crack he was talking about.

"Yeah, I see it now, but it isn't something that would have caused a problem. I think the problem's going to have to be in the buoyancy compensator. An O-ring failure would either leak air into the water, not into the octopus, or maybe cause bad air."

"With bad air he'd have gotten a little loopy. He'd do dumb things. Like fill his BC and drop his weights," Marcus said.

"True, but it would take longer for it to reach that point. He wasn't down more than ten minutes, based on what I've been told. It couldn't have kicked in that quickly."

"George, the problem is probably in the inflator. Maybe it's in the Schrader valve. Sand can get stuck in that and keep it open."

The Schrader valve looked fine. There wasn't any sand in it. We spent nearly an hour looking at the valve. I finally spotted the problem.

"Marcus, look here." I shined a light pen on the inflator hose. "There's a small hole in the air inflator hose coming from the octopus, and another right next to it feeding into the vest. Air leaking from the inflator hose poured into the vest inflator. It was basically in free flow, and there wasn't anything Dylan could have done to stop it."

The connector from the breathing system to an air tank is known as an octopus. There are multiple hoses coming from the octopus. One runs to the primary regulator, the mouth piece that the diver breathes from. Another runs to a secondary regulator, in case of a malfunction in the primary regulator. Another, depending on the style of the system, runs to the inflator control to put air into the vest. The system Dylan used combined the alternate regulator and the inflator. The end of the inflator can be used as a secondary regulator for breathing. That reduces the number of connections, the number of moving parts, and streamlines the diver making them more efficient. These types of secondary regulators aren't as easy to breathe from as the other types. It's a trade-off. I have a secondary regulator that is the same type, the same brand and model, as my primary. I'd rather have the ease of use, plus I have at times had other divers run out of air and having a good secondary regulator makes it easy to share my air tank. We don't have to exchange regulators, what a lot of people have heard called "buddy breathing."

"How could these holes get there?" Marcus asked.

"I don't know. And why wasn't it in free flow before he got in the water?"

"George, it should have been in free flow as soon as he turned the air on at the tank."

"There's something sticky here. It's kind of like glue. Maybe it's some kind of adhesive that was corroded by the salt water?"

"Do you think Dylan had a problem and tried a repair job on his own?"

"No. I think Dylan knew his limitations. He was a pretty smart guy, and handy with tools. He also knew that when his life could be on the line it would be best to rely on an expert."

"For an amateur to try fixing their own dive gear is like asking an ex-wife to pack one's parachute. The results aren't likely to be favorable," Marcus said.

What do you know, the kid's got a sense of humor.

"Marcus, I think that I've never heard you make a joke before. I'm certain you've never talked about skydiving before."

"I tell jokes, you just don't catch most of them. Larry though, he told me a story about a friend whose wife suspected him of cheating on her. The friend was a skydiver. He came home from work one day, picked up his skydiving gear, and went to the airport. When he got there something didn't feel right. He opened his pack on the ground and found that his wife had unpacked his main chute and cut it into a bunch of strips, then shoved it back."

"Larry didn't tell me that story." I said. "He's had several new ones lately."

"So, how do you think this happened?" Marcus asked.

"Someone else did it."

"Who would do that? And why?"

"I don't know. It would have to be someone with access to the equipment room and who wouldn't draw attention if seen in there."

"George, that room is open most of the day. Any of the guests can go in there to change clothes. Larry goes in a couple of times a day to get data from his dive computer for his log books. But why would someone do this?"

"I don't know, not yet anyway. But there's something else that bothers me."

"I know, even if that happened, why would he drop his weight belt?"

"Exactly. If this happened to one of us we'd be dumping air, using the dump valve at our left shoulder as fast as it was coming in, and could control our ascent enough to avoid decompression sickness. Dylan wasn't as experienced as either of us, but he wasn't a novice either. So why didn't Dylan do that, and why would he dump his weights?"

"Doing so was suicidal. I didn't see any significant changes in him lately to suggest he was contemplating suicide."

"Neither have I, Marcus. Of course, we haven't known him all that long. It would be an awfully painful and unreliable way of doing that."

Marcus shook his head. "I heard about a dive operator in Hawaii a couple of years ago doing the opposite. He put on a lot of weights after a dive, without his vest on, and waved goodbye and jumped in. At first the people on the boat thought he was fooling around. They found him at the bottom, about one hundred and twenty feet down. That makes more sense than doing this."

"Marcus, whose idea was it for this dive to be at The Crack?"

"I am not sure but I think Misty suggested it. Then again, Larry likes diving there. He likes the big fish, the groupers that hang out down there. He saw a black tip shark in there once."

"Okay. Well, Marcus, for now, let's keep this between us."

"And check our equipment more carefully every dive."

Chapter 35
Thursday, December 28th, 4:30 P.M.

"Hey Larry, can we talk for a couple of minutes?" I was at the base of the steps to his cabana.

"Sure, come on up." He was wearing a pair of swim trunks and lying on the hammock reading the latest Stephen Coonts' book. I took a seat in the only chair on the porch.

"I need to know what happened yesterday. Tell me what you saw."

"I told Charlie everything already. It's the same story," he said.

"I understand, but I need to hear it from you, if you don't mind."

"I didn't really see much. There was a little bit of chop, not much, but you know how I hate being on the surface."

"I know. We make it a point to get you under real fast."

"Yeah, and I was the first in the water, after Dylan anyway, and we started down immediately while the Cavutos were getting in. I was at the top of The Crack with Dylan and saw that Misty was in the water and making her way down to the entry point. Dave and Dagan were next to me and followed me into the hole."

"You were first?"

"No, we followed the plan. Misty went first, then me, then Dagan, and then Dave. Dylan was last."

"Did everyone wait for Dylan?"

"No, it was getting a bit claustrophobic down there, and Dagan was having buoyancy problems. So Misty swam out the bottom of the swim-through, I followed, and they were behind me. I looked back into the hole after Dave was through and saw Dylan. He was on the sandy bottom but looked like he was inflating his BC."

"Inflating it?"

"Looked that way to me, but he could have been trying to stop it from inflating."

"Then what happened?"

"I got Misty's attention. I thought something was wrong with Dylan."

"So you saw Dylan was having trouble first, not Misty?"

"That's right. She looked in, waited a few seconds...I don't know...maybe fifteen seconds or so...and then swam into The Crack to see if she could help."

"Could you see Dylan once Misty swam in?"

"No, she blocked my view. I could see a lot of air bubbles coming up through the top of The Crack."

"Did you see him release his weight belt?"

"No, I couldn't see him once Misty went back in. She was facing him and I saw a blast of air bubbles above the entry point, and then saw Dylan coming out of the entry point, real fast. He bounced off the side of the reef a little bit. Then he was gone."

"Scary stuff, huh?"

"A little, but I've seen uglier stuff before."

"Really? Like what?" Larry occasionally surprised me, but until he mentioned his ex-wife and son Christmas night I always thought he'd lived a sheltered life.

"When I was little, maybe five or six, someone driving through the neighborhood hit a neighbor's dog. It was hurt badly injured. My father went into the house and got one of his handguns, a twenty-two. He gathered up some of the other kids about my age, you know, we were all into playing cowboys and Indians or playing army with toy guns then, to watch. He shot the dog, putting it out of its misery."

"He did that when you were that young?" It just seemed really cold for such young kids.

"I remember the event, and the dog's suffering ending, more than the results of him shooting the dog in the head. I don't remember any of my friends having any nightmares about it. Me either. But he taught us what real guns can do, that when someone gets shot they don't get back up a few minutes later. That got reinforced a few years later."

"How so?"

"We'd moved about twenty miles and I had a friend in this new school. He lived in the projects up the road from the school. The only black kid I ever knew named 'Chip.' Anyway, after school one day we went to his place to play and when we got there his parents were fighting. His dad was drunk. I don't know what the fight was about, but his dad pointed a gun at Chip's mother. Chip stood in front, and his dad shot him. I dropped down behind a sofa. I heard his mother scream, then another shot, and then footsteps as Chip's father ran out of the apartment."

"Were they dead? What'd you do?"

"I went next door and got a neighbor and they called the cops and an ambulance. Chip was shot in the stomach. He was out of school for more than six months and when he came back he still couldn't eat real food, or even the crap we had at school. His mother wasn't hurt bad."

"What do you think of guns now?"

"I see them as a tool. I'm a big supporter of the Second Amendment and the right of individuals to have a gun. I exercise that right by not having one, but won't deny the choice to others provided they're otherwise law-abiding and sane. I know how to shoot. At least, I used to be proficient. I haven't used one in over twenty years."

"You saw something pretty scary. I'd hate to have seen something like that at that age." *I saw worse, but at least I was in my early thirties.*

"When I was a kid, between eleven and seventeen, I was in the

Civil Air Patrol. Are you familiar with them?"

"I've heard of them, but don't know what they are."

"They're like the Boy Scouts, but the Air Force runs it. The idea is to give kids a taste of military life and teach something about aviation. They're also really into search and rescue, as well as camping and mountaineering."

"Camping and mountaineering? You don't strike me as the mountain man type."

"I have friends that would disagree. In fact, one of my best friends said something after the FBI arrested the Unabomber. He said I was the kind of guy that could live in that little cabin, all alone, and go into town once or twice a year. I like my comforts too much, but I can live without people most of the time. And, yeah, we did a lot of camping in the Appalachians. I learned to rappel down cliffs at Carderock Park, near Washington, DC."

"What kind of search and rescue did you get involved in?"

"Anything from floods to airplane crashes to searching for missing people. We helped evacuate people in a flooded area in my hometown, Frederick, Maryland, after a hurricane dumped a foot of rain. A few months after my twelfth birthday I got my first call to participate in a ground search after an airliner crashed into a mountain in Maryland. There were a lot of dead bodies, lots of limbs and body parts. Mostly they just used us to control traffic nearby, to keep the media away."

"Pretty gruesome stuff for a twelve year-old."

"I saw more at other crashes after that. At the local airport, a few times a year, we'd have to go looking for missing ultra-light aircraft. A lot of them crashed into the corn fields nearby, usually with a fatality. I also got called out to search some woods along the Potomac River after two girls went missing. For two years, in addition to the Civil Air Patrol, I was in the Junior Fire Department."

"What's that?"

"When I was in high school we lived in a town that was surrounded by farming communities. In the Junior Fire Department, volunteer teenagers worked shifts, usually early evenings and weekends so that it didn't interfere with school activities. They'd ride along with the professional firemen and help do things like control traffic, run water hoses and connect hoses to fire hydrants, and do clean-up after a fire. A few kids every year were offered the opportunity to ride with the ambulance crews. I completed basic and advanced first aid and got my CPR certification and I earned that assignment. I couldn't administer drugs but I could help bandage up people, put on splints, that kind of thing."

I sat silently, wondering about this. It sounded plausible, but I had trouble reconciling it all with the Larry I knew.

"With that kind of experience, how'd you wind up in computers?"

"All I really wanted to do as I was growing up was to fly. The Civil Air Patrol helped with that. I soloed on my sixteenth birthday and got my private license exactly two years later. I went in the Army after graduating from high school. I reported for basic training about two weeks after the baby was born. I mentioned the other day that my wife and baby were hundreds of miles away. I spent that first year at Fort Benning in Georgia, learning to fly helicopters."

"So what happened with the Army, and flying?"

"For more than two years I flew wherever they told me to. I was assigned to a base in Florida, part of the Special Warfare Group. As co-pilot on a Blackhawk helicopter I flew assault teams to places we weren't supposed to be. I've been to parts of Central America that aren't ever going to be on my passport."

"You flew covert operations missions?"

"Yes, but don't let me fool you. I never, ever, got out of my ship. I'm the world's biggest coward. When bullets were flying I wanted to get in quick and out quicker. I did what I had to do, I served honorably and all that, but I'd never be the kind of heroes I transported."

"So, what happened?" I asked again, this time chuckling a little at how easily he could call himself a coward.

"About a year before my enlistment was due to end I started having some health problems. It turned out I had diabetes. The Army wouldn't let me fly suicide missions with diabetes. They took it really seriously."

"So, you couldn't fly anymore?"

"Not like that. I could keep my private pilot's license but the medical evaluations got more serious. I could never be a commercial pilot. But in the Army, flying was no longer an option. I still had a year left on my enlistment to complete. They offered me training on computers and I found it came easy to me. I left the service when my time was up and moved on."

"You grew up in Maryland. How'd you wind up in Texas?"

"My father was an engineer in the electric power field. He was working on a contract job at a utility company in Beaumont. I needed a job and they were looking for an operator with experience with large systems like the ones I'd worked with that last year in the Army. They made an offer and I moved."

"You went from the fire and into the frying pan. Beaumont's on the Gulf coast and I know it's incredibly hot and humid there most of the year."

"Beaumont sucked the life out of me. It was hot, humid, and flat. I hated living there. The only thing that made it tolerable was that the women outnumber men about seven to one and they're damned good looking. I stayed for six years, six weeks, and six days."

"Six-six-six. Isn't that a bad omen or something?"

"The mark of the beast, the devil, they say. I started drinking heavily while I lived there, and stopped working out. A while back I ran into someone from high school, he was on a conference call, and he recognized my name. Once we determined that we'd gone to high school together he asked if I was still running. My response was 'Not since my divorce was final' which is funnier but in truth it was when I got my discharge. While I lived in Beaumont I took up skydiving, for a little while."

"There's no way anyone would ever get me to jump from a perfectly good airplane," I said.

"There's no such thing as a perfectly good airplane, they've all got some defect. George Gobel was on the Carson show once and said he'd been a paratrooper for four years in the war but never once jumped out of a plane. Carson asked how that could be. 'The sergeant pushed my ass every damned time.'"

"He was a classic."

"Yeah, he was. Anyway, on one of my jumps I fractured an ankle and didn't realize it until later, when I was under a canopy on my next jump. Because of the adrenalin of that first jump I didn't even realize I'd messed up my foot. A few months later I saw one of my jump instructors nearly go in."

"Go in?"

"His chute never opened. A skydiver has a small pilot chute in a leg strap. When the jumper is ready to open his chute he'll reach down to his hip, pull that pilot chute out and toss it into the wind. A cord from the pilot chute pulls the pin holding the main chute in the pack and it, in turn, pulls the main chute out. In his case, his leg strap was twisted and the pilot chute couldn't pull the pin out to deploy the main chute."

"What happened?"

"Way too late he deployed the reserve chute. He went between two power lines and the reserve chute was just starting to come out. It wrapped around the power lines. That was enough to stop him from hitting the ground. The phrase 'going in' refers to hitting the ground without a fully opened chute."

"Diving is a lot safer than skydiving. At least you can always swim back to the boat. I don't care how much you flap your arms, you aren't flying back to the plane."

"Back then I worked with two guys. One was a skydiving instructor. The other was a scuba instructor. The skydiving instructor always had lots of good-looking women around him. The scuba instructor was a clown. I didn't have much confidence in him. Anyway, they'd often have this argument about which was more fun, cheaper to do, and safer. The argument grew old. Finally their boss said they had to settle it once and for all. They came to the conclusion that 'neither one is any fun when you run out of air.'"

"Cute. Which do you think is more fun?"

"For me, scuba. At least it is here, where the visibility is fantastic. Skydiving was a blast, or 'airgasmic' as a friend used to say, but I'm a bit of a klutz, and that's the wrong sport for those of us that are uncoordinated."

"Well, I'm glad you took up diving. Kim and I like having you come here."

"Do you like having me here enough to not charge me for the trip?"

I smiled. "No, not that much. Well, I'll let you get back to your book. I'll trade you the latest Cussler novel for that when you're done if you're interested. And, Larry, thanks."

⊰❖⊱

I walked away from that with a different view of Larry. He'd been more of an adventurer than I knew. He had rappelled, camped, and did search and rescue work as a teenager. Later, as an adult, he even tried skydiving. And that stuff about the Army and being a coward. I don't believe anyone that would call themselves a coward would be flying in that type of unit.

Anyone that comes to Mountain To Sea, anyone who makes their first vacation trip out of the U.S. and goes to a primitive resort like ours, is, by definition, out for an adventure. That he chose to come back here rather than go to other resorts in other countries just meant he liked calculated risks, not that he was risk adverse.

❦

I talked with Dave and Dagan too. Like Larry, they couldn't see Dylan once Misty swam back into the hole. It was a pretty narrow passage. They couldn't see Dylan so they didn't see him dump his weights. They hadn't noticed much at all. They were experiencing sensory overload.

Chapter 36

Thursday, December 28th, 5:30 P.M.

I had a knot in my belly and it was really beginning to tighten. I walked out to the dock and tinkered with the motor on the *Sensencula*, trying to tune it but mostly just trying to think. I didn't want to reach the conclusion I was coming to. Someone with the requisite knowledge, and unquestioned access to my equipment room, intentionally damaged Dylan's inflator hose so that it would go into free-flow, leading to his death. Someone also stabbed Bernie in his chest using a weapon that I couldn't identify to make it look like he'd had a heart-attack. Someone also got onto Jack and Sherry's deck during the storm Saturday night and moved a railing so that if either one leaned against it they'd fall and be injured or killed.

Who? And why?

I'd known Larry Carlson for a few years, yet until Christmas night that he'd been married and had a son. I'd only now learned he'd been in the Army, and about the violence he saw as a kid. What other surprises might he have, and what motive would he have for any of this? He'd had access to my equipment room. I let him change in there before and after each dive, and he'd go in a couple of times a day to get information about his dives from his dive computer to enter into his logbook. According to Beth, Larry said he'd completed an equipment maintenance course. Could he have learned enough to sabotage Dylan's gear? Probably so, but why would he? He's a big guy. He doesn't move stealthily. Even if he had motivation, I don't think he could have snuck onto Jack's porch undetected, with or without a storm. He's an easy going guy, too. Last year there was another guest, one from Alaska, who Larry didn't like. Two dives they made together and two incidents in which the other guy got careless and kicked Larry. The third incident was the whale shark trip we made. We had two dives planned. Ten minutes into the first dive the other guy kicked Larry's mask off. It was lost in water more than a thousand feet deep. Larry made it to the surface okay but didn't get a good look at the whale sharks or the big bull sharks there feeding off the snapper spawn. Without a mask, Larry couldn't make the second dive we planned. He didn't fight with the guy, curse him out or anything. Larry just decided to not go on any additional dives with the guy during the rest of the week. I hadn't seen him get angry at anyone, except maybe himself on those times he got spooked and got back in the boat, on any of his five trips. He hadn't had any problems with anybody here, not even Kevin.

Kevin O'Reilly was still an obvious choice, if only because he'd been such a brute. I didn't know of any motivation, at least for either Dylan or Jack and Sherry. He hadn't fought with any of them that I knew of. His squabbles with Bernie weren't worth killing for. Besides, he's a brute. He'd use something like a hammer or a large knife. He wouldn't be discrete. I didn't find anything when I searched his room that might have been used as a weapon.

Antonio Terrazzo bothered me. First, for all the humor in it, and even acknowledging there are skinny TV chefs like Bobby Flay, there's truth in the saying "Never trust a skinny chef." He's good with knives, and has access to some in the kitchens. He'd gotten along with everyone, except maybe Kevin and if I were to suspect everyone that had a problem with Kevin I wouldn't have anyone left. I didn't see a motive and didn't know what was used to kill Bernie.

I thought about Eric White. He certainly stood to gain from Bernie's death. He said he'd be in line to take Bernie's place as a partner in their law firm. He'd been against their involvement in fighting

Martinez' new resort and, if Michelle was right, may have taken some money from Martinez. He always spoke of Martinez, either directly by name or indirectly, in hushed tones, as if afraid of Martinez, and he was suspicious about Bernie's heart-attack. Could he have stabbed Bernie with something? I still didn't know what the weapon was, but why would he have done anything to Jack or Sherry? Why would he do anything to Dylan, and could he have sabotaged Dylan's gear?

I'd limited my thoughts mostly to guests, but what of my staff? Certainly they all had access to the equipment room. Dylan had the easiest opportunity to replace the railing, but why would he? He got along well enough with Bernie and his family. And with his death, which I didn't believe was an accident, he wasn't a suspect.

Misty? None of the divers on Dylan's last dive could see him once she'd gone back into The Crack. Could she have removed his weight belt? Wouldn't he have been able to stop her if she tried? What motive would she have? She had easy access to the equipment room. Did she have the skills to make the alteration to Dylan's BC? Probably, most dive masters know a lot about the equipment they'll use. They'd been together at least a few times since Dylan's arrival, but she'd been with others too. I didn't see jealousy or their past relationship as a factor. She has a mean streak, and she's had some real darkness in her background. She had impressive fighting skills, and speed, but none of the incidents involved a fight. What motive would she have?

Beth? She'd have met Jack and Sherry, and Bernie and the rest of the Mountain To Sea guests in Belize City the morning the boat brought them to the island. She'd known Dylan for a few years, at least professionally, and recommended him for the job. She hadn't had any conflicts with anyone while here and I've known her for so long that I couldn't conceive of her hurting anyone, unless we count breaking hearts.

I thought about the guides. I try to keep the same guides, the good ones anyway, from season to season. Some work out, like Gator, and come back every year. Others don't come back. It's part of their career choice: their sense of adventure keeps them moving from resort to resort, always looking for new adventures. No one on my staff had criminal backgrounds and I ran credit checks for all of the American employees, just to make sure I didn't have to deal with creditors that might want to garnish wages. I didn't see any motivation for any of them.

⨳

The winds were picking up again. Another late afternoon storm was heading our way. My boats were all tied up on the downwind side of the dock as the growing waves moved them together. We got a lot of these short storms this time of year. The skies darkened, the wind picked up, and the waves grew. I could see the storm, the line of rain, approaching. I saw the first flash of lightning, heard the thunder clap.

Jeremy stood on the other side of the dock, in ankle-deep water, cleaning fish. He looked over his shoulder, saw the rain line in the distance. "Five minutes and we'll be getting wet," he said.

"And twenty minutes from now it'll have passed."

I watched as he put a couple of strips of fish on a plank to keep Kim's two cats occupied. Every time they'd finish what he gave them they'd put their noses close to the fish he was cleaning and he'd cut off another couple of strips for them. The guts and head of the fish he'd throw into the water. He'd been at it a while and there were already a small nurse shark and a southern stingray swimming along the sea grass to scarf up the remains. Jeremy and I were both used to that, neither the shark nor the ray would be any danger to us. Sharks will eat rays, but with plenty of free fish guts the shark wasn't a threat to the ray.

Chapter 37

Thursday, December 28th, 5:15 P.M.

I walked down to the Mountain To Sea dining hall. The nightly volley-ball game was well underway. The two sides were evenly matched, at least in numbers. I wasn't in the mood for a game anyway. As I walked into the dining hall I saw Antonio and Felicia working closely.

The kitchen and food preparation area was raised up about two feet from the sandy floored dining area. I couldn't see over the counter.

"Do you have enough of the lobster for everyone?" I asked. I'd had a couple of my Belizean staff go free diving earlier in the day to harvest lobsters.

"And then some. We've also got a lot of crabs and some prawns to mix in. I think these lobster rolls are going to be really good," Antonio said.

"Come, have a taste," Felicia said. She dipped a small spoon into a gooey mess.

I climbed the steps into the kitchen and tasted the mix Felicia held out for me.

"Wow. I can taste the lobster and crab. What else is in this?"

Antonio beamed. "It's got onions, celery, flour, a seafood broth made from the shells of the critters that we put in here, some garlic, and a bunch of local herbs that Felicia is introducing me to."

"It has a lot of garlic, too, George. Antonio here likes a lot of gar-lic," Felicia said.

I could taste the garlic. Felicia wasn't kidding about that.

"How about bread for the rolls?" I asked. Normally we have some

203

sandwich bread available and some tortillas. Neither seemed right for lobster rolls.

"Antonio is teaching me how to make a different kind of bread," Felicia said.

"Have you ever had the cheddar rolls at a Red Lobster? This bread will be something like that. It's got a little harder crust, we need that to support the seafood mix. We don't have any cheddar so we'll find out how Monterey Jack works instead," Antonio said, holding up one of the submarine shaped rolls.

"What's that in your other hand?" I asked.

"This? It's a flavor injector. A couple of minutes before the rolls are done we're taking a little bit of the seafood mix and injecting it below the upper surface. They'll still have to cut the roll and put some of the mix in, but this will be a little extra. I like putting surprises into my creations."

"May I see that?"

Antonio handed me the flavor injector.

"I've never seen one of these before. Did you bring this with you on your vacation?"

"No, I don't carry tools from my kitchen with me on vacation. Felicia had some. Why?"

"Felicia, is this the only one you have?"

"No. I brought three of the injectors and about a dozen of the disposable canisters. We used a few of them the other day with the Christmas ham. Is there a problem, George?" Felicia asked.

"Problem? No. I've just never seen one of these. How does it work?" I asked.

"Let me show you," Antonio said.

He took the injector back from me, opened the disposable canister and stuffed some of the lobster mix into it, put the cap back on, and attached the injector's syringe. He held one of the still hot, not quite done rolls in a gloved hand, inserted the syringe into one end and shoved it a few inches down the roll. He pushed the plunger with one finger while he slowly extracted the syringe.

"See, if it works right we'll have a small tube, a quarter to a half inch in diameter, of the mix just below the crust. Now, we've got to get these rolls stuffed and back in to finish cooking," he said.

"May I see the roll for a moment?"

"Be careful, George. It's hot. Put on a glove."

I did and Antonio placed the roll in my hand. I looked closely. The syringe left a small hole in the end where it had been inserted. It wasn't huge, but much bigger than a medicinal use syringe. The hole might have been between an eighth and quarter-inch in diameter.

About the size of the puncture wound I saw on Bernie's chest.

"Felicia, you said you had three of these, and a dozen of the disposable canisters. Can you find the other two syringes?" I asked.

She rummaged through a drawer. "Here's one. Antonio's holding the second. I, I don't see the third one."

She rummaged through a couple of other drawers and dumped several utensils from a small bucket where the kitchen staff keeps them.

"I don't know where the third one is. We used all three on Christmas Day. It's got to be around here, somewhere. I hope nobody threw it away after Christmas Dinner. They're hard to find in stores."

"They're not very expensive, but they're hard to find. I order mine online," Antonio said.

Antonio took the roll from my hand and put it on a cookie sheet with some others and went back to stuffing rolls. When he took it from me I noticed something I hadn't before.

"That's an interesting tattoo on your arm, Antonio," I said.

"She's pretty, ain't she? A souvenir from my days in the Navy."

"When was that?"

"I'm a bit older than most of you. It was in 1970 and lasted almost three years. I failed to follow Dr. Spock's very good advice."

"What advice was that?"

"He advised young people. 'Don't get caught in the draft.'"

"What kind of ship were you on? Were you a cook?"

"No, I wasn't that lucky. I was a gunner on a patrol boat. The 'brown-water navy' they called it."

"You mean like John Kerry?"

"That traitor? Yes, the same boats. Different times."

I let the comment drop. I've met a few people that served in the brown-water navy, the boats that ran the rivers of Vietnam. Anytime John Kerry gets mentioned you risk a fight. I voted for him in 2004 myself, but wasn't really a supporter.

"Felicia, did you have all three of the flavor injectors after the dinner dishes were done Monday night?"

"I don't know. I don't do the dishes. The guides do all the dinner dishes. I'm sure it's around here somewhere."

"That's okay, I'm sure it'll turn up sometime."

I couldn't compare the size of the puncture wound from the flavor injector to that on Bernie's chest. I hadn't actually measured the hole on his body. It seemed like the right size.

Chapter 38

Thursday, December 28th, 6:30 P.M.

After dinner on Thursday I went into the office, locked the door, and looked through my personnel records. I didn't keep much in the form of records but I had an application form for each of my American staff members. I got the name of the airline that Misty had once worked for and looked them up on the internet. We had a two-way satellite-based internet service called Starband that worked reasonably well for us. It was faster than dial-up, not that that was an option out here anyway.

Canyon Air was a two-plane operation out of Kingman, Arizona. From what I could find on the internet, it operated from 1985 until last spring. In April there was a crash involving their larger plane, a Cessna Caravan. The stock picture of a Caravan showed a high-wing with two engines. It was configured to carry ten passengers. Their smaller plane was a Cessna Skymaster. I recognized the picture of the Skymaster. A high-wing plane with two engines; however, with the Skymaster the two engines are located in front of and behind the cabin in a push-pull configuration. I remembered Danny Glover flying one in *Bat 51*.

The pilot in command of the Caravan died in the crash. He was also the owner, he and his wife. I couldn't get much information from the internet about the crash or what caused it. Fortunately, I knew someone who could help. It took a few minutes of digging through our guest records but I found the name I needed, and his contact information.

Glenn Kline had been a Mountain To Sea guest two years earlier and we certified him for diving. He had never dived before coming out here and planned to just do the Discover SCUBA class and make one or two dives. Same for his wife, Alison, but they got hooked. The first time they saw the grey angelfish and parrotfish and blue wrasse they fell in love with diving. Both passed their PADI Open Water certification by the end of the week.

It was only about eight here on the island. That's Central time. Glenn was an FBI agent based out of Las Vegas. So calling him now would probably be okay; they were only an hour behind us.

"Hello?"

"Glenn?"

"Yes, who is this?"

"Glenn, it's George Schroeder, from Over The Edge in Belize. How are you?"

"George? Man, I haven't heard from you since my trip a couple of years back. How are you? Is everything okay?"

"I'm doing fine, and so is Kim. But I have a problem and I need some help."

"Sure, what can I do for you?"

"A Mountain To Sea guest died Monday night. His wife couldn't wake him Christmas morning. The Maritime Police think it was a heart attack. I'd like to believe that."

"But you don't."

"Sunday morning we had an accident. A guest at Mountain To Sea leaned against a railing. It gave way and he fell, breaking his neck."

"Two in one week? Bad luck, I guess."

"There's something else. We'd replaced that railing two weeks earlier. When this accident happened it looked like the railing had been installed wrong. We always put the head of the bolt on the inside of the porch, that way if it does get loose pushing against the railing pushed it tighter. In this case the bolt heads had to have been on the outside, and the nuts not attached. A couple of days later I found a ratchet wrench in the sand next to the cabana."

"So, either someone was exceptionally careless or this was intentional, and the person responsible disposed of the wrench immediately. That's a sign of a professional."

"It is?"

"You see movies where a killer peels off their gloves and walks blocks only to throw their weapon into a river or trash can, right? Well, the professional doesn't do that. They dispose of the weapon right there at the crime scene. It won't be traceable and won't have fingerprints. There's no risk. But carrying it some distance increases the likelihood of a chance run-in with a cop that discovers them with the weapon."

"I'm not comfortable thinking there's some professional here."

"It could be coincidence," Glenn said.

"Yesterday we had another accident. One of the guys working for me died in a diving accident."

"Anyone I knew?"

"I don't know. He only started working for me a couple of months ago but he used to be a park ranger at the Grand Canyon."

"What's his name?"

"Dylan Bellamy. Do you know him?"

"No, but that doesn't mean anything. I've met a few of the people at the park when investigating immigration stuff, a lot of the illegals run through the canyon. I don't know most of those guys."

"He knew Misty, one of my dive instructors, from the States."

"Is Beth still working for you?"

"Yeah, Beth's here too." *Man, every guy that has ever been here asks about Beth.*

"Anyway, Misty used to work for an airline called Canyon Air. She worked for them at the time of a crash that put them out of business. I can't find much information on that crash. Do you know anything about it?"

"As a matter of fact, I do. The flight that crashed was carrying some members of the U.S. District Attorney's office and a friend of mine." Glenn's voiced had changed. It got deeper, quieter, and more businesslike.

"What were they doing on an aerial tour?"

"Canyon Air ran aerial tours but also did some local charter flights. The D.A.'s office chartered the flight to take the D.A., two of his assistants, a couple of D.E.A. agents, and an F.B.I. agent from Vegas to Phoenix with a side trip to Kingman on the way out, and planned to stop in Lake Havasu on the way back."

"What happened?"

"Nobody really knows for sure. The pilot, the owner of the airline, requested landing instructions for Kingman and reported his position as being about thirty miles out. That was at about ten-thirty that morning. An attempt to contact him five minutes later failed. They weren't heard from again. The plane, and the remains of the passengers, were found that afternoon on Mt. Tipton."

"Is the cause of the crash known?"

"What they said was 'mechanical failure of unknown nature.' The National Traffic Safety Board never determined what went wrong. They say the electrical system was completely shut down and there were signs of a cylinder being blown."

"So it was an accident, but nobody knows exactly what failed?"

"Yeah, and believe me, we wanted to know why it happened."

"Why would the Attorney General's office be doing charter flights like that? I would think flying coach would be cheaper."

"The people on that flight were prosecuting a major drug dealer, a guy from Central America."

"Do you know his name?"

"Yeah, it was Carlos Benito Martinez. Know him?"

"I know of him. He owns several small resorts in Belize and Honduras. He owns one over on Victoria's Caye. They recently put in a helipad."

"And you say that someone that worked for Canyon Air at the time of the crash is now working for you?"

"Yeah, she's been here for about four months. She leaves this weekend for a new job in Indonesia."

"The timing is interesting, isn't it?"

"Yes, it is."

"Give me her name again? And what was the name of the park ranger?"

"Her name is Misty Lawler. His name was Dylan Bellamy. And there's another connection you should know about."

"What's that?"

"The guy that died Monday night is, was, a lawyer. He was working in Belize to stop a massive new resort from being built."

"What's the connection?"

"Martinez is the developer of that resort."

"That doesn't sound like a coincidence, does it?"

"No, it doesn't. Glenn, I didn't point it out to the local authorities, they thought it was just a heart-attack, but Bernie Stamps was stabbed in the chest with something. I don't know for sure what. It was something small, but larger than a medicinal needle. Our chef this season has something called a flavor injector that looks like the right size, and one of the three she brought with her is missing. It's a flimsy plastic though. I'm not sure it would pierce human skin and get past the rib cage."

"Is there anything else?"

"There's another item of interest. Another guest here this week used to go to high school in the same little town that Misty's from. He says there wasn't anyone by that name in the town, that the only family by that name lost a daughter."

"I'll see what I can find out about them. Is your email address still the same?"

"Yes, but there's more. The week you and Teri were here, wasn't Larry Carlson here too?"

"I don't remember him if he was."

"I think he was. He's in his late forties, fat, pretty easy going but kind of quiet. He'd been here before."

"Okay, I think there was someone like that there that week. Why?"

"Glenn, he's back this week and he's had a few surprises for me. Just stuff in his background I never heard before. He'd been married and divorced early. He'd been in the Army, as a helicopter pilot doing special operations stuff. It could all be true, but it's just that much of these things don't square with how I've seen him the past few years."

"So you'd like me to check him out too?"

"Yeah, but if you can I'd like you to check out someone else too. We've got a guest this week from California, a guy named Antonio Terrazzo. He owns a restaurant and is a chef. He's also a Navy vet from the Vietnam era. There's just something not sitting right, but I can't say what it is. He doesn't dive, snorkel, or kayak. His wife said he can't swim but he said he can, he just doesn't want to. That flavor injector I mentioned as a possible weapon—well, he was using one in the kitchen."

"Okay, I'll get on the system tonight and send you whatever I can."

Chapter 39

Thursday, December 28th, 9:00 P.M.

I shut down my computer and walked down to Mountain To Sea's dining hall. A few of the guests were still there. I saw Lisa and Antonio Terrazzo at one table, playing gin. At another table Jerry and the two sisters, Carolyn and Alicia, were playing Scrabble. Gator sat at another table, playing his guitar. At another table, as far from the others as they could get, sat Dagan and Dave Cavuto talking with Sticks. I'd encouraged Sticks and Beth both to try to get some advice from the two. With Sticks and Beth looking at buying my resorts they'd benefit from all the input that a financial analyst and reporter could give. Getting to know them well here might be a good long-term relationship.

"Hey, boss, is everything alright?" Gator asked when he looked up.

"Yes, as far as I can tell. I thought I'd come over and check in, just making sure everything is peaceful," I said.

"I hadn't seen you since you got back. We're doing fine up here. Everyone else has turned in for the night. We just have these few party animals over here still up," he said, nodding toward the three guests playing games.

"It's time for us to call it a night, I think," Antonio said.

Within a few minutes the five guests had all packed up and headed off for their respective cabanas.

"George, are you alright? You're really looking worn out," Gator said after it was just he, Sticks and I left.

"It's these accidents. Twenty years with no serious injuries and now two dead and one serious injury. I just don't know what's happening.

What are we doing wrong?"

"Accidents happen, boss. We're all careful. What's that saying? 'Sometimes you're the windshield, sometimes you're the bug.' Twenty years, that's a fantastic run for safety."

"George, we've got the best safety record in Belize. Stuff happens," Sticks added.

"Maybe so, but I'll be glad when this week is over."

～✤～

We hung out for another twenty minutes or so, just gossiping about the guests and people we've known.

"Time to call it a night, I guess. I'll see y'all in the morning," I said as I got up and started walking back to my place. I took the scenic route again, still hoping to see the dolphins playing in the moonlight in close to shore.

I saw them, four young dolphins, playing in about twenty feet of water just fifty yards or so offshore, near the last of the guest cabanas. They didn't stay long after I arrived and I began walking toward my cabana. I stopped once, thinking I'd heard something moving in ground cover close the guest showers. Nothing moved. I heard nothing else, no unusual noises. Maybe I'd heard some iguanas, or some big hermit crabs. The trails are lined with parallel dots, hermit crab tracks.

The lack of sound, that was unusual. I started walking again. I reached a junction of three trails. The junction doesn't have much tree coverage and I stopped, looking at a nearly full moon. I thought that if I weren't so tired it would be a great night for stargazing. Kim likes to make up tales of her own about the stars. She begins with the various tales of Orion and then makes new tales, trying to establish new configurations from stars in different constellations. She's got an artist's sense of creativity. I don't think that as a child she kept her crayons within the lines.

I started walking again, passing under a couple of palm trees. I heard something move, something behind me. I started to turn around. I saw motion, but I don't know what kind. I heard the thud, felt the impact, saw stars but not the ones in the sky, and the lights went out.

❖

"George, can you hear me?"

I looked up, into Kim's eyes. I blinked a few times. "What happened?" I asked.

I lay partly on the trail, partly in the ground cover. My right side hurt, as did my head. I felt around, first running my right hand across my skull. I could feel a bruise, a good one, and something sticky. Blood? I brought my hand to my nose and it smelled metallic. That's the smell of dried blood. Then I ran my hand down my side. I felt moisture of some kind, blood maybe? I also felt several sharp objects.

"Beth and I came looking for you. You fell, your side is bleeding a little. Your head was too, but it's stopped." She had her hand on my shoulder.

"Beth?"

"She went to get Marcus and Jeremy. Can you sit up?"

I struggled, but I sat up. I got dizzy. "What happened?"

"I don't know. There's a coconut over here, split in two. Maybe you finally got bonked on the head by a falling coconut."

After twenty years?

"My side? What cut me there?" I felt around, gingerly. I pulled something out of my side. A piece of one of the conch shells we line all the trails with.

"You broke a few of those shells when you fell."

Beth arrived, with Jeremy and Marcus.

"George, we're going to help you up, alright? You can lean on me,"

Jeremy said.

I tried to get up on my own but got dizzy and fell to my knees. I felt them reaching under my arms, stopping me from falling face down again. They lifted me up. I leaned on Jeremy. Fortunately he's about my height and build. Marcus is almost a foot shorter than either of us. They helped me get to the bench at the foot of the stairs to my cabana and sat me down.

Beth and Kim disappeared upstairs. Beth came back down with the medical kit. She and Marcus took my shirt off and started to bandage the little cuts. I winced several times as they pulled shell fragments out. I winced again as they applied the peroxide to open cuts. A few minutes later Kim came back down.

"Eddie's on his way over with Arthur, the neurosurgeon staying there. They'll be here in a few minutes, George. Just relax," Kim said.

"I don't need him. I'll be fine."

"Well, they're on the way already so we'll let Arthur tell us that you're okay."

"What time is it?" I asked.

"About ten-thirty," Beth said. "Marcus, would you get the dock lights lit up? Let's make it easy on Eddie."

"I was out at least half an hour?"

⁓✧⁓

It was about ten minutes later I heard Eddie's boat. I looked between Kim and Beth and saw the spotlight at the bow of his boat. A minute or so later they tied the boat up to the dock. Eddie I recognized. He's about my age and size, with sun bleached-blonde hair down to his shoulders. The other man, Arthur, apparently, followed him along the dock.

"Hi, George, I'm Arthur Fish. I met your wife a few days ago. So, how are you doing?"

I looked at him. Kim was right, he is young. When I think of a neurosurgeon I think of older guys, at least in the late forties. This guy was barely thirty. Thin, six foot plus an inch or so, I couldn't quite tell since I was seated, and he had a decent tan.

"I'll be okay. I'm a little dizzy. I'm sorry they interrupted your vacation again."

"I haven't sent you my bill yet. Then you'll really wish they hadn't called me. But I'm here, so let's take a look."

He used a penlight to look at my eyes and felt my head. He shone the light on my bruise.

"That's pretty nasty. How'd that happen?" he asked.

"We found him lying on a path in the middle of the island. There was a coconut, split into pieces, on the ground next to him. We think it fell and hit him on the head," Kim said.

"Hmmm, I don't think that did it. These trees aren't really that high. I don't think they could fall enough to have this much impact," he said.

He looked at the bandages on my side. "What happened here?" he asked.

"He fell on some conch shells. They broke and we've pulled several fragments out," Kim said.

"George, look at me," he said. I was having some trouble focusing. My head really hurt. The little cuts on my side, they weren't bothering me much.

I tried to focus.

"George, how many fingers am I holding up?" he asked.

"Arthur, I really hate to have people giving me the finger. I see one finger."

"Okay, how about now?"

"Were you a Boy Scout too? I see three fingers."

"I was, and I held up three fingers, just like our old salute. The first time though, I had two fingers up. When was your last tetanus shot?"

"I don't know, three, maybe four years ago. Kim, that was right before our Cenotes trip. When was that?" I asked. We'd made a trip to do cave diving in the Cenotes, a huge cave system in Mexico.

"About four years ago," she said.

Arthur stood back, then leaned forward and ran his hand over my scalp again. "I can see in your medical kit over there you've got some topical antibiotic cream. I'd suggest putting some of that on those cuts on your side and keep that area bandaged for a couple of days. Reapply the cream a couple of times, maybe three times, a day for the next week."

"Otherwise, I'm okay?" I asked.

"Well, I'm not sure. I think you've got a mild concussion, but it doesn't seem too bad. You're aware of your surroundings and Kim agreed with the timing of your last tetanus shot so you've got an awareness of time."

"A concussion? I've had one or two before," I said.

"I recommend not diving or doing anything intense the next few days. Get some rest, and keep a bandage on that head of yours. George, I want to talk with you alone for a minute."

He looked around and ran everyone off. Kim didn't want to leave but he insisted.

When we were alone he sat down next to me. "George, don't take the possibility of a concussion lightly. You might be dizzy, and have difficulty focusing on your thoughts for a day or two as well. But George, the reason I wanted you alone is this. I really don't believe that bump on your head could come from a coconut falling. These trees just aren't that high and they aren't going to fall that hard. I think someone hit you with a coconut."

"Arthur, I know that, but please don't tell anyone else. I didn't see who it was, but I know I was assaulted. We've had a few accidents here this week and I don't want anyone getting more spooked than they already are."

Arthur let the others come back and he said "I think Eddie and I can go home. Eddie, can you bring me back over here sometime around mid-morning to check in on George?"

"Sure, no problem," Eddie said.

"George, Kim, we'll be back around nine-thirty or so. If you have some aspirin I'd suggest taking a couple and keep some water handy."

I shook Arthur's hand and thanked him. As they pulled away Jeremy and Marcus helped me to my feet and up the stairs to my cabana. I sat on the bed.

"Jeremy, do me a favor and go get Sticks for me," I said.

"Right away, boss," he said and the two of them left. I heard Beth and Kim murmuring outside and Kim came in.

"I've got some aspirin and some cool water here. Take a couple of these and get some rest," Kim said.

I took three aspirin and drank about half the bottle of water. "I'll lay down in a minute. I asked Jeremy to get Sticks. I want to talk with him for a couple of minutes."

⚘

Sticks arrived in less than five minutes. "Jeremy just told me what happened. Shouldn't you be sleeping?" he asked.

"Yeah, but we need to talk."

"What about?"

"It wasn't an accident."

"What?"

"I thought I heard someone, or something, moving in the brush. I stopped once and couldn't see anyone. Then I heard someone behind me. I turned but all I saw was something moving, and then I was out.

Someone hit me with that coconut, Sticks, it didn't fall from a tree."

"Are you sure? I mean, we've had a few accidents this week. Maybe you're just getting spooked?"

"They weren't accidents," I said.

"What do you mean, they weren't accidents?"

"Someone took the railing off Cabana Five and reattached it with the railing and bolts on the outside of the porch and left the nuts off. That's the only way it could have just come off like it did when Jack leaned against it."

"Who would do that, and why?"

"I don't know yet, for either question. But Bernie's death wasn't a heart-attack. He was stabbed with something small. I'm not convinced yet, but I think whoever it was used one of the flavor injectors that Felicia had in the kitchen."

"Again, George, why would someone do that? Are you sure you're not just getting paranoid?"

"I'm sure, and then there's Dylan. Somebody punctured the inbound air hose from the tank to the inflator valve and the outbound air hose from the valve to his BC. They're right beside each other, as are the punctures. They used a water soluble adhesive to cover it up. When the saltwater dissolved the adhesive the inflator went into full inflate mode."

"You're talking about murder, George. Dylan and Bernie were both murdered? Who was it, George?"

"I don't know. I'm thinking we have a pro on the island. I'm leaning toward either Misty or Antonio. Keep an eye out," I said. My head was pounding.

Sticks left, no doubt confused and thinking that I was going crazy. Kim had been standing on the porch, alone, listening in.

"Why did you share your suspicions with Sticks?" she asked.

"Other than you, he's the only person that couldn't have done it.

He wasn't here. He never met Jack and Sherry, or Bernie's family and the Whites. He came over on the boat that took you, the Whites and Bernie's family to the mainland. He hadn't been here long enough to get access to Dylan's dive gear and alter it."

Chapter 40

Friday, December 29ᵗʰ, 05:30 A.M.

I didn't sleep well that night. It seemed that every time I'd drift off to sleep I'd have another nightmare, wake up, and drift back off again only to have the nightmare replay.

❧◆❧

The attempted break in at my family's dental office was on a Tuesday night. Every day for more than a week, even on Saturday since we had office hours every weekend, the bikers would come by and harass our customers. They'd stay for a while and then leave just before the cops got there.

On Thursday, a week after the break in, my parents were going to join Grace and me for a live performance of *Peter Pan*. It was a school play and Austin was one of Captain Hook's pirates.

Grace picked up my mother and brought Austin to the office in our Jeep. She parked next to my dad's newest Cadillac. He'd always been into displaying his wealth. He even spent money on vanity plates that spelled out 2TH DOC. Mom's car had plates that read TOOTHDR.

We had planned to go to dinner from there. Just as we were fixing to close the shop Karl Sparks came in with an emergency. There was some blood on his uniform blouse.

"Karl, what happened?" I asked.

"My partner and I had to bust a couple of guys and one of them took a swing at me. He was a big guy."

"He'd have to be to hurt you." Karl was a good six-foot three and probably weighed two hundred and forty pounds.

"I think he was on something. I don't know what. Anyway, he managed to get a few good shots in. I think he knocked a couple of teeth loose."

"Karl, go down the hall to that second door on the left. I'll be right in."

I put my hands on Austin's shoulders. He looked up at me with a smile.

I looked at my father and said, "Dad, why don't you take everyone to the restaurant? Go ahead and order dinner. This will probably take me less than half an hour. If I'm more than thirty minutes behind, I'll just catch-up with you at the school."

"Are you sure? I can stay and take care of this if you'd like."

"Thanks for offering, Dad, but Karl's an old friend of mine."

"Okay, I'll go get my coat and we'll be ready to go." Dad walked down the hall to his office to get his suit jacket. It was one of the differences between us. He wore a two-piece suit, long-sleeved dress shirt with a button-down collar, a bolo tie and a pair of dress boots to work every day. He'd leave the suit jacket on a hanger in his office while working on patients. Me, well, I typically wore khakis and I had several single-pocket polo shirts I had made with our practice's name and logo embroidered on them, along with a comfortable pair of ropers.

I tucked a bib around Karl's neck and sat on a stool. I heard the back door click shut as my family left.

"So, Doc, I hear that punk's friends have been around. You know, he's been in prison in three different states. He'll be an old man by the time he gets out this time."

Karl was nervous. When I had him open his mouth and started to look around I could see he hadn't had any dental work done in a long time.

"Yeah, they're trying to intimidate me into dropping the charges."

I moved my mirror around, trying to figure out what the most urgent problem was. I pulled the mirror out and turned to get a probe.

"Are they threatening you?"

"They said someone might get hurt. Mostly they've just been scaring off my patients. Open wide for a minute."

"Have they actually hurt anyone?"

"No. They ran their bikes in circles around Grace's Explorer, shouting something, she wouldn't say what. That was the day before yesterday, just before she picked up Austin at school."

"How long did that go on?" Karl was stalling.

"Not long. This is Texas and she has a concealed weapons permit. She pulled out her thirty-eight and lowered the driver's window to display it and they cleared out."

He stopped me. "Doc, it's going to get worse. Stand firm. Don't give in to their threats."

"I won't. Now, open wide."

⚜

The concussion from the blast knocked photos from the waiting room wall and broke glass in storefront windows throughout the block. Karl and I ran outside only to see a car on fire: my father's car. I ran toward it but a secondary blast, from the gas tank, sent another concussion wave that knocked me down.

⚜

There were no survivors. I buried my parents in the Schroeder family plot within Concordia, a historic cemetery in El Paso. There was a very large turn-out. Dad was well-known in the community and his buddies from El Paso's Lions clubs and the city's Chamber of Commerce came out. Mom's friends from church and a couple of charities she was involved in filled half the church.

Andrew asked to have Grace and Austin buried on the reservation. It was a more somber, more private service, after which Andrew and I had a long talk while walking across reservation land.

"George, are you a Christian?"

"Yeah, but you know I've never been very active in the church. Why?"

"The men responsible for these deaths, they cannot go unpunished."

"The police say they know it was this bike gang, but they can't say who planted the bomb."

"The police? They won't do anything. Doesn't your own bible say to take 'an eye for an eye?'"

"Somewhere, yeah. What are you suggesting?" I stopped walking and looked him in the eye.

"You know what I'm suggesting. We must have justice for their deaths. The police aren't about justice."

"We don't know who built the bomb." I was nervous. I've always thought that "an eye for an eye" only left a bunch of blind people.

"And we won't know as long as the guy that broke into your office is in jail. Drop the charges."

"Drop the charges! Now? After his friends killed my family?" I turned away from him and started walking back to my Corvette.

"Yes, George. He'll lead us to his friends and we'll find out who built the bomb."

I drove home and just wandered around in the emptiness. I called my office manager and had her cancel all appointments for the next two weeks.

"Two weeks? George, what about everyone here?"

"I'll pay their salaries, don't worry. I'm just not ready for patients."

On the third day Andrew came to the house. I let him in and he sat on the sofa, facing me. "Well?"

"I don't know if I can do it. We're talking about murder."

"No, we're talking about justice. That's what it is: justice for your parents, justice for Austin, and for Grace. It's justice, George."

"I don't know if I can do it."

"We, George, we can do it. And we must."

I dropped the charges against the guy that broke into my office. Within hours a group of bikers arrived at the El Paso police headquarters. A small plane flew several thousand feet above the city and followed the caravan of motorcycles as they drove into the desert.

⚜

"George, we know where they're holed-up. It's public land off I-10 about fifteen miles east of town."

"Okay, Andrew. Now what do we do? Kill all of them? There must be at least fifty of them."

"No, not all of them. But we'll get the leader, and the guy the police let go. We'll get them to tell us who made the bomb."

"As easy as that?"

"No, it won't be easy. Neither of us is stupid. But we know where they are, and we can sneak up on them. We'll get one at a time."

My stomach was rolling. "When?"

"Tomorrow night. We've got a front moving in, maybe even some rain, but for sure some clouds to cover our tracks. But I need to go to your office for a few minutes.

Chapter 41
Friday, December 29th,
6:00 A.M.

T rue to his word, Glenn gathered information on Misty and Dylan
and sent it to me via email.

George,

It was good to hear from you last night. I just wish it had been for more en-
joyable reasons. I also wish I had better news to pass on.

The Canyon Air crash was about ten months ago. I wasn't part of the team
that investigated. I talked with a friend who was the FBI's member on that
team. There were also FAA, NTSB, and DEA representatives.

The NTSB just gave their official ruling last month: mechanical failure resulting from a total electrical system failure of unknown origin.

Team members interviewed all Canyon Air employees. As you know, it was a
family run business. The owner, Curtis Haggar, was the chief pilot and died in
the crash. His wife, Peggy, was the business manager and handled the books.
Their oldest son, Douglas, was also a pilot and flew on the aerial tours. This
particular flight was a charter and Curtis Haggar always flew those.

The U.S. District Attorney's office routinely booked charter flights with
Canyon Air. They'd been doing a weekly shuttle between Las Vegas and
Phoenix as part of the Carlos Martinez investigation.

Canyon Air had three full-time employees at the time of the crash. Their lead mechanic was a guy named Jake Thomas. He worked for them for eight years and is now working for the Arizona State Police as an aircraft mechanic. Robin Marcuss was an assistant mechanic. He worked for them for three years. Previously he had been an aircraft mechanic in the Army. He's currently working for Southwest Airlines in Las Vegas.

The third employee was your dive instructor, Misty Lawler. Not much is known about her. She showed up looking for a job a few days after her predecessor, Carole Sellers, went missing. Ms. Sellers has never been heard from. That was two months before the crash. By the way, in her job application she indicated she had been in the Air Force for four years where she was an MP. I haven't been able to get her military records yet.

Misty's job was a little bit of everything. She sold tickets, handled luggage, and helped Peggy with whatever paperwork needed to be done. She also cleared tours with the Park Service. That's how she and your guy, Dylan, knew each other. She had access to all of Canyon Air, including their hangars.

There isn't anything known locally about where she went after the crash. She was there for a week or so, during the investigation, but once the widow said she was closing the airline Misty disappeared. Evidently she made her way to Sunrise Caye to work for you.

The team investigating the crash really wanted to find signs of someone tampering with the aircraft. There had been rumors that Martinez had ordered a hit on the D.A. but there wasn't any evidence.

I checked out Larry Carlson. He was married and divorced and was a helicopter pilot in the Army. He was stationed at McGill Air Force Base in Florida for a couple of years. That's a key base for the Special Forces, mostly Rangers and Green Berets. I was there in the late 1980s myself but he was out of the service by that time. He had an honorable discharge. He had a couple of DWI's in the early 1990s but otherwise has a clean record. He's got a Top Secret clearance, apparently that's pretty standard for his computer consulting work with the government including the Secret Service, Department of Defense, and Nuclear Regulatory Commission.

Antonio Terrazzo is married and owns a restaurant. They've got three kids, two daughters and one son. He has no police record, and an honorable discharge from the Navy. In Vietnam he spent almost two days in the water, trying to survive, after his patrol boat was hit by a rocket propelled grenade. I suspect he can swim but being in the water reminds him of that time.

Let me know if I can help any further or if you have something my agency would want to know about.

Glenn

It was still early in the morning. The sun wasn't even completely up yet. I wasn't ready for our morning run, my head still ached and I heard a constant hum. Kim suggested that she and I walk, instead of run, and that, preceded by a glass of freshly squeezed grapefruit juice helped. As we completed the first lap the pain and humming in my head faded.

We passed the Mountain To Sea kayak palapa and something didn't look right. There was a rounded groove in the sand leading to the water's edge. Someone had taken a kayak out during the night. I stopped and counted kayaks. They were all there. I resumed my walk. By the time we made another loop around the island the grooves had disappeared, at least near the water's edge. One of the Mountain To Sea guides had raked the beach, clearing it of debris, but the groove near the shelter was still visible.

When Annette, our cook this week, let me know that breakfast was ready, I picked up my favorite conch shell and blew the dinner horn. I felt lightheaded, just from taking in that deep breath and blowing the horn.

I went into the dining hall and found Misty already there. Misty was almost always the last one to show for breakfast. She once claimed to be allergic to morning.

"You're up early?" I said.

"Guess I'm getting nervous about leaving tomorrow. I couldn't sleep last night. How are you feeling?" she asked.

"It'll take more than a falling coconut to put me out of action. My head's too hard. I've got a headache but I'll be fine. Are you looking forward to seeing your family?"

"Yeah, a little, but I'm dreading the cold."

"Your family is in Iowa, right?"

"Well, it's only my kid sister, Rachel. She's in Illinois but only a few miles from the Iowa state line."

"What about your aunt and uncle?" I asked. I remembered her story about her mother dying and her father abusing them.

"My uncle died a few years ago."

"What about your aunt? Is she still alive?"

"Yeah, but we don't talk. I don't talk about her. There's a lot of pain, for both of us."

"What's the weather like there?" I understood enough now to change the topic.

"I checked on the web yesterday. It's cold, with highs in the low twenties and around zero at night. They had a couple of inches of snow."

"Yep, that's cold alright."

"I'll only be there a few days anyway. I plan to stay for four days and then leave for Indonesia."

"When do you start there?"

"Not until late January, but I want to do some sightseeing and take my time."

❧❖❧

After breakfast, and three more aspirin, I walked down to the Mountain To Sea dining hall to see how many people wanted to dive today. I wore a ball cap to cover the bruise. The fewer people that knew about my getting hit the better.

The Mountain To Sea schedule had them taking the boat back to Belize City tomorrow. They would not get into Belize City in time for any flights back to the States. They couldn't fly home until Sunday. Since they wouldn't be flying for at least twenty-four hours they could get in a final dive if they wanted to. Most of my diving guests try to get in one last dive.

"Hey, Gator, how's it going?"

"Okay, I guess. With Gene gone we've all had to pick up some chores. I've got trash-burning duties today. How's your head, boss?"

"I'll be okay. Trash-burning detail, huh? Isn't it great to be a manager and to know how you're putting that degree in business administration to use?"

❧❖❧

I went into the dining hall and talked with the guests. I noticed Kevin wasn't around. He hadn't missed a meal all week but was always sitting by himself. None of the other guests seemed to like him. I'd barred him from diving anyway, so I scheduled two dives for that morning and one in the afternoon.

"Hey, Gator, have you seen Kevin this morning?"

"No, I haven't, but I wasn't looking for him. We had another little incident last night. He got a bit drunk and mouthed off to a couple of people."

"Any fights?"

"No, I escorted him out of the dining hall about seven-thirty and that was the last I saw of him."

"You might want to check on him, just in case. By the way, do you know if someone took a kayak out early this morning?"

"No, I haven't seen anyone over there and I've been up since sunrise. Why?"

"On my run this morning I noticed a couple of grooves in the sand, like someone had dragged a kayak out."

"No, but other than Kevin I've seen everybody at breakfast today. I'll check on Kevin after I'm done with the dishes, boss."

<hr/>

It was about nine-thirty when I saw Gator and two other guides walking down the beach. I'd just sent a small group out on a dive with Beth and Marcus.

"What's up?"

"Well, I checked in on Kevin. He wasn't in his cabana. I also checked the dining hall again and the bathrooms. Now the three of us are walking the island to see if he might have walked down to the far end."

"Make sure you find him."

"Is he in any trouble with you?"

"No, but I don't like not knowing where our guests are. I've got a bad feeling."

"Four accidents this week are enough, boss. Are you sure you aren't just a little spooked?"

"I probably am, but let me know when you find him."

About an hour later Gator and the two other guides, Marlene and Joanne, came by my office. "We haven't found Kevin and we've searched the whole island."

"It's only thirteen acres, there isn't much to search."

"He isn't here, boss."

"Are all of the kayaks and windsurf boards accounted for?"

"We've got two kayaks out right now, but I know where they are. The two sisters from Minneapolis, Alison and Carolyn, went to the marine research facility on Victoria's Caye. All of the wind boards are accounted for too."

"Marlene, there's a storm coming in. Go find Sticks and tell him to paddle to Victoria's Caye and escort the two ladies back. I want everyone on the island and hunkered down when the storm reaches us."

Marlene jogged off toward the Mountain To Sea dining hall.

"Gator, is there any chance he went snorkeling alone?"

"I don't think so. He hasn't gone all week except for that first afternoon when we took everyone out to The Aquarium."

"Wonderful. Well, I'll give the Maritime Police a call."

Chapter 42

Friday, December 29th, 11:00 A.M.

Charlie arrived just before lunch.

"Have you found him yet?" Charlie struggled as he tied his boat up and stepped onto the dock. A strong wind was blowing in from the west and the waves, even here in the sheltered area of the lagoon, were picking up. My diver-down flag was fully extended, pointing east.

"No, we've searched the island. We've also searched Susan's and Tradewinds Cayes."

"Where are your boats?"

"I sent both of my boats out looking for him. Jeremy and Beth went to Tradewind Caye with a couple of Mountain To Sea's guides to search the island. The water's shallow enough between us and them he could have waded or swam there. Marcus and another Mountain To Sea guide are cruising along The Wall in case he went snorkeling out there."

"Could he have gone off in a kayak?"

"No, all of the boats and wind boards are accounted for. But when I was out for my run this morning I saw grooves in the sand by the Mountain To Sea kayaks. I thought someone had taken one of the boats out during the night."

"Did someone?"

"Nobody admits to it."

❧❖❧

A few minutes later Marcus pulled the boat up to the dock.

"I went all the way down to Victoria's Caye and doubled back to

Tradewind Caye. There's a whole lot of ocean out there and no sign of Kevin. I saw a couple of snorkelers off Victoria's Caye but they were guests there. I suggested they get back to their island before the storm hits. It'll be here in a few minutes," he said as he pointed to the southwest.

I followed his extended finger. A waterspout stood half a mile out and the storm was heading our way. My guess was it'd pass north of our island but hit Tradewind Caye. The water was about to get real rough.

❧❖❧

Beth came back from Tradewind Caye. "We went over the whole island. He wasn't there. We saw a couple of sharks, black tips, swimming through the channel."

"Which direction were they heading?" I was thinking we might not want to dive around that end of the island this afternoon, assuming anyone wanted to dive after the storm passed. Black tips usually avoid divers but they're big and can be aggressive.

"They were moving kind of slow, but heading from the Aquarium back to sea."

❧❖❧

Charlie wanted to walk around the island once himself. I went with him. When we walked by the kayak area we went up to the palapa. I pointed out the grooves I'd seen, or at least what was left of them. The grooves ended right under Sticks' boat. It was a Lexan canoe, made of a clear acrylic, kind of like a glass-bottomed boat. It allowed people in the boat to see into the water as though they were looking through a dive mask.

"Someone has used Sticks' boat," I said to Charlie.

"Which boat? How do you know someone used it?"

"Sticks' boat is the clear one up here. He doesn't let guests use it. He always suspends it with the opening facing the ground so that water won't puddle up in it and birds won't build a nest. It's hanging right side up." It was also the only canoe or multi-person kayak on the island.

We pulled the boat down, rolling it a little so that the bottom of the boat was into the wind.

Charlie pointed toward the front of boat's seating area. "George, do you see blood?"

"Yeah, and that looks like hair." Brown hair.

"George, isn't Kevin's hair brown?" Charlie asked.

"Yes."

"George, I think we should take the boats and search the water around The Aquarium. I don't think we have an accident this time."

"Okay. You're thinking about those big sharks that Beth and the others saw, aren't you?"

"You don't normally see black tips there, do you?"

"No, mostly nurse sharks, barracudas, and an occasional eagle ray."

❦

Jeremy took one boat, along with Beth and Gator, while I drove the other boat. Marcus and Charlie were with me. Off to the south I could see three kayaks coming from Victoria's Caye: the two sisters, Alicia and Carolyn, with Sticks leading the way. They were paddling fast, trying to keep up with Sticks and he was trying to beat the storm.

As Jeremy's boat approached the entrance to the Aquarium, Beth began shouting and called us over.

"There's a lot of activity over here. I see dozens of barracudas, two nurse sharks, and even a couple of rays. There are at least two mantas down there!" Beth said.

"What has them so excited?"

"I don't know, George. I can't see through the mass to see what it is they're feeding off of. We'll have to go in."

I was hoping it was a dead manatee. It would have to be something big to draw in this many big fish. But manatees seldom come this far out from the mainland. It isn't unheard of, but it's about as seldom as seeing the saltwater crocs. Then again, there's been a saltwater croc at Victoria's Caye lately.

I pulled our boat up next to them. We were maybe thirty yards from the entrance to the Aquarium but well outside the normal path for snorkelers coming from either Sunrise Caye or Tradewind Caye. The water around here is fifteen to twenty feet deep. Usually it's pretty calm, the coral acts as a buffer to the wind and currents. The waterspout was still heading our way and the wind in front of it was getting strong, maybe thirty miles per hour, and even within the pro-tection the aquarium's coral wall provided the waves were big enough to move our boats.

"Wait, before you jump in. Using your masks, can you see any better?"

Beth and Marcus both leaned over the side of their respective boats, faces in the water and breathing through their snorkels.

Marcus came up first.

"There's something big on the bottom."

"What about the sharks?"

"Nothing but nurse sharks."

Beth was up again. "All I see are nurse sharks, and a manta. It's a big one." She spread her arms as wide as she could, as if suggesting the manta's wingspan was at least as big as hers. She grasped a railing along the side of the boat as the wind and waves rocked the dive boat.

"Okay, Jeremy, see if you can scare off some of these critters."

Jeremy revved the motor. The noise and splashing sent the barra-cuda and nurse sharks away. The manta pulled away too.

"Alright, Marcus, dive down. See what's there." I was fairly certain I knew what, or who, it was.

⤙❖⤚

"It's Kevin. The fish haven't left much."

Charlie borrowed Marcus's mask and snorkel and dove down. When he came up he said, "I think I need a camera. I should probably take a picture before we retrieve the remains."

"Gator, go back to the dock and ask Kim for my digital dive camera and also bring back my mask and snorkel. Tell her I need a couple of sheets, too. Don't tell anyone what we've found."

Beth and Gator nodded that they understood.

In less than ten minutes Gator returned with the items. Marcus handed me a knife and a mesh bag we use to store items we take from the sea during a dive. "You'll need these."

"Spread out the sheets. We'll use them to wrap the remains." I looked around and saw a crowd of Mountain To Sea's guests standing around by the hammock palapa, watching us.

I went into the water with Charlie, despite my headache. The concussion from last night's blow still had me a bit uneasy but this wasn't a task I could delegate.

I took several photographs from different angles. Kevin, wrapped in fishing line, was wedged under a coral head. The line was attached to several dive weights, about twenty-pounds worth. There were bones that had been torn from the torso by the sharks. All that was left was his head and upper torso. All of his appendages had been torn off. One eye socket was empty. My guess was an octopus had gotten to that eye.

I cut the fishing line and suppressed the urge to vomit while I pulled his torso loose from the coral. A couple of garden eels came out of his chest cavity and swam away. I gave in to the urge, further fouling the water and giving me a sharper pain in my head. We stirred up a lot of sand, covering some of the bones in the process.

Charlie climbed into the boat. He stood over the spread out bed sheets and pulled the body out of the water.

"I'll be back up in a minute. I think I saw something we'll need." I had to suppress the urge to vomit again. Not so much because of the scene but the from the exertion and my concussion. I dove back down and retrieved a dive knife I'd seen on the sandy bottom. I also retrieved some bones, any I saw within about an eight-foot radius from the coral head.

We covered the remains and pulled up next to Charlie's boat. Charlie and I climbed out of our dive boat and into Charlie's larger boat. Marcus and Jeremy lifted the sheets up and we moved the body onto Charlie's boat. Jeremy moved our boat to the other side of the dock and tied it up.

"Gator, come over here, please."

"What can I do to help, boss?"

"Charlie, you probably ought to search Kevin's cabana."

"Yes, I should. I don't think I'll find anything interesting."

"Me either, but you'd probably be in trouble with your bosses in Belmopan if you don't look around. I want Gator to help you, and as you search the cabana I want Gator to pack up his stuff."

"Okay by me, I guess."

"Okay by me too, boss."

"Gator, take some paper with you. Make a complete inventory of everything you guys find. And find Sticks for me. Tell him to come over here."

<hr />

I got to work. I exposed the body again. Now that we were out of the water I could see it more clearly. Charlie and Gator came back in less than twenty minutes. I'd already covered the remains again, partly to prevent other guests from gawking and partly to keep bugs out of the wounds.

❦

"I found nothing interesting. His cabin had no weapons, no drugs, and his wallet had $387 in U.S. money and a couple of credit cards, so he wasn't robbed," Charlie said.

"Gator, do you have all of his stuff packed up?"

"Yeah, he only had the one duffel bag. He packed light."

"I remember that he didn't have a lot of clothing. Where's the bag?"

"My cabin."

"Go get it, please. Make sure your inventory is complete, including money and any papers he had. Make a second copy. One is for our records and the other's for Charlie. Charlie will have to take the stuff with him when he takes the body into Belize City."

Gator ran off to do as I'd instructed.

"Charlie, I want to show you something." I uncovered the body. "See this wound? His throat was cut, but not from side to side like you'd see in the movies. The knife went in just below his Adam's Apple. He couldn't scream or cry out. He bled into his lungs."

"George, who does the knife you found belong to?"

"It looks like one of mine. I have several. I'm not sure how many. I keep them with the rest of the dive gear, under my office." It's pretty standard stuff. Any experienced diver would be likely to have one like it. We had a dozen or more divers with at least some of their own equipment here.

"So anyone could have used it?"

"Yes. I keep the room locked at night but during the day the dive and boat staff all come and go as they need to. So do some of the guests, those that bring their own gear with them."

"Okay, well, I guess I should ask everyone if they saw anything. Can you get all guests and staff, from both resorts, together?"

"Sure, Charlie."

It took about an hour to get everyone together at the Mountain To Sea dining hall. All of the flaps on the south, west, and north sides of the dining hall were down. The squall was in full force, driving sheets of rain that felt like hundreds of simultaneous pin pricks against bare skin. With most of the tarps down the tent was stuffy. The tension and mood didn't help.

"Everyone, this is Officer Charlie Johnson of the Belize Maritime Fisheries Police. The Maritime Police have jurisdiction for all crimes in the cayes. We have something to tell you." I was nearly shouting to be heard over the wind and rain.

"It's Kevin, right? He's dead, isn't he?" Lisa Terrazzo spoke nervously. She sat next to her husband, Antonio.

"Yes, I'm afraid so. Charlie has some questions for everyone. Charlie?"

"I'm very sorry to say that your friend is dead. Unlike the other events this week, this was not an accident, somebody killed him. I need your help. When was the last time any of you saw him?"

Jerry Douglas spoke up. "Shortly after dinner last night. Most of us were here, in the dining hall, playing cards. Kevin was drunk and got mouthy again. He wanted to fight. Gator walked him back to his cabana."

"That was about seven-thirty last night. I left him at the stairs to his cabana. He was okay," Gator said.

"Who did he want to fight with?" Charlie asked.

"Anyone, really, but I was the target of his anger," Dave Cavuto said.

"Did anyone see him again after that?" Charlie asked.

Everyone looked at Beth. "I did."

"When did you see him?" Charlie asked.

"It was about eleven o'clock, maybe quarter past. It was after Eddie and that doctor left. Misty and I were on our dock, talking. We saw Kevin standing on the Mountain To Sea dock. I think he was taking a leak. When he was done he sat down and lit a cigarette."

"Was he alone?"

"Yes. Misty and I sat there for maybe another fifteen minutes before we called it a day."

"So he was still there when you went to bed?"

"Yes."

"Both of you?" Charlie was looking at Misty.

"Yes," Misty replied.

I had another knot in my stomach. Misty was the last person to see Kevin.

"I was out on the dock about midnight. He wasn't there then," said Marlene.

"What were you doing on the dock so late?" Gator asked.

"I had the late shift, dish duty. After that I went out on the dock to do my yoga exercises."

"Marlene, did you see anyone else while you were doing your yoga?" I asked. I didn't have to shout this time, the wind and rain were already dying down. The waterspout itself was already moving out to the open sea.

"You know, I thought I saw some movement on the ground in the kayak palapa. I wasn't sure. I stopped and watched for a few seconds but when I didn't see anything else I went to bed. Someone could have been lying on the sand."

⚜

Charlie had nothing else to go on. He left to take Kevin's remains and possessions to his headquarters in Belize City.

Chapter 43

Friday, December 29th,
1:30 P.M.

I downed a few more aspirin and a bottle of water. I lay down for a few minutes, trying to get some rest but it just wasn't going to happen. I grabbed a garden rake and walked down to Bernie's cabana. Along the way I saw Sticks and asked him to join me. My head was still hurting and I'd had a couple of dizzy spells.

"What are we looking for?" Sticks asked.

"I found Dylan's missing ratchet wrench in the sand outside Jack and Sherry's cabana while on my little treasure hunt with the two kids. If whoever moved the railing that night tossed the wrench down did so to avoid maybe being caught with it then maybe whoever killed Bernie might have done the same with whatever they used."

"You're certain we've got a serial killer here?" He leaned on the rake.

"I'm certain we have at least one killer here, yeah. Since I'm not certain yet what the murder weapon was we might as well poke around."

"Aren't you worried about getting a crowd watching us?"

"Not really. I think everyone is in the dining hall, afraid to go off on their own. I'd like to get some people off the island, have them go diving or something, but I understand their reluctance."

"How much of the area do you want to rake? We can't do the whole island."

"Just start at the base of Cabana Ten and we'll go as far as Cabana Twelve. We'll start along the shore and work our way to a point even with Cabana Eleven's doorway. If the killer tossed the murder weapon as they came out of the cabana it would fall between the cabana door and the water."

"How deep do you want me to dig?"

"Not far at all, just drag the tines through the sand. I doubt they'd have taken the time to bury something."

Sticks dragged the rake along the shore all the way from the base of Cabana Ten to Cabana Twelve, made a 180 degree turn, and overlapped by a couple of inches. Back and forth he went. I walked along the water's edge after he'd made a couple of passes in case I saw something the rake might have exposed. He was on his ninth pass when I saw something about a foot offshore, a brief glint of sunlight bouncing off metal, almost halfway between Cabana eleven and Cabana twelve.

"Hold up for a minute," I said.

I stood, and searched for the glimmer I'd seen a moment earlier. I saw the glint again and stepped out into the water. I knelt down, leaning on some drift wood, and reached into the water. My hand drifted in the right area, fingers just breaking the sand. I grasped something and stood up.

"What is it?" Sticks asked as he lay the rake down.

"It looks like a coat hanger. The two ends of the hanger are wrapped tightly around each other." I touched the point they formed. It was sharp.

The entwined section was at least an eighth inch thick at the point and maybe a quarter inch thick an inch or so up from that. About six inches from the tip the hanger bent ninety degrees, ran a couple of inches and doubled back past the tip another couple of inches, then back again. It resembled a cork screw.

"What do you think?" Sticks asked.

"I think we found the murder weapon."

"Murder weapon? What murder," a voice said.

I turned around. "Larry, how long have you been standing there?"

"I just walked up. I came looking for you. I'm bored. I've read every book I brought with me. Beth and Marcus have said they'll take me on a dive if it's okay with you. But back to my question, what murder?"

I hesitated. I really didn't want to scare anyone any further, but Larry wasn't stupid and he'd heard me correctly.

"Let me ask a different question. Wasn't this Bernie's cabana?" Larry asked.

I nodded.

"So it wasn't really a heart-attack?"

"No, I saw a little dried blood on his chest, just about where the sternum is located. Do you know where that it?"

"From my CPR classes some thirty years ago, yeah, it's right about the center of the chest, just at the base of the lowest part of the rib cage. It's right over the heart. In CPR classes they taught me to locate it and that's where you do the chest compressions."

"That's right, and I saw a little dried blood there. I almost mistook it for a mole," I said.

"We know someone killed Kevin. Now you're thinking the same person killed Bernie? Why?"

"That's the big question that's been bothering me. Who, and why? Knowing either would help figure out the other."

"Well, everyone over here is cowering in the dining hall. Down at Over The Edge it's the same thing, the Wrights and Erin are all in the dining hall. I'm bored. How about that dive? You might as well ask at Mountain To Sea if anyone wants to make a dive."

"Do you really think anyone else will want to dive?"

"What else can they do? Sit around staring at each other, wondering if somebody in the room is going to kill them? Or run to their cabanas seeking privacy but lacking the safety in numbers? Sounds like a horrible way to spend the next eighteen hours to me."

This was the Larry I expected. No sense in panicking, and practical. While it wasn't cowardice to hide with everyone else in the dining hall, doing so would just add to the stress level.

"Okay, I'll ask if anyone else wants to dive. If it's just you though then the answer's no."

✦

I was surprised, but when I put the question to the guests, all huddled in very small clusters in the dining hall, Dave and Dagan Cavuto wanted to dive. Beth and Marcus inspected each diver's gear, even going so far as to have each swim submerged there in the lagoon. Jeremy headed out with the Cavutos, Larry, and Joe and Terri Wright. With Beth and Marcus along, I felt as comfortable as I could about this dive. Marcus chose the dive site, Beth's Garden, since it's the closet to the island in case of a problem.

While the boat was out I sent an email to Glenn telling him about the coat hanger I'd found. He responded almost immediately with a text message:

I'm in the air. Expect the cavalry to arive by helicopter at Sunrise Caye with a Belizean official at 09:30 tomorrow morning.

Autopsy being performed on Bernie Stamps today. Medical Examiner tested your suggestion of a flavor injector and ruled out as too flexible and too weak to penetrate into the heart. Will advise of your wire hanger finding.

"See you in the morning. Stay safe."

✦

I stood on the dock as the dive boat returned, slightly more than an hour after it left. "How was it?" I asked the group.

"Just what I wanted it to be, George," Larry said.

"You guys were gone a long time." I extended a hand to help Terri and then Joe climb onto the dock.

"We all kept it pretty shallow. My dive computer says my max depth was thirty-five feet," Larry said.

"With that shallow a dive you wouldn't go through your air as fast," I said.

Beth looked up at me. "I think that under the circumstances everyone is a little nervous and wanted to keep it shallow, just in case of a problem. It was a fun dive. We even had a couple of dolphins swim past."

"Dolphins? Alright, did they play with you?"

"No, they swam up from the deep, breached the water, swam back past one more time and then left," Larry said. "It was cool, but I couldn't get a picture of them. It happened too quickly."

Chapter 44
Saturday, December 30th, 5:30 A.M.

Iwoke up Saturday morning filled with a sense of dread. I sat up, kicked my legs over the edge of the bed, and leaned forward. I didn't want to get up.

Kim reached over and held my hand. "It'll all be over in a few hours," she said.

"I know." I wasn't very convincing.

"You've done everything you could. It isn't your job to do law enforcement out here."

"I'm in charge out here. After all, I'm the King, remember?" I gripped her hand just a bit tighter for a moment and tried to smile. I looked outside. The sun was rising, but thick clouds blocked much of the light and a fog, unusual for this time of year, shrouded the island.

⊱✦⊰

I'd replayed it all night.

Andrew and I drove his four-wheel drive Jeep into the desert, pulled off I-10 and went north about a mile and parked it. We each carried a hunting rifle but Andrew had a 45 caliber handgun and a couple of knives. He also had a bag, the contents of which he didn't show me.

We walked toward the bikers' camp and found a spot on a hill-side where we could watch them. They had a pretty good party going, complete with barbeque and lots of booze. They partied into the night but most were passed out by about midnight. I was able to recognize both the guy I caught breaking into the office and the guy that led the group harassing my customers and I noted which tents each went into.

We made our way into the camp. I took a position next to the tent the guy I caught was in. Andrew went into the tent and came back out almost ten minutes later. I heard a crunching noise, what I thought was a bone being broken, and nothing else. He had a bag with him as he came out, with something heavy and wet in it.

We made our way to the leader's tent. Andrew opened the smaller bag and pulled out a couple of large syringes. He went into the tent. I heard a muffled sound, a woman's moan, then nothing.

Three minutes passed, and the tent flap opened. "Give me a hand with this guy," he whispered.

The guy was unconscious. I put my hands under his armpits, cradling his head between my forearms. Andrew picked up his other bag and grabbed the guy's legs. We carried him off without waking anyone.

We put the guy in the Jeep and drove a few miles further into the desert, onto reservation land.

"What's this?" I asked when we stopped. I could barely see, it was so dark, but in front of me was a large hole in the ground next to a large pile of dirt.

"The Bureau of Indian Affairs is building a small medical office about half a mile from here. I borrowed some equipment for a while yesterday." Andrew smiled, then pushed the guy out of the Jeep.

The guy hit the ground with a thud, and then moaned. He was starting to come around. I watched as Andrew kicked him a few more times. With each kick the guy would roll over, edging closer to the pit.

We waited about thirty minutes. I could see the first slivers of daylight breaking out.

"What do you think, George? Is it time to wake him up?"

"Yeah, judging from his moaning he's almost awake. Got any water to throw on him?"

"There are a couple of bottles of water in the Jeep but I think that's a waste of good water."

Andrew unzipped his pants and urinated on the guy.

"Who are you?" he asked, struggling. Andrew had bound his hands using some cable ties.

"You know who he is," Andrew said, pointing to me. "As for whom I am, well, my name is Andrew. You killed my family when you killed his." Andrew kicked him again and again, until the guy was on the edge of the pit.

"I didn't kill them."

"Maybe so, but you know who did. Now, what's your name?"

"They call me 'Sarge.' I don't know who killed your family. Let me loose." He wriggled, trying to free himself.

"Sarge? Why do they call you that?" Andrew kicked him again, pushing him into the pit. Sarge fell, landing on his right side, about six feet to the bottom of the pit. I thought I heard bones break, or at least crack. He was silent for a moment, then began groaning and cursing.

"Because I was in the Army." He squirmed and moaned and managed to sit up in one corner of the pit. The pit was about eight feet long, four feet wide, and six feet deep.

"Well, Sarge, I was in the Army too," Andrew said. "So here's some intel for you. You're miles away from your buddies. They might not even know you're gone yet. Then again, they might. It doesn't much matter, really. They aren't going to find you out here. And I think you know who made the bomb."

"I'm telling you, it wasn't me." He was trying to stand but not getting anywhere. The drugs hadn't fully worn off and his muscles weren't cooperating.

"I didn't say it was. I said you know who did. And you're going to tell me," Andrew said.

"Why, you're not going to kill me."

"Yeah, I will. You're a dead man. How quickly, and how painfully, you die is still undecided. Now, tell me who built the bomb."

He stopped trying to stand. "No."

"What was your friend's name? The guy that broke into the Doc's office?"

"Butch. Why?"

"Butch is dead. If your friends know that you're gone, they probably know he's dead too."

"Why should I believe you?" He was getting defiant. He must not have understood his predicament. Maybe he thought we were kidding, or we didn't have the guts to go through with this. I might not have, but he didn't know Andrew.

Andrew just stood there, not saying a word, for several minutes. He looked up, turning his face to the sunrise. With the sun's low angle he cast a shadow, keeping the pit in darkness. He took a couple of steps to one side.

"So, Sarge, were you in 'Nam?"

"Yeah. You?" He was squirming a bit more.

"Yeah. I saw some scary stuff there. You?"

"Damn right, I saw a lot of scary stuff there. I learned a lot from Charlie. Let me out of here and I'll show you," Sarge said.

"I don't think so. I learned a lot from Charlie, too. One of the things I learned at Benning Charlie reinforced."

"Benning? You were a Green Beret?"

"No, I was in the Rangers. Anyway, what they taught me, and what Charlie already understood, is that you never give your enemy an even chance. So while letting you out could be interesting it's not a smart move. I'm not afraid of you but I'm not dumb."

"You're afraid."

"Not really, but I learned a lot too." Andrew walked over to the Jeep, grabbed the larger bag from the back along with a Coleman cooler.

I looked at the cooler. "What, are you going to give him some water?"

Andrew looked at me, a hard grin on his face. "No, but I do have something else for him in there. In a minute though."

He took the larger bag, untied the opening, and stepped to the edge of the pit above Sarge.

"Here's proof that Butch is dead." He dumped the bag out and Butch's bloody, severed head fell from the bag into Sarge's lap.

The screaming lasted several minutes. When Sarge stopped screaming Andrew stepped back up to the edge of the pit. "Is that proof enough?"

"Don't kill me. I didn't do it." Sarge sobbed as he began to grasp his situation. While screaming he'd put his body through all kinds of contortions, managing to get Butch's head off his lap and kicking it to the far side of the pit.

"That's a given. I AM going to kill you. The question remains how slowly and how painfully. Butch here, he was asleep and barely felt anything. Do you want to die quickly and painlessly?"

"I don't want to die," he wailed.

"You will. Living isn't an option. You led that gang, and they killed our families. So you have to die. Now, tell me, who made the bomb?"

"I don't know."

"You're lying. Look, see this?" Andrew held up a syringe. "I got some good stuff from the doc's office. You'll just drift off to sleep and never wake up. You'll never feel any pain. If you tell me now who made the bomb."

"Fuck you."

"You're not my type, so I think I'll decline the invitation, thank you. But this stuff, hey, that's the easy way out. Maybe you want to do it the hard way."

Andrew went to the cooler and retrieved a sack and placed it on the ground. He also grabbed a couple of bottles of water and tossed one to me. I saw the sack move.

"The desert has a lot of nasty stuff living out here. Scorpions, for example. Ever been stung by one, Sarge?"

"No." He tried not looking at Butch's head, but his eyes kept drifting back to it. So did mine.

"I have. Doc, you've been stung by them too."

"Yeah, it hurts like hell. But just one scorpion sting, that won't kill most men." I wasn't sure where he was going, but Andrew's sack had moved again. It held more than one or two scorpions.

"Remember that camping trip, you were what, nine maybe? A scorpion was in your sleeping bag when you climbed in. Stung you on your balls, if I remember right." He laughed and took a drink of water.

"Yeah, it still hurts." My hand automatically went to my crotch.

"Remember what we found in your sleeping bag the next night?"

"I sure do. I'd rather get stung by the scorpion again than mess with that." I knew now what was in the sack: rattlesnakes.

At that, Andrew poured a little water on the sack and then kicked it into the pit. Two rattlesnakes made their way out of the sack. One took up a position next to Butch's head. The other coiled at Sarge's feet, it's rattle clearly sounding.

"Get them out of here, man!" Sarge pleaded.

"Your best bet is to sit real still. Let them get calmed down a bit. Now, who made the bomb?"

"Eric the Red. That's his name. Now get me out of here."

"What does he look like?"

"He looks like Willie Nelson, only with bright red hair. He was a bomb-disposal guy in Vietnam. He rides a big, dark-red Harley with a sidecar."

"I don't remember seeing anyone that looked like that in your camp last night. Doc, did you see anyone like that?"

"Not that I remember." I moved closer to the pit, pushing some dirt in, angering the snakes.

"He has a place in the city. Get me out of here, please, man, I'm begging you."

"Where do we find this guy?" Andrew kicked a little more dirt in, angering the snakes again. He smiled at me. It was an accident when I did it. He knew what he was doing.

"There's this bar, place called The Boulevard. It's off MLK in the southeast part of town," Sarge said.

"Why do we care about a bar?" Andrew asked as he kicked a little more dirt into the pit.

"You can find him there. He goes there almost every day around three. Now, get me out of here," Sarge pleaded.

"So, now what?" I asked Andrew, not looking into the pit.

Andrew pulled his pistol and shot one of the snakes, the one still coiled next to Butch's head. The other snake uncoiled and bit Sarge on the leg. It coiled up again in a corner. Andrew kicked in some more dirt and the snake struck again, this time biting into Sarge's left arm.

"What now?" I asked.

"Now we go find Eric the Red. Let's go." Andrew killed the second snake. I could hear Sarge sobbing and crying out for us as we walked to the Jeep and we pulled away.

"Aren't you worried someone will find him?" I asked.

"No, nobody will be out here anytime today. We'll be back soon enough."

We drove into town. Our first stop was a carwash where Andrew washed the Jeep, making sure there were no traces of blood or hair, anything that might provide DNA matches for Sarge or Butch.

"George, there's a chance this guy, Eric the Red, might recognize you. He won't know me, and I can go into that bar without drawing much attention to myself."

I hung out at a McDonald's across the street. Andrew went into the bar at two-thirty. There were only three bikes in the parking lot. Andrew's Jeep was in the fast food lot.

It was about four o'clock when I saw a blood-red Harley with matching sidecar come down the street. The driver looked like Willie Nelson, with shiny hair and beard. He parked the bike, looked around, and went into the bar.

I waited five minutes, as planned, and pulled the Jeep out into the street, stopping right in front of the bar's door. The door opened. Eric the Red led the way with Andrew, holding his gun in his left hand down along his pant leg, following closely. There was something else in Andrew's right hand but I couldn't make out what.

"Okay there, Eric, now get into the back of the Jeep," Andrew said quietly, looking around.

"No." He stood still, his back to Andrew, staring at me. "Hey, I know you. You're that dentist."

That was as far as he got. I saw Andrew put a syringe into Eric's neck.

"You know, you're using up all my best sedatives."

"It's a good thing we're about done, too. It took three doses for the guys inside. I had to get the first one when he went to the head. I got the second one when the bartender went into the stockroom. I used another dose on the bartender when he came out of the stockroom.

Andrew pushed Eric's limp body into the back seat and fastened the seat belt. "Wouldn't want to get a ticket for not using seat belts, you know. Now, back to the pit, and drive carefully. We don't want to get stopped by any cops."

Eric was still out cold when we arrived back at the pit. There were no signs anyone had been around. I walked up to the edge of the pit and saw Sarge. He was still alive, his eyes moving slowly. His face was swollen and he was breathing with difficulty. He saw me. I sensed he was pleading, whether it was to help him or put him out of his misery, I don't know. I didn't much care anymore.

"George, keep an eye on this guy. I've got to get down there for a minute." At that, Andrew jumped down into the pit. I saw him pull a knife out of his pocket. He climbed back up, with the plastic cable-ties he'd used to bind Sarge's arms.

"Just in case anyone ever finds these bodies, we don't want it clear they were executed."

"What do we do with this guy?" I didn't see how a corpse-less head could be viewed as anything but an execution.

"Push him off the Jeep and we'll let him crawl into the pit when he wakes up."

I handed my gun over to Andrew and did as was told. It was about twenty minutes before Eric started to come around.

"Where am I?" he asked, looking around. The sun was starting to go down.

"The middle of nowhere," I answered.

"Or, for you at least, the end of the road," Andrew added.

"Who are you? What do you want with me?"

"In town, you recognized me. Do you still?" I asked.

He tried to focus his eyes. "The dentist?"

"Yeah, the dentist. You killed my family."

"No, I didn't. You've got the wrong guy. You want Sarge, he did it."

"Interesting, we got Sarge. He said you made the bomb."

"I didn't know what he was going to do with it. If he says otherwise, he's lying."

"But you didn't care, either. Maybe you thought it was going somewhere else, to kill someone else. Maybe you knew. I don't care," I said.

"I didn't know." He was looking for help—and realizing there wasn't any to be found.

"See that pit over there?" I asked, pointing a few feet from him.

"Yeah. What about it?" He was trying to use his legs, they were still rubbery but he could move them.

"Get in it. We'll make it quick. Maybe even painless," I said.

Andrew kicked him, repeatedly, rolling Eric the Red to the edge of the pit. Another kick sent Eric into the pit.

"If he manages to stand-up, shoot him in the leg. I'll be back in a few minutes." Andrew drove off in the Jeep.

Twenty minutes later I heard the sound of a vehicle coming up. Andrew's Jeep.

"I had a hunch there wouldn't be anyone left at the bikers' camp. There was just one tent, and there was a headless corpse in it."

I helped Andrew pull Butch's body out of the Jeep and dump it into the pit. Eric started yelling. He'd been talking, looking at Sarge's swollen body and the dead snakes. He hadn't noticed the head in the corner before. All of Sarge's various contortions had piled dirt around Butch's head.

"Okay, back in just a few minutes. Don't let him out of there, Doc." Andrew walked off.

A few minutes later I heard heavy equipment. A bulldozer.

"Let me guess, you borrowed it again?"

"Yeah, we're getting to damned old to move all this dirt by hand."

The bulldozer moved the mountain of dirt into the pit, burying Eric the Red and a still breathing Sarge. He drove the bulldozer over the pit a few times to pack it down firmly before returning the bulldozer to the new medical office site.

Chapter 45

Saturday, December 30th, 8:00 A.M.

The Mountain To Sea guests would be leaving after lunch. The *Tropical Breeze* was bringing the coming week's guests and should arrive around eleven-thirty. This week's guests would get back to Belize City at about four o'clock. They could not fly back to the States until Sunday.

The Over The Edge guests were also leaving Saturday after an early lunch. None were going to be flying out that afternoon. Jeremy and Kim would be taking the four of them to Dangriga in the *Sensencula*. Erin Walker and Larry Carlson were each spending Saturday night in Dangriga and then flying to Belize City and then onward to the States on Sunday. Teri and Joe had their boat docked in Dangriga.

The sun finally burned through the fog to reveal clear skies. The wind shifted again, now a gentle breeze, maybe five to ten miles per hour, blew in from the west. The fog left moisture on the palm leaves, every now and then the breeze would send droplets onto anyone below.

At either resort there would be nothing much to do this morning. After yesterday's storm passed we had very calm seas and blue skies. At Mountain To Sea we would allow people to take the windsurf boards and kayaks out but only if they stayed within sight of Sunrise Caye and came back in when they saw the ship approach.

We would, under normal circumstances, offer a dive on Saturday morning. Given the deaths that week I assumed everyone would be anxious to get off the island and while on the island stay together.

They'd figure there is safety in numbers. The guests and staff could all convince themselves that Dylan's death and Jack's injury were accidents. They could even believe that Bernie's death was a heart attack. There was no mistaking Kevin's death for anything but a murder.

I found Larry swimming laps between the two docks. "Hey Larry, don't get yourself too tired out."

He stopped swimming and stood in the lagoon, near the end of the Over The Edge dock. The water was waist deep. I could see he had swim fins on. "I'd rather be diving this morning. I know it's been a rough week but there's no telling how soon I will get another chance to dive."

"I don't think anyone else is going to want to dive," I said.

"Maybe not, but have you asked? George, it just seems to me that we've all spent a lot of money on this trip and there's no way of telling how soon anyone can dive again. Seems like a waste to just sit in the dining hall and wait."

"Okay, I'll ask the others."

"If you get others to dive, are you coming with us?"

"I wish I could, but I've got some work to do before y'all leave. I've been meaning to ask you something." I still had a headache. My stomach had settled and the headache was just a steady pain, it didn't throb.

"What's that?"

"Well, Beth and Kim noticed it before I did. We've all noticed you've made more dives than usual. This morning's dive, if we make one, gets you the twelve-dive package discount."

"I've been working out a little. Not much, but I lost about fifty pounds this year." He walked toward the shore, leaned against the dock and removed his fins. Then he grabbed a towel and dried off.

"It shows. Fifty pounds? Man, that's great. How did you do it?" We both took seats in the Adirondack chairs.

"Well, it was a combination of eating a little better and exercising a bit more. Just a bit more, though. Mostly it was just walking. I bought a recumbent bike last summer, a trike actually."

"A trike? What do you mean?"

"It's got three wheels, in a tadpole design. You know, like a tadpole has its two legs out front and one tail. This trike has two wheels in front and one in back. It's a blast to ride."

"That sounds interesting, you'll have to show me a picture of it. So, what made you do it? What made you get healthier?"

"You know, when people go to support groups like Alcoholic's Anonymous they have this common saying: 'I got sick and tired of being sick and tired.'"

"I've heard the phrase."

"Well, that's sort of the case with me. I'm self-employed, and the weight and diabetes combined keep me from being able to buy a good health-insurance plan. I have to get off at least another thirty pounds or so just to have a chance to qualify for a private plan."

"That blows. You don't have any insurance now?"

"I've got a catastrophic care plan. It doesn't pay anything for routine office visits, and the drug prescription plan is worse than paying full price at Wal-Mart. It beats not having anything, but costs about the same as a good private plan."

"And you've lost the weight by walking?" I saw an osprey flying along the water a little further down the lagoon.

"One of my customers has an office about a mile and a quarter from my old apartment. I started walking there and back a couple of times a week. When that wasn't much effort anymore I moved to another apartment that's half a mile further each way. Round-trip it's a three-and-a-half mile commute, fully dressed and with a fairly heavy backpack with my laptop in it."

"Three to four miles a day adds up, I guess."

"Yeah, plus one of my customers and I go to lunch twice a week at one of three restaurants, each of which is nine-tenths of a mile from the office. So that adds another one-point-eight miles."

"Not bad, and it's paying off. How many laps have you been swimming while here?"

"I think it's about a hundred yards and I've been swimming ten laps each morning. So I'm guessing it's about two-thousand yards each morning?"

"Yeah, it's close to that. Your motivation was the cost of health insurance?"

"That's part of it. I bought a book by John Bingham. Have you ever heard of him?"

"No, can't say I know the name."

"He writes for one of the big running magazines. He calls himself 'The Penguin.' Anyway, he wrote a book called *No Need For Speed* in which he says the speed someone runs isn't really important, or how well they run for that matter. What counts is that they keep moving."

"Okay, I guess that makes sense."

"He said something in his book that really registered with me. It was about the self-talk we all have, that part of us all in which we tell ourselves we can't do something. I may not have this exactly right but it goes like this:

'We look at ourselves at age thirty, forty, or fifty and see all the evidence we need to justify caving in. We see a belly where our waist used to be. We can't see our feet. We struggle to walk up the steps or play with our children. We look in the mirror and see more of what we are and less of what we want to be. Many of us get trapped in our own bodies. We're prisoners of what I call 'sedentary confinement.' Worse, we are our own guards and wardens. We are the ones who won't commute our sentences.'"

"And that really made a difference for you?"

"Yeah, well, I'm often amazed at how many of the people I work with, my clients' technical staff, complain about their management, about businesses in general, 'the suits' that run their companies. But they won't take the initiative to go out on their own or make an effort to move up. It's mostly their own self-talk: they tell themselves they don't know enough to be successful, to find a way to sell their services. I think most are just weak and lazy. Then I see myself doing the same self-talk when it comes to working out. So I've been trying to change that self-talk."

"Well, I'm not sure I agree with you about your clients but what you've been doing is working. Keep it up. Maybe next year we can put you through a Rescue Swimmer course?"

"Maybe, but I'm not really interested in the responsibility for other people that certification requires. I hope to be another fifty pounds lighter the next time we get together."

❧❖❧

I checked in with the Wrights and they were both interested in making another dive. I walked down to the Mountain To Sea dining hall and found all of the guests just sitting around, talking in small groups or playing card and board games. Antonio was in the kitchen, cutting up fish for lunch. He'd had a part of preparing every lunch and dinner since Sunday.

"I know this might seem odd, but since the ship won't be here for a few hours yet, does anyone want to go on a dive?" I asked.

I saw Dave and Dagan look at each other. "It beats sitting around here," Dagan said to Dave.

"Are you sure?"

"Yeah, at least we'd be doing something."

I wound up with several people wanting to dive.

❧❦❧

I gathered my dive masters. "We've got seven people wanting to make one last dive. That's too many for one boat. Why don't we break it up into two groups? Beth, you and Marcus take the four people from Mountain To Sea out to Victoria's Caye Wall. Misty, you and Kim can take Larry and the Wrights out to Southwestern Caye. He said something last night about not having seen a moray this trip and we all know where one hangs out. Keep it shallow; try to keep everyone above fifty feet so they can stay down as long as possible. Give these folks a really long dive."

"I've packed all my stuff already," Misty said. "I'm ready to leave."

"Misty, I need everyone out there today. You can use some of the rental equipment. I don't want any of the guests to have a problem, so I want everyone out there."

I asked Juan, one of the maintenance guys working at Mountain To Sea, to drive the second boat. He's done that for me before, and does a pretty good job of following the bubbles. Usually that job would fall on Dylan.

❧❦❧

I wanted Misty off the island for a while, so sending her out to Southwestern Caye took her away for as long as possible. The boat left the dock right at nine-fifteen. I figured that gave me an hour at least, maybe ninety minutes. I was expecting company somewhere between nine-thirty and ten.

I heard the helicopter. We didn't have a helipad on Sunrise Caye, but the British Royal Air Force emergency copter had landed on the beach in front of the Mountain To Sea dining hall.

Three men got out of the helicopter and walked over.

"Glenn, I'm glad to see you."

"I'm glad to see you too, George." He pointed to one of the men with him. "This is Special Agent Ted Baer from the FBI's Washington office. And this is Captain Jonathan Black from the Belize National Police."

I shook hands with each man. "Man, it must have been a challenge growing up with that name, Ted."

"Yeah, my mom was pregnant with me and the guy at the carnival couldn't guess her weight. She won a giant stuffed animal. I'm glad she didn't win the velvet Elvis. Then again, Elvis is my middle name. So I really am Ted E. Baer."

"No kidding? On the other hand, she could have been a zookeeper responsible for the pandas."

"I've heard every Teddy Bear joke there is. At least women like a great big, huggable teddy bear."

"So, where is she?"

"I'm sorry for wasting time, Captain," I said. "Misty and some others are on a dive off Victoria's Caye. I figured I should get her off the island before you arrived."

"Good idea. May we search her cabin?" He shouted as the helicopter lifted off the beach and flew in the direction of Tradewinds Caye.

"Sure, it's right this way. She said earlier that she's completely packed and ready to go."

"Go? Where is she going?"

Glenn spoke up. "Captain, I thought I'd told you that she was scheduled to leave today. She has a new job in a few weeks in Indonesia."

❧❦❧

They searched her cabana efficiently, unpacking Misty's bags and repacking them.

Agent Baer held a wire hanger. "Does everyone have these?"

"Every cabana has two or three. Why?"

"George, after our call the other night, we had an autopsy done in the States on Bernie Stamps. You were right about a puncture wound. Our pathologist confirmed your guess yesterday about the wire hanger. She shoved it into his chest, right at the sternum, and swirled it around. It shredded the heart and punctured a lung."

"There should be one or two in what was the Stamp's cabana. I didn't look; however, I have the one I found in the water yesterday in my office."

"We'll want that before we leave. It probably doesn't have any prints on it but maybe it can get entered into evidence. We also had an autopsy done on Dylan Bellamy. It was an embolism, like you said. I don't see any way to prove he did, or didn't, drop his weights."

"I know. There weren't any eye witnesses except Misty. The others say their view of what was happening was blocked by coral or Misty."

Ted held up a cell phone. "I'm curious about the cell phone. Why would she have this out here?"

"Belize has cell phone towers throughout the country. The technology was coming out when the national phone company made the decision to wire the country so they invested heavily in cell and digital technology. The tower in Dangriga reaches out here and there's a relay tower on Tobacco Caye."

"Oh, can you call the States from here with them?"

"Sure, but I use the voice-over-I/P connection when I call the States. That way I don't have to pay the long-distance charges. The cell-phone service here is very expensive."

"May I see that phone, please?"

Agent Baer handed Misty's phone to Captain Black. "She made a call this morning. The last number dialed is a number in Belize. I'll find out who she called."

He stepped outside and placed a call to his headquarters. Three minutes later he stepped back inside.

"She called a resort in Placencia."

"Which one?" I asked.

"The Toucan."

"I'm not familiar with that one. Who owns it?"

"Carlos Martinez."

Chapter 46

Saturday, December 30th, 11:00 A.M.

We walked outside, headed back to my office, when I saw the *Tropical Breeze* approaching. It was almost an hour earlier than usual.

"I'm sorry, gentlemen. I've got some work to do. Glenn, while I take care of Mountain To Sea business, why don't you take these guys to our dining hall?"

At Mountain To Sea's dock, I oversaw the boat's unloading and looked over our new guests. I verified the boat was empty and left Gator to oversee loading for the outbound guests and staff. I gave the new guests the tour of the island.

As we got to the Mountain To Sea dining hall, I saw one of our dive boats coming back in from the south. I turned the group over to Reggie, this week's lead guide, and hurried over to my dock.

"So, how was the dive?" I asked nobody in particular.

"Oh, it was fantastic!" Alicia gushed. "There were thousands of Wrasse, they swam all around us." I helped her climb up onto the dock and took Carolyn's hand.

"We saw another nurse shark and a couple of hawksbill turtles. I don't want to leave; I want to go back for another dive!"

"We can probably arrange another week here if you'd like. Mountain To Sea has one empty cabana this week."

"Alicia's family probably wouldn't like that, and neither would my husband, but it sure is tempting."

It felt good thinking that one dive could, for a few minutes at least, let them not think about the deaths this week.

"If I can't tempt you then we should probably get you folks down to the dining hall quickly. The new group came in a while ago and the rest of the folks from Mountain To Sea have finished loading the boat and are having lunch."

The four Mountain To Sea guests were halfway to their dining hall when Beth said, "Jeremy said there was a helicopter that landed and took off here. What's happened now?"

"It's a long story, but everyone on the island is okay and we have visitors. Someone you know."

⚜

All of our guests would be leaving today and, other than their dive gear, all of their bags were already packed and sat on the end of the dock. Erin, the writer, wandered the island taking pictures. Jeremy and Marcus loaded the bags into the *Sensencula* along with crates of empty bottles and bundles of our laundry. I rejoined Glenn and the other two in the dining hall.

⚜

Time passed slowly. The dive site I'd sent Misty and the others too was only about ten minutes further away than the Victoria's Caye site. So I figured they'd be gone maybe twenty to twenty-five minutes longer. After thirty minutes had passed I knew something wasn't right.

I looked at my wrist, as if I actually wore a watch. "They should have been back by now."

"Maybe they stopped in at Southwestern Caye, so that Misty could say goodbye to Eddie and the guys over there," Beth said.

"Maybe, but I think Kim would have called. Besides, we need to get our guests back into Dangriga and pick up the people coming out here today. Kim wouldn't have wanted to delay the trip any longer than necessary."

"So what do you want us to do? Go look for them?"

"Glenn, I think that's precisely what we should do. Jeremy, we're going to take the dive boat. Fill up the gas tank on the *Sensencula*, then find Erin and get her on the boat. You can meet us at Eddie's on Southwestern Caye. Gentlemen, please come with me."

❧❖❧

I threaded the dive boat through the break in the coral that separated Sunrise Caye from Victoria's Caye and opened the throttle as we headed south. I've been diving and sailing these waters for two decades and could find the Southwestern Caye wall buoy in the dark if I had to.

We passed the far end of Victoria's Caye and Southwestern Caye appeared on the horizon. As we cleared the near end of the island I focused my eyes on where the dive buoy was. I cut the motor to an idle about a hundred yards from the buoy. We looked around.

"No boats," I said.

"I think I heard something." Glenn was leaning over the edge of the boat, staring and trying to pick up whatever he'd heard.

"I heard it too. It's coming from over there." Agent Baer was pointing toward the buoy.

I saw movement at the buoy and moved the boat slowly toward it. We were maybe sixty feet away when I saw him.

"It's Juan. He's in the water, hugging the buoy."

I pulled as close as I could. Captain Black stripped down to his shorts. He dove in, swam over to the buoy and put an arm around Juan. He crawled back to the boat where Glenn and Agent Baer pulled Juan, and then Captain Black, into the boat.

Juan was exhausted. Even in the warm waters of the Caribbean, hypothermia can set in quickly. The water temperature was in the upper seventies but that's more than twenty degrees below the human body's temperature. An hour and a half in this water without at least a minimal wet-suit would sap almost anyone's strength.

I held Juan's head up and gave him a bottle of water. He took several sips, and tried to speak.

"Juan, where's the boat?"

"Misty…" and he pointed toward the island.

I started toward the motor.

"Wait…" He struggled to talk. He waved his arm toward the open sea.

"Wait? For what?"

"The others—" he gasped, taking a bit more water.

"What about the others?"

He waved one hand, toward the open sea.

Glenn stood up, raising a hand above his eyes to shield the glare. "I think he's saying the others aren't in the boat."

Juan was nodding and gesturing toward the sea.

"Oh God, no. Juan, were they in their dive gear still?"

He nodded. "Si, dive suits and vests." He was still waving his arm out to sea.

I cut the motor.

"Why'd you cut the motor?" Glenn asked.

"Two reasons. One is to hear anyone trying to get our attention. The other is to determine the direction of the current." It took a couple of minutes but the front of the boat turned toward the northwest.

As I started the motor I said, "Keep your eyes on the water to our southeast." I turned the boat, proceeding slowly, not much more than an idle.

"Why that way? The current turned us toward the island," asked Agent Baer.

"The current pushes the broadest surface away, leaving the front of the boat facing into the current, minimizing the resistance to the current. That means the drift is to the southeast."

We crawled along the surface in a widening zigzag pattern, but generally followed the drift, constantly scanning for any sign of someone in the water. Five minutes passed, then ten.

"There's a boat coming," said Agent Baer, pointing behind us.

I turned to look. "That's Jeremy with the *Sensencula*."

I stopped the boat, waiting for Jeremy to pull alongside.

Captain Black climbed onto the *Sensencula*. Glenn and Agent Baer picked up Juan and passed him over to the captain.

"Erin, see if you can find a blanket in those bags and get Juan warmed up. Jeremy, take them back to Sunrise Caye. Have someone get Juan into some warm clothes, and start a fire if they need to. Then get back out here and help with the search. Captain, I think you should call your helicopter."

"Do you want the helicopter to take him to the mainland?"

"No. I want the helicopter to help search for the others."

"The *Tropical Breeze* left the island about twenty minutes ago," Jeremy said.

Jeremy headed back to our island.

"They've been in the water for two hours, at least."

"I know, Glenn, but they were all wearing wet-suits. They should be okay." I don't know how convincing I was. I wasn't too convinced of that myself.

※◆※

About ten minutes later the police helicopter flew overhead. It flew a circle, about a mile in radius, and began flying in a series of tighter circles. It came to a hover about a hundred feet above the surface. I headed toward it.

"There, I see something," Glenn said.

I followed Glenn's gaze, a little short of where the helicopter was hovering.

"It's a sausage. Kim always has an inflatable signaling device, along with a plastic whistle." She wasn't waving her arms; the sausage was just floating on the surface. The other three divers were still afloat a few feet from her. At least they were together.

The helicopter climbed as we pulled the divers into the boat. Terri Wright was breathing but unconscious. Joe was dead. Larry and Kim were both conscious, shivering and their teeth were chattering.

"Get them out of their wet-suits!" I shouted as I opened the throttle and headed toward Southwestern Caye, the nearest land. The wet-suits help warm the water that gets caught between the suit and the body but once out of the water they'd be better off exposed to the warmth of the sunlight.

"I think she's trying to say something!" Glenn yelled.

"Take the wheel," I said, looking at Agent Baer.

I knelt beside Kim, holding her tight, rubbing her arms to generate some heat and increase her circulation. She took a sip of water and said, "Terri and Joe..."

"Joe is dead. Terri's breathing."

"Larry..." Kim sobbed.

"He's okay," I said. He was sitting upright, taking water that Glenn gave him.

"We got in the water first. Misty was in her wet-suit. She asked Juan to help her...with the tank. He stood up to help her..." Kim took another sip of water "She pushed him over the side of the boat. Then she drove off. She just left us. Juan...?"

"We found him hanging onto the buoy. He'll be okay." I looked up and saw the water color was changing ahead. That meant we were getting close to The Wall, back to shallow water.

"The dolphins…" She was tiring.

"Dolphins? What about dolphins?"

"Circling us…me…" She passed out.

❧❦❧

"Ted, are you familiar with these boats and waters?"

"I've never even been in a boat before."

I took the wheel, figuring he'd drive us onto the coral and tear a hole in the hull or rip out our motor. There are a couple of miles of coral heads rising up to the surface, or close enough to rip the hulls of any fast-moving boats to shreds. There are also mangrove trees near the break in the reef through which Eddie's boats make their way to the sea. Passage through this section requires a series of slow slalom-like maneuvers.

"Hey, George, since when is there helicopter service to the resorts?" Glenn asked me.

"Huh?" I followed his gaze. "About a year ago Eddie started letting a service fly guests out here for about $900 per flight. His guests come and go on Wednesdays and that isn't their service's helicopter."

"So, whose is it?"

"I don't know."

After we plucked Kim, Larry, and the Wrights out of the water, the police helicopter climbed to about five hundred feet and was gone, flying north toward Sunrise Caye. I assumed Captain Black had called to be picked up. This new helicopter was lower and had probably flown directly there from the mainland. We were still a mile from Eddie's dock when the chopper made a sharp turn, hovered briefly, and set down—head into the wind—on Eddie's dock. Three men climbed out. Even from a half mile out I could see two of them were armed.

"I don't think they've seen us. Nobody appears to be looking our way. Ted, let me have those binoculars for a minute," I said.

"Here they are. Looks like the two guys have Uzis."

"Yeah, and does the guy in the middle look familiar?" Glenn asked.

"Yeah, he does," Ted said.

I brought the boat to a stop. I let the motor idle, figuring we weren't going to be heard over the helicopters idling jet engines and rotor noise. Glenn handed me the binoculars. I recognized the logo on the side of the helicopter: a hammock strung between two coconut trees with shark fins around it.

"Martinez," I said.

"We recognized him from pictures. The question now is how do we get on the island without being seen?"

From behind me I heard something. I looked at Larry, sitting up. "George, that bitch drove off as soon as the four of us were in the water. We never did make our dive. These tanks are mostly full," Larry said.

A group of people came out of the Victoria's Caye resort's dining hall. A petite figure ran out in front, seemingly shouting something. The two armed gunmen fired a few rounds above the crowd, sending several back into the dining hall and others diving into the sand.

"I don't know how to dive," said Agent Baer.

"Well, Glenn and I do." I reached into the boat's console and retrieved two small containers.

"Glenn, these are water-tight, at least for a few dozen feet. They'll hold your service revolvers and keep them dry."

"I'm going alone."

"No, you're not. I'm going with you. Ted, I need your gun."

Agent Baer started to argue with me, but stopped and pointed. The police helicopter was approaching the island. They probably didn't see us under the mangrove canopy. The police helicopter hovered about seventy-five feet above the water, taking what little breeze was blowing sideways. Captain Black's voice could be heard from a speaker:

"This is Captain Jonathan Black, commander of the Belize National Force. Lay down your weapons. You are under arrest."

The two armed men glanced at each other, then at Martinez. They raised their guns, pointed at the helicopter, and fired. Several rounds hit the aircraft's fuselage and cockpit. The pilot pulled up on the stick, climbing and turning to the left—away from us—as he climbed.

I helped Glenn put on Joe Wright's dive gear. Then I put on Terri's gear. Just before we slid over the side I grabbed Agent Baer's arm.

"Give us five minutes and then use the binoculars. You should see us under the dock. We'll give you the okay sign."

"What's the okay sign?"

"There are two. One you already know: that is touching an index fingertip to the adjoining thumb tip with the other fingers up. For divers, putting one hand on top on your head is the same gesture. That should be easier for you to see."

"Okay, got it."

"Hopefully they won't see us. Take the boat into the lagoon to the left of the dock. If they start shooting at you, just turn to the left and you can go several hundred yards before you encounter more coral heads. You'd be out of range for those guns." I wasn't sure of the truthfulness of that last sentence.

Just before I went under I saw the police helicopter coming back. It was higher this time, pointed into the wind, making for a tougher target to hit. Glenn and I dropped down to about ten feet and began swimming toward the dock. I kept him moving slowly to minimize his breathing. I didn't want our air bubbles giving us away.

I could see the dock clearly from twenty feet out, even lying on the bottom in ten feet of water. That works both ways, if they looked our way they'd have seen us too. We made the last few kicks and surfaced under the dock and under Martinez's helicopter. We could stand under the dock; the water's depth was barely chest high. I heard more shooting and looked up. Martinez's men were shooting at the police helicopter again. The chopper moved off, made another circle, and set itself up in another hover a bit further away.

I pulled my dive gear off, including turning the air off at the tank. Glenn followed my lead. I attached the two dive vests to each other and lashed them, and our fins, to one of the dock supports. It wouldn't do for them to float into the open or to let the tanks clank against each other, letting the bad guys know we were there.

We opened the dry storage containers and retrieved our guns. Glenn faced the mangrove trees and put his right hand on top of his head. He held it like that until we saw the boat pull out from the mangroves.

There was movement above us. I moved to one side of the dock and peeked out. I saw Eddie run out onto the dock. He grabbed Misty's arm. She stepped into him rather than trying to pull away. Instead, she grabbed him by the arm and bent over, pulling him forward and flipping him over her and down on the dock, hard. She dropped down to one knee, pulled a dive knife from her boot, and thrust it into Eddie's abdomen, twisting it. She pulled the knife out, wiped it a couple of times on the leg of Eddie's shorts, and laughed as she climbed into the helicopter's cabin.

Martinez was climbing back in as well when one of his gunmen stopped him.

⚹

My dive boat had just come around the jetty and was heading toward the dock. Misty stepped back out. I could hear her shout to Martinez: "That's Sunrise Caye's dive boat. I don't know who that guy is."

"It doesn't matter who he is. Or rather, who he was. Kill him," he ordered his men.

They fired toward the boat. Baer turned the wheel sharply and pushed the throttle down hard. The boat swerved as it sprayed water up onto the dock. It was gone quickly, but I saw Agent Baer slump forward as if hit.

I started to move out from under the dock, just as Glenn and I had planned out on the boat, but he grabbed my arm and pointed out to sea. The police helicopter was coming closer again, as if to position itself above Martinez's chopper and prevent it from taking off. The two gunmen fired again, this time hitting the police aircraft multiple times. The pilot pulled away, climbed to the left again, taking even more hits. Smoke came from the engine, and the craft pitched forward and tumbled into the water.

Misty re-entered the helicopter, followed by Martinez. One of the gunmen circled around to the other side of the helicopter. Glenn and I looked at each other and made our move.

I ducked my head to clear the dock, took two steps and fired. I wasn't a cop. I didn't give a damn about giving warnings and playing fair. I just wanted to stop these guys and they outnumbered and outgunned us. I remembered Andrew's words so long ago about never giving the enemy a fair chance. Shooting the guard in the back didn't bother me a bit—I fired three rounds into his back. He jerked a little as each round hit, and fell onto the dock.

Glenn did much the same. That guard fell forward, onto Misty. Glenn began climbing out of the water, as if trying to get to the helicopter and Martinez. Glenn's a big guy and the dock was too high above the water for that kind of maneuver. Both Misty and Martinez opened fire. I turned my gun toward the pilot and fired until I saw blood and he slouched forward.

I was feeling pretty smug for a few seconds as I figured that with the pilot out of commission they couldn't get away. That lasted until I saw Misty move into the front seat and push the pilot's body out of the way. Martinez pushed the dead guard's body out of the cabin. It hit the dock and rolled into the water on top of Glenn.

It wasn't the prettiest take-off I'd ever seen, but Misty managed to get it airborne and banked to the south, toward Honduras. Honduras. They didn't have extradition treaties with the United States or Belize. Glenn and I fired the last few rounds we had.

My dive boat was coming back in. Larry was at the helm. Behind him was the *Sensencula*. I yelled for Jeremy to pick me up. We went to where the police helicopter crashed. It was in shallow water. The pilot was dead but Captain Black was sitting upright in the co-pilot's seat when we got there. He had his cell phone in his hand.

Monday, February 2nd, 10:00 A.M.

"George, it's Glenn. He wants to talk with you." Kim knelt down on the dock and held the phone out for me. I was standing in the lagoon, putting a new prop on the *Sensencula*. I set my tools down and took the phone.

"Hello, Glenn, how are you?" I walked toward the beach.

"I'm fine. The real question is: how are you doing?"

"Fair to middling, I guess. It's been a month, the media circus has left, but so have a lot of our bookings. Is there anything new with your case?"

"There are still no signs of Catherine Berry, I mean Misty. Maybe her body washed out to sea, or a shark got her."

"I don't think so. The helicopter crashed a few miles from the shoreline. Martinez's body was intact within the chopper. If sharks had gotten Misty they'd have gotten him too."

"George, we'll keep looking for her. If she's alive, we'll find her."

"Got anything new on her?"

"Yeah, we've done some digging. That guy, Kevin, was right. Misty Lawler really did die at age five. We used some photos you and some of your guests provided and determined that Misty Lawler was really Catherine Berry. She came from another town near Coal Valley, just across the Iowa line, and was the real Misty Lawler's cousin. She used her cousin's ID to enlist in the Air Force because of a couple of drug convictions and an assault charge. She did one four-year hitch and left with an honorable discharge."

"What about her family?"

"Her mother died when Misty—I mean Catherine, was about ten. She died in a car wreck. Catherine's father was driving, and he was drunk."

"What did she do in the service?"

"Believe it or not, she was an MP. She spent a lot of her time guarding aircraft and spent a lot of time with aircraft mechanics. I guess with her looks, none of them much cared why she wanted to hang out with them. She was qualified as an expert marksman with rifles and handguns. She was also a third-degree black belt in some form of martial arts. She got her scuba training through the service too. She even got her private pilot's license for fixed-wing aircraft while stationed in Japan, and for helicopters after returning to the States."

"Do you have any idea how she got hooked up with Martinez?"

"While in the service she had a relationship with an underwater demolitions team guy, someone that washed out of the Seals. He was a bad guy, got a dishonorable discharge, and later served time for a contract killing. We know he worked for Martinez. He's told us that she killed some minor-league dealer that was stealing from Martinez."

"Why did she come here?"

"The same reason she went to Arizona. Martinez hired her. By the way, last week the state police in Nevada found a body they think is the woman that disappeared from Canyon Air. We think that Misty, I mean Berry, killed her and got herself hired so that when the opportunity came she could cause a crash that would kill the District Attorney and his team."

"And killing Bernie Stamps?"

"Martinez hired her to kill the lead lawyer interfering with his plans for the resort. I don't think he cared if the resort made money; it was just a good way to launder his drug money. I understand Stamps made his reservation there last summer?"

"Yeah, I think he made it back in June. The Christmas and New Year's trips fill up early."

"We think Martinez got the Stamps' travel plans from someone he worked with."

"Eric White would be my guess. He stood the most to gain and, according to Bernie's daughter Michelle at least, Bernie thought that Eric had taken some money from Martinez."

"Could be. We've got someone investigating that further."

"But that doesn't explain Dylan? Why kill him?" I asked.

"He'd probably be the first to draw a connection between her work for Martinez there—that is killing Stamps—and the crash that killed the DA. That or, from what you've told me, maybe it really was some kind of lover's quarrel. We'll never know, unless we find her alive somewhere."

"For what it's worth, a few days after you left I found a bottle of children's glue in my equipment room. That cheap stuff they let kids in daycare use. I'd never have that here. It's water soluble and useless on an island. I'm guessing that's what she used on his inflator hoses."

"Could be. If she used it there and left it in the equipment room that would make sense. It might not ever get noticed."

"What about Kevin O'Reilly? Let me guess, it's because she didn't know he'd already told me she was lying about her name?"

"That would be my guess. I've checked, he lived where he said he did and knew the Lawler family. Nobody back there liked him and apparently nobody's really missing him."

"I believe that, still, he didn't deserve what he got."

"Few do. By the way, according to Catherine Berry's sister, their father used to beat them."

"Hmm, okay, maybe that's why she reacted the way she did when Kevin pushed one of the kids. It's another part of her story that held true."

"Yeah, maybe. So, business is off, huh?"

"Yeah, we've had a lot of cancellations. We're being painted by the American media as being a haven for drug lords. I'm not sure Sticks and Beth will recover from this."

"What do you mean? Sticks and Beth weren't hurt."

"Sticks is buying Mountain To Sea. Beth and her husband, Mike, are buying Over The Edge."

"What are you and Kim going to do now?" Glenn asked.

"When the sales are complete, and both should close in the next week or so, we'll be moving back to the States. Remember the dolphins that surrounded her? Like the one's that surrounded Teri a couple of years ago at The Crack?"

"The dolphins that surrounded Teri? That's how we found out Teri was pregnant."

"They did it again. Kim's pregnant."

"Pregnant? Congrats, man! Hey, I've got some vacation time coming. I know a lot of law-enforcement people that would like to thank you for what you've done, and when I tell them about your place I think I can drum up some business, especially if you give a law-enforcement discount. Teri's ready for a vacation. I bet we can get her mother to watch the baby for a week. How about she and I come down two weeks from now?"

"Two weeks? Yeah, I think we can fit you in. As a repeat guest you get a ten-percent discount. I guess we can start a law enforcement discount too, maybe another five percent."

Kim frowned at that. She was the business person in this partnership.

"You know, Beth is still here. We can put you through a Rescue Diver class."

Credits:

CPSIA information can be obtained at www.ICGtesting.com
Printed in the USA
LVOW112051220512

282842LV00003B/7/P